A Royal Christmas Wish

LIZZIE SHANE

A Royal Christmas Wish
Copyright 2019 @ Lizzie Shane

Print: 978-1-947892-44-6
eBook: 978-1-947892-48-4

www.hallmarkpublishing.com

Table of Contents

Dedication

For Jane Noelle and Amilia Brook—may you
always believe in impossible things.

Chapter One

"WAKE UP, SLEEPING BEAUTY!"

I groaned as eighty decibels of enthusiasm landed on top of me in the form of my roommate.

"Today is the day we take New York by storm!" Margo crowed while I burrowed deeper beneath the covers in self-defense, hiding under my pillow as she continued to bounce. "The day all of our struggles turn into charming stories we can tell about how we overcame adversity to triumph magnificently." I braced my feet on her hip and attempted to shove her off the bed, but my feet slid off her slippery pajamas. She seized on my moment of distraction to yank the pillow away from my face. "Watch out, world, we're coming for you! Margo Gonzalez with her audition and Jenny James with her interview."

Oh, no. "My interview." My eyes popped open and I stopped my oh-so-subtle efforts to remove Margo from the bed. "What time is it?"

The light in my room was entirely too bright for seven a.m.—which was when my alarm should have gone off. I scrambled for the bedside table, searching for my phone.

"Seven-oh-five," Margo said. "You left your phone in the kitchen and when I heard the alarm, I figured you needed a more hands-on wake-up system. Also, your sister called."

Seven-oh-five. Margo had flipped on the overhead light; that was why my room was so bright. My ability to breathe returned. I wasn't late. Yet. "Which sister?"

"I dunno. The perfect one? You want breakfast?"

"As if that narrows it down," I grumbled as Margo bounded out of the room without waiting for an answer.

My sisters Chloe and Rachel—the doctor and the mayor—were the twin paragons of our hometown. Rachel had been student body president practically from birth, and Chloe had taken the local Mathletes team to a national championship before graduating early and completing med school at the top of her class. They'd each married their high school sweetheart—one of whom was literally the boy next door—and moved back home to work at their dream jobs and raise perfect children.

And there I was, just Jenny. Still trying to figure out what I wanted to do with my life.

Though maybe this interview would be a start.

I scrambled out of bed and dressed quickly, bypassing the color that dominated my closet and buttoning up in what had become my standard interview uniform: a sleek gray power suit. It was supposed to make me feel confident and professional, but as I tugged nervously on the cuffs, I wondered if the outfit was jinxed. I hadn't had a lot of luck with interviews so far...but this time would be different. This time, as Margo had said, we were going to take New York by storm.

Emerging from the narrow confines of my bedroom, I detoured around the poofy white explosion of tulle currently taking up so much of our living room that it should start paying rent. Margo's wedding dress was too big to fit in either of our microscopic New York closets, so it had become our de facto third roommate—camping on the couch.

By the time I hit the kitchen, Margo was dishing up pancakes and dancing along to the Christmas music coming from her iPhone speakers. "You're a saint," I told her as she handed me my phone.

"Enough of a saint for you to grab my costume for tonight when you pick up yours?" she asked hopefully, pouring me some coffee. "I'm supposed to meet with the caterer after my audition."

I groaned—half with bliss at the pancakes and half with dread at the thought of the party tonight. "I forgot we had to wear costumes. What are we this time?"

"Santa's elves. But with any luck, this will be the last time we have to serve hors d'oeuvres in elf gear. By next Christmas, I'll be a famous actress and you'll be a wildly successful..." She cocked her head. "What's this interview for?"

"Editorial assistant for a publishing house."

One of Margo's eyebrows popped up. "That's the new dream job?"

"I like books," I said, a little defensively. Because yes, I did like books. But I'd had so many interviews for so many jobs in the past two years that it was hard to keep them all straight—and I'd also never expressed any interest in working in publishing before, so Margo's skepticism was somewhat warranted. "Maybe I'll discover the next J. K. Rowling."

Margo rallied quickly, raising her orange juice in a toast. "To the next big thing in publishing."

"Who is going to pick up the next big thing on Broadway's elf costume when I grab mine," I added.

Margo's dark eyes filled with gratitude. "You're the best. And you're going to rock that interview."

"Thank you," I murmured, trying to absorb some of her confidence.

At least some good had come from my as-yet-unsuccessful attempts to find my place as a New York power player. Margo never would have met Harish if she hadn't been rushing to the rescue with a clean blouse after I'd spilled coffee all over mine right before my interview with his company. The poor man had taken one look at my roommate and been smacked hard with the love stick. He'd invited her to his office Christmas party, kissed her under the mistletoe, and the rest was history.

There was nothing quite like mistletoe magic.

Harish had later lobbied for me to get the job, but after the way I'd flailed during the interview, I wasn't surprised when they decided to go another way.

It was crazy to think that was a year ago—and I was no closer to figuring out what I was going to do with my life. Or where I was going to go when our lease was up at the end of January. Margo would be moving out after her winter wonderland-themed New Year's wedding, but she'd promised to pay her share of the rent until the lease expired. After that...

I really needed this job. I couldn't keep doing odd jobs for the rest of my life. I'd come to New York to prove something—and so far, all I'd managed to prove was that I had an impressive ability to bomb interviews.

Margo caught my hand, sensing my insecurity. "It's gonna be great," she assured me. "*You're* going to be great."

"I hope so. I can't be a catering server forever." I glanced at her over my pancakes. "I'm surprised you're still working the party tonight with all the wedding prep going on."

"I need the cash," she admitted. "Weddings are expensive—and I refuse to have Harish think I'm marrying him for his money. Of course, when I'm a wildly famous actress I'll support us both." She winked, but I knew her well enough to see the bravado covering her own nerves.

"You're going to kill this audition," I assured her, squeezing her hand back. "Break a leg, Bernhardt."

"You too." She grinned. "Or maybe I shouldn't say that. You have a tendency to take those things literally."

I rolled my eyes, but I couldn't argue. My clumsiness was legendary. It only got worse when I was nervous—and trying desperately to make everything go right—which made interviews particularly hazardous. "I'll try not to break anything," I promised her.

"Good. You've got this," Margo assured me.

I tried to hold on to her faith in me forty-five minutes later, as I walked into the lobby of a posh Manhattan high-rise for my interview.

The heels of my sharp, interview-only ankle boots

clicked across the polished floors as I approached the security guard and gave him my name and ID, earning a visitor's badge in return. As I shrugged out of my overcoat, I watched the regular employees swiping their passes to gain access to the elevator bank. I tried to picture myself as one of them.

Would I feel purposeful? Accomplished? Would I finally be able to quit all the odd jobs that allowed me to make rent? Or at least quit a couple of them? Would I know that I was doing what I was supposed to with my life? And someday, after a few promotions, would I maybe even be able to afford a cute little studio that allowed pets?

I rode up in the elevator, trying to picture myself in this place, in this job, searching for some sense that this was where I was meant to be. The elevator doors opened and I slipped out past the serious people in serious suits going to higher floors. I quickly spotted the large glass doors etched with the name of the publishing house and smoothed my jacket, whispering a little pep talk to myself as I approached. When I stepped through the glass doors, the office was quiet, almost like a library, and my nerves returned full force.

The receptionist smiled when I gave him my name—which I chose to take as a good sign—and handed me a clipboard. "These are just a few forms to speed up the process. You can take a seat through there and someone will be with you in a few minutes." He pointed through an archway to one side. "Good luck."

I accepted the clipboard with a smile, went into the next room, and sat down, trying to remember how to breathe properly.

The rest of the seats were empty, and I found myself picturing the other people who had occupied those chairs while waiting for their interviews. People who had undoubtedly been more qualified and prepared than me.

I focused on the forms in my lap, trying to calm the twist of nerves in my stomach, but the first words I saw were *Relevant Experience* and the roiling in my abdomen only got worse. Did dog walker count as relevant? One of my clients' dogs was named Charles Dickens—that had to count for something, right?

I left *Relevant Experience* blank for the time being, turning my attention instead to the parts I could answer. Name. Address. Education. I had just finished writing Liberal Studies in the space for my major when a woman with a warm smile stepped through the archway.

"Jenny James?"

"That's me." I scrambled to my feet as the woman's smile broadened and she extended her hand.

"I'm Kate Telly. I'll be conducting your interview today."

"Great!" I juggled my coat and the forms, shifting them to one side so I could shake her hand, instantly second-guessing the enthusiasm of my response. Should I have been more measured? Coolly confident? And how hard was I supposed to squeeze her hand? I'd heard that handshakes were important—the ultimate first impression—but how did you know if you were giving a good first impression or a terrible one? I studied her face for some clue, until I realized I'd been holding her hand for too long and abruptly dropped it. I looked away, blushing and fervently wishing I could replay the last few minutes and be less awkward and self-conscious.

"Right this way."

I fell into step behind the interviewer as she led me through the hush of the office. It was early and the office staff were still arriving, greeting one another and sliding behind their desks to check their email and start their days. I could do this. I could belong here. At least, that's what I told myself as I followed the interviewer into a small office and took the chair facing her desk.

Bookcases lined two of the walls, overflowing with books of every variety. Behind Ms. Telly, giant windows provided a view of the high-rise next door. Her desk was cheerfully cluttered with photo frames and knickknacks, but she cleared a space at the center and extended a hand for my forms. "Let's see what you've got."

I flushed, feeling like I was back in high school and had forgotten my homework. "I didn't have time to finish..."

"That's no problem," Ms. Telly assured me. "This just gives us a starting point. So." She accepted the clipboard I reluctantly handed over and scanned the top page, zeroing in on the few blanks I'd managed to fill. "What exactly is a major in liberal studies?"

It's what they give you when you change majors every six months and they just want to find some way to graduate you in four years based on the hodgepodge of classes you've already taken.

Embarrassment thickened on my tongue. "It's, uh, it's a little of everything."

"Interesting. As you imagine, we see a lot of English

degrees." She smiled encouragingly, as if my major made me unique rather than unfit for the job.

I tried to smile back, tugging at the cuffs of my suit jacket, the one I'd bought because it made me feel professional. Now, I just felt like I was playing dress up. An imposter in gray wool.

"All right, let's get straight to the fun part," Ms. Telly continued. "What first inspired you to pursue a career in publishing?"

"I, um..." The truth clogged in the back of my throat, blocking all other words, but I could *not* say that I just needed a job, *any* job, and my post-grad career counselor had all but washed her hands of me, throwing this at me in a last-ditch effort to find me something. "I like books?"

Ms. Telly beamed. "That's why we're all here, isn't it? Book nerds unite!"

She was so nice. So incredibly nice. I'd been to interviews with people who were bored or distracted, who had taken one look at my unimpressive resume and mentally dismissed me before we even began, but Ms. Telly was doing everything imaginable to put me at ease and it only made me feel even more like a fraud.

"Which five books would you say had the greatest influence on your life, and how?" she asked with the tone of someone who had asked that question a thousand times, and I swallowed nervously, glancing around the room at the walls *filled* with books.

Suddenly, all I could think was *Harry Potter was awesome* and *I really liked Pride and Prejudice.* I didn't belong here. I wasn't going to discover the next big thing in publishing. I'd never even read *Wuthering*

Heights. You had to have read *Wuthering Heights* to be an editorial assistant, didn't you? That had to have been some kind of rule.

"Um…"

"I know. It's hard to pick just five. Don't overthink it. First instincts."

"*Wuthering Heights*?"

Oh, no. Why had I said that? What if she asked me something about it? Did I even know any of the characters' names?

Ms. Telly nodded, smiling. "Interesting. And how do you feel it impacted your life?"

"Well, you know, the characters were very, um, good." Good was noncommittal, right? It could apply to just about anything.

She nodded, making a note on my forms. "And was it gothic romance in general or *Wuthering Heights* in particular that resonated with you?"

"Oh, you know, generally, the gothic." Why was I lying? If I'd said *Harry Potter*, she might not have thought I was highbrow and fancy enough to work there, but at least I would've known what I was talking about.

"Any other influential works?"

"Yeah, um, Charles Dickens."

Oh, no. It was just getting worse. I knew I'd read some Charles Dickens in school, but at the moment, I couldn't remember a single title. The fact that I walked a dog named Charles Dickens did *not* make me qualified to work in a publishing house. What was I *doing* there?

"Great." Ms. Telly seemed to sense I was floundering and pivoted. "Let's move from the classics into the future. What do you believe is missing in the literary landscape of today and how do you see yourself filling that gap?"

My heart beat faster and my hands started to sweat. I didn't know anything about the literary landscape of today. This was wrong. All wrong.

I stared at Ms. Telly as my mouth seemed to fill with sawdust. She belonged here, surrounded by all these books. While I was a fake.

Tears pricked the back of my eyes and I swallowed hard, refusing to fall apart in the middle of the interview. Words blurred in my mind and a buzzing sound filled my ears. I must have answered somehow, but the rest of the interview was like an out-of-body experience. Before I knew it, the very nice Ms. Telly was rising from behind her desk and shaking my hand again. She escorted me back to the front of the office where the receptionist gave me a smile and I caught a glimpse of another woman in the waiting area, wearing her interview best, her pen flying over her forms like she couldn't write her answers fast enough.

She looked qualified. Like the kind of woman who deserved a job like this. Who *wanted* a job like this. She'd probably been striving for this job since kindergarten just like Rachel and Chloe and Margo and everyone else who knew what they wanted out of life. *She'd* probably read *Wuthering Heights*.

Ms. Telly promised they'd be in touch, though we both knew they wouldn't. I forced a smile and thanked her before escaping through the glass doors. The elevator opened the second I pushed the button and I stepped inside, clutching my coat in front of me with both hands and silently kicking myself. The elevator was empty on my ride back down to the lobby—as if to remind me that everyone else was on their way up and I was the only one going in the wrong direction.

I peeled off my disposable visitor's badge and tossed it into a trash can on my way out of the lobby. As I stepped out onto the sidewalk, the cold air and distinctive scent of New York hit me in the face. The smell and noise of the city had always made me feel excited, with that if-you-can-make-it-here-you-can-make-it-anywhere feeling humming beneath the surface.

But as today proved, I couldn't make it here.

I felt foolish as I started uptown on autopilot, walking rather than taking the subway. It was still early. My phone rang as I walked, and I groaned when I saw my sister's name on the screen. Of course. Her timing was as perfect as ever.

"Hello, Rachel."

"When's your interview?" my sister said, completely bypassing any normal sort of greeting. "Are you headed there now? Remember: project confidence."

It was tempting to lie. So incredibly tempting. But Rachel would know. I was a horrible liar. "I wasn't projecting anything other than incompetence. I already bombed it."

"Oh, Jenny." Rachel sighed heavily. "What was it this time?"

I veered around a group of tourists gawking at the Plaza Hotel and jogged a little to catch the light at the crosswalk. "I froze, okay? Because I always freeze."

"Maybe you didn't come across as badly as you thought. You always think you're doing terribly."

"I told her I love *Wuthering Heights*, and when

12

she asked why, I said that the characters were, and I quote, 'good.' That's it. That's all I could think of."

"*Do* you love *Wuthering Heights?*"

"I've never *read Wuthering Heights.*"

Rachel groaned. "Oh, Jenny."

"Why did you call me so early this morning?" I challenged, trying to distract her as I skirted the edge of Central Park, dodging the lingering piles of snow on the sidewalk from the last storm. "Why were you even awake at five in the morning your time?"

"My daughter has decided she doesn't believe in sleep." I heard the exhaustion in her voice. "And I wanted to wish you luck on your interview. Don't change the subject. Why did you tell them you loved a book you've never even read?"

"Because if I'd told them the book that influenced me the most was *Harry Potter*, they would've laughed me out of the office."

"You don't know that. And isn't it better to fail as yourself than succeed by trying to be someone you aren't?"

"I didn't belong there, Rach," I insisted. "Even before I started lying about books, it didn't feel right. Publishing just isn't my thing." At least I hadn't broken anything or spilled anything on anyone. It was all about the little victories.

"Did you really give it a shot, though? Or did you sabotage yourself by counting yourself out before you even walked through the door? Again."

"Rachel..."

"Has it occurred to you that maybe you're putting too much weight on this decision? Pick a job. Any job. I feel like you're waiting for lightning to strike and a giant neon flashing sign saying *this is who you are* to appear, but life isn't like that. Sometimes figuring out what you're meant to be is about making a choice, not waiting for a sign."

"Says the woman who has known what she wanted to be since birth. Besides, I'm not waiting for a sign."

"Are you sure?" Rachel challenged. "Are you even dating anyone?"

I frowned at the phone. "What does that have to do with anything?"

"It's all part of the same problem. You're waiting around for some fairy tale and until you realize that isn't possible you're never going to let yourself have something real. No one gets the fairy tale. There's no such thing as perfect. Not with jobs and not with guys."

"I don't want a fairy tale," I protested. "I don't. I just... I want to know where I belong. I want to *feel* like I belong. You've had that forever. I just want it to be my turn. And yes, I want someone to kiss beneath the mistletoe, who falls madly in love with *me*. I want a guy who looks at me the way Eliot has always looked at you. And the way Danny looks at Chloe. Like Mom and Dad, and Margo and Harish. Is that really so much to ask?"

"Of course not, but we just worry that you're waiting for Prince Charming when he doesn't exist."

"I'm sure all the real-life princes in the world would be horrified to hear you say they don't exist, but I promise I'm not holding out for one."

I didn't want a prince. I just wanted someone who gave me that *zing*. That feeling that I was exactly where I needed to be with the person who fit me like a puzzle piece.

Speaking of princes...

I glanced up, taking in my surroundings and smiling as I realized that I'd automatically navigated to the one place guaranteed to make me feel better. I turned up the street. "Though I am on my way to meet a prince right now."

"Jenny—"

"I know, Rachel," I interrupted my big sister. "Whatever you're about to tell me, I know. I love you, but I'm going to fix my own life, okay?"

"Maybe if you came home. New York isn't for everyone—"

"Goodbye, Rachel."

I disconnected the call before my sister could continue her lecture. I didn't need to hear her tell me that I couldn't really afford to live here on my own after Margo moved out. That I should retreat back to our hometown in Iowa with my tail between my legs—a failure. The one James girl who'd never made anything of herself.

I didn't want to think about any of that.

I pocketed my phone, moving faster now that I knew my destination. I was on my way to meet a prince, and that was all that mattered. The one male in all of New York who looked at me with absolute devotion.

I pushed open the doors to Paws for Love and the jingle bells over the door rang, drawing the attention of the volunteer working inside.

"G'morning, Mercedes."

"Hey, Jenny," she called out, giving me a quick smile before turning her attention back to the lopsided

Santa hat she was trying to balance on a pit bull mix's head. "You here to see your prince?"

"That I am," I confirmed, unbuttoning my coat. "Do you need a hand first?"

Mercedes and I both volunteered at Paws for Love. Lately, she'd been updating the website with adorable holiday-themed photos in a campaign to find more of our furry residents forever homes during the holidays. This time of year, so many New Yorkers felt stressed or lonely and could use a little more love in their lives, but there were always more furry angels in the shelter looking for love than there were families to adopt them. Lucky was one of our newest residents. The one-eared pit bull mix gazed adoringly at Mercedes, his little tail wagging frantically at the attention so his entire body seemed to shiver with happiness.

"No, thanks, I've got this guy," Mercedes assured me, stepping back to pick up her camera as Lucky wriggled with the effort not to leap up and follow her. "Have fun with his highness."

"I will."

I typed the code into the door and headed toward the kennels. Real estate in the city was always at a premium, so the dogs were tucked in two or three to a run. They yipped when they saw me, wagging and bouncing as I called greetings to each one. I plucked a red ball out of a toy bin as I passed and tucked it into the pocket of my winter coat with a smile already growing on my face.

I'd begun volunteering at Paws for Love six months ago, but five weeks ago, everything had changed when I'd met *him*.

A bona fide prince.

No matter what Rachel and Chloe might think, I haven't been holding out for Prince Charming. But when he walked into my life, everything changed.

I rounded a corner and there he was.

"Hello, Your Highness!"

My prince looked up at the sound of my voice, his eyes lighting at the sight of me, filling with an affection so sincere it couldn't be faked—

And then he barked.

Chapter Two

OKAY, YES, MY PRINCE WAS a dog, but he was also the sweetest dog on the planet.

The love of my life was in the second run from the end, spinning tight little circles of joy as I approached his pen. Prince Harry, a little ginger mutt, was about as far from pedigreed as you could get, but somehow that only made him that much more perfect.

"How are you today, Prince Harry?" I asked as I came up to his pen and plucked his leash off a hook.

I officially volunteered two days a week at Paws for Love, but I'd also worked out a deal with the shelter's managers that said I could come in any day I wanted to give the dogs a little extra exercise. And if I had a slight tendency to play favorites, well, who could blame me? He was a prince, after all.

And the one creature on the planet who always made me feel like I could do anything.

Prince Harry poked his nose against the chain link, licking tiny puppy kisses on my fingertips before plunking his rear end on the ground as soon as I reached for the gate's latch. He was so smart—he'd figured out on only our second outing that he needed to sit for the leash. Ever since, he'd behaved perfectly, always waiting with his little tail swishing across the ground. Lucky was his latest roommate, so Prince Harry was alone in the run, trying his best to stay still for the leash even though he was bursting with excitement.

"Should we go to the park today, Your Highness?" I asked—and he leapt up with a wriggle of delight, convincing me as he always did that he understood every word I was saying.

I wasn't exactly dressed for dog walking, but I had a couple of hours before I needed to pick up the elf costumes and get to my next job, and I desperately needed some Prince Harry time. If I'd been able to afford a pet, I would've adopted Prince Harry like a shot, but living in the big city was a lot more expensive than I'd anticipated when Margo and I had hatched the idea to move there. Until I could afford to keep him, volunteering with the shelter was the next best thing.

Prince Harry and I stepped out on the sidewalk and he instantly heeled, his little face tipped up to me, so eager to please. "What a good boy," I praised, guiding him toward one of the portions of Central Park that had been designated as dog-friendly and hurrying to get there before the off-leash hours ended.

Before I'd moved to New York, I'd seen Central Park in movies—or at least, the parts of it teeming with horse-drawn carriages and tourists—but I hadn't realized how *massive* it was. Or that my favorite part of the city would become a quiet little stretch of the park where I could throw a ball with a certain ginger mutt.

I waved to Edwin, the Puerto Rican Santa setting up his red bucket at the entrance to the park, singing "Winter Wonderland" in a beautiful tenor. He waved back with a smile, never breaking off his Perry Como impression. It had snowed a couple days ago and there were grimy piles of snow at the edge of the streets, but in the park, the white stuff was still mostly white, stretching out across the fields until it really did seem like a winter wonderland.

This part of the park was quiet in the mornings, just a little hill and a stretch of jogging paths occupied by the serious runners, the kind who always seemed to be training for a marathon. It was peaceful here, unlike the hectic rush of the rest of the city, and I tried to breathe it in—and forget about my disastrous interview.

As soon as I bent and unclipped his leash, Prince Harry bounded into a pile of snow, sending it flying in the air. I laughed and fished the red ball out of my pocket—and Prince Harry instantly came alert, vibrating with excitement, his entire focus locked on the toy.

"You want the ball?" I asked him and he crouched eagerly, head down, rear end high, tail wagging wildly. "This ball?" I tossed it and it barely flew five feet before disappearing into the snow. Harry dove after it, his entire front end disappearing for a moment into the snowbank before he emerged victorious, the ball in his jaws.

He raced back to me, showing off his prize before dropping it at my feet and crouching again in anticipation. It was impossible not to feel lighter in the face of his enthusiasm, even as I tried not to dwell on the *Wuthering Heights* disaster...or the fact that spending time with Prince Harry *was* the closest thing to a date I'd had in months.

Dating in New York was... intimidating. And I knew Rachel meant well, but she and Chloe always made me feel like it was my fault I hadn't found a boyfriend yet. My parents were a matched set and my sisters had both grown up with their husbands, but there were only so many eligible men in our small town and none of them had ever given me butterflies. I wasn't looking for Prince Charming, but I at least wanted that zing.

The legendary mistletoe zing.

Mistletoe was sort of a thing in my family. My father tells the story of how he knew he was going to marry my mother the first time he kissed her beneath the mistletoe. Eliot had just been the boy next door until he'd kissed Rachel beneath the mistletoe at the Christmas dance when they were fourteen—and they'd been together ever since. Danny had been the high school quarterback and not at *all* Mathlete Chloe's type, until he'd managed to charm her into a kiss beneath the mistletoe at the Christmas dance their junior year.

And even *Margo*, who wasn't even related to us, had fallen for Harish after a mistletoe kiss. It was like the magic had skipped right over me. I just wanted it to be my turn. I knew I was supposed to be a strong, independent woman whose happiness didn't depend on any man, but couldn't I have one little Cinderella moment beneath the mistletoe?

I'd watched love stories happening around me my entire life, and I just wanted to find my person. My partner. Someone to kiss beneath the mistletoe—and then, down the road, argue with about centerpieces and paint colors and baby names. I wasn't waiting for him, not putting my life on hold, but I did want the husband and the kids eventually, and sometimes it felt like it just wasn't going to happen for me.

I'd thought in New York I was *bound* to find my guy. There were literally *millions* of men here. One of them had to be meant for me. But the women all seemed to be supermodels and CEOs, the men all seemed to be in a hurry to get to the top, and I hadn't been able to find anyone willing to slow down long enough to see if we might be zing-worthy.

Margo and I had moved to the city together after graduation. Yes, it had been more her dream than mine, but I hadn't expected to feel so lost here. For a girl who'd never quite figured out which dream to chase, New York was intimidating in its possibilities. There were so many incredible opportunities here, but I'd spent the past two years screwing up interviews and paying my share of the rent with a variety of menial jobs.

Prince Harry whined from his crouch, refusing to allow me to mope, and I picked up the ball, now damp from snow and dog slobber. I wound up like a pitcher in Yankee stadium, grinning down at the dog. "You ready?" I asked Prince Harry, who held himself perfectly still, an eager canine statue ready to burst into motion. "You sure you're ready?"

I threw the ball as hard as I could, since the snow would stop it in its tracks where it landed, but as

Prince Harry whirled toward it and began leaping through the snow, the ball hit pavement, bouncing high into the air and flying toward the jogging path—where dogs were *not* allowed—with Prince Harry hot on its trail.

"Harry! No!" My heart launched into my throat as I bolted after him.

Visions of disaster flashed in my mind. Prince Harry plowing into the prima ballerina from the NYCB production of *The Nutcracker*, spraining a knee worth millions and breaking the hearts of all the children who would no longer be able to see the show. Or worse, Prince Harry tripping a litigious Wall Street lawyer, who would break his leg and sue Paws for Love, closing the shelter so all the dogs would have nowhere to go, punishing poor Prince Harry for the consequences of my stupid throw.

As if to taunt me, the ball kept bouncing wildly and Prince Harry scampered after it, loving the game, with no idea we weren't supposed to be on that path. I raced in his wake, out of the dog area, down the hill, off-balance in my high-heeled boots which were *not* designed for this, moving so fast I was practically flying, so focused on Prince Harry I didn't see the jogger coming around a corner—

Until I was broadsiding him, my momentum carrying both of us off our feet, sending us flying into a snowbank.

"Oh!"

"Uhngh!" I'd landed on something entirely too firm to be snow. The man beneath me grunted with the impact.

Mortification swamped me as I tried to clamber off

him, earning another grunt when I pushed down—which was a good sign, right? If he was grunting, then at least I hadn't killed him.

"I'm so sorry! Are you okay?" *Please let nothing be broken.* "Sir?" I lifted myself high enough to check for injuries and found myself looking into the bluest eyes I'd ever seen.

"Are you all right?" a deep voice tinged with a slight accent asked, but I'd lost my powers of speech.

Crystal-blue eyes with a dark gray circle outlining the edge of the iris and fringed by the thickest, darkest lashes imaginable stared up into mine from a distance of inches and for a moment, my breath caught in my throat as the outside world seemed to fade away...

Only to return with a thunder of footsteps as a group of joggers rushed toward us. "Are you all right, y—"

"I'm fine," the man beneath me told the joggers in a stiff accented voice, holding up a hand to wave them off before arching a brow at me. "Do you mind?" he asked—and I realized I'd been gaping at him like an idiot while hovering over him so he couldn't get up.

"Sorry! I'm so sorry!" I babbled, scrambling to one side. The joggers, a group of men in matching black running gear, had fallen back to the opposite side of the path, pretending to stretch and watching me as if I might start tackling more unsuspecting runners. I couldn't really blame them. Why did I have to be such a human train wreck? "Does anything hurt?" I asked, kneeling at my victim's side—and getting my first good look at him when I wasn't fixated on his dreamy eyes or tackling him into the snow.

He really was unfairly good looking. Tall and fit,

your basic dream guy—and posh, with fancy designer jogging gear and his thick, dark hair styled perfectly. Everything about him was basically perfect, which only made me feel like more of a walking disaster.

He glanced at me warily as he sat up, rubbing a hand across the sharp plane of his jaw. "All parts functional," he replied and the accent tugged at me; something vaguely European that seemed to wrap the words in luxury. "And you?"

"I'm fine. I'm so sorry," I said. Once the words started, I couldn't seem to stop. "My dog—it wasn't his fault. I threw the ball too hard and it bounced, and he didn't know he wasn't supposed to chase it, he's always been allowed to chase it in the park before, so how would he know we weren't supposed to be on the jogging path—"

He studied me, as if suspicious of the barrage of words. Why did I have to body slam someone so intimidatingly perfect and composed? "Your dog?" He seemed skeptical as he came to his feet, looking at me as if he was wondering exactly how many bricks short of a load I was—though he still extended his hand to help me to my feet.

I took the offered hand, which lifted me effortlessly to my feet, and I felt my face heat as I dusted the snow off my tailored gray pants. "I was chasing my dog—well, a dog." Belatedly realizing that didn't make me sound any more rational, as if I just ran through the park chasing random dogs and attacking joggers, I blushed and rushed on, "I promise I don't normally tackle strangers in the park. And I promise there's a dog." Prince Harry reappeared then, bounding over

25

the snow with the ball clutched in his mouth, and I pointed at him with a rush of relief. "That dog."

The jogger's shoulders lowered a notch at the sight of Prince Harry—canine confirmation that I wasn't *completely* out of my mind—and for a moment I almost thought I saw his lips twitch. "Looks like he got it."

Prince Harry bounced in front of us, proud of himself for vanquishing the renegade ball, and I wasn't sure whether I should praise him for returning with it or scold him for chasing it—though I was the one who had thrown it for him to chase, and he didn't know he was supposed to stay off the jogging path. I settled for patting him on the head and murmuring, "Good boy, baby," as I clipped the leash back onto his collar.

Prince Harry dropped the ball at my feet, though he didn't go into his crouch, confused by the combination of the leash and the ball, which we'd never had out at the same time before.

"I'm so sorry—" I began again, but the jogger gave me a look that froze the seventeen millionth apology in my throat and bent to search for something in the snow—which put him right on Prince Harry's level. The dog enthusiastically snuffled his ear and I started to apologize and pull him away, but the jogger was already rubbing his head affectionately, earning puppy kisses in return.

Which of course made me melt into a puddle of goo. He liked dogs. Of course he did. He was perfect. The kind of man who hadn't threatened to sue when I broadsided him into a snowbank and instead asked if *I* was okay.

"Cute mutt," he said, bending his head toward Prince Harry's.

"He's up for adoption," I offered.

The jogger looked up, surprise in his eyes. "You're trying to get rid of your dog?"

"He isn't actually my dog." As much as I would selfishly hate it if I never saw Prince Harry again, I wanted him to have a good, loving home of his own. "I volunteer at a shelter near here and this little guy is my favorite."

"Sounds like you should adopt him." He continued rubbing Harry's ears, earning a look of devotion.

"I can't have pets. My apartment doesn't allow them."

"So move to a different apartment."

I laughed. "As if it's that easy. Do you know how much broker fees are in New York?"

The jogger gave Harry one final pat and plucked an iPhone out of the snow. I mentally crossed my fingers that it wasn't damaged as he wiped the moisture off it and straightened. "If you want something to work, you make it work," he said—as if it was only a matter of wanting a thing badly enough. And maybe for men with the latest iPhone and designer running gear it was as easy as that. His watch probably cost more than I made in a month.

"Sometimes it's about more than just making it work. Not all of us can afford a pet in New York," I argued, "but that doesn't mean we aren't working hard. Most of my friends are working two or three or even four jobs to pay rent."

His eyebrows bounced up, as if he wasn't used to people arguing with him, but interest gleamed now in his eyes as they met mine. "I'm just saying it's about choices. If you really wanted a dog, you could move to where the rent is cheaper—"

"I'd still have to worry about vet bills and dog food, not to mention finding time to actually *see* him in between working all hours to pay my bills. Add in commute time to and from this magical apartment with the cheap rent that allows pets, and I'd never be home to take care of him. How would that be fair to a dog?"

"You could work remotely. Lots of people do."

"As a dog walker and catering server? I hear there's a lot of demand for that," I teased.

"I'm just saying there are options. You could look for another job. One that's more conducive to owning pets."

"And *I'm* just saying it isn't always as easy as that. It's awfully easy to say it's just a choice when you aren't the one who has to make it work." I saw the smile on his face and realized I was having a hard time keeping a smile off my face as well. There was something about matching wits with him that was really *fun*.

"Are you always this passionate?"

"Not always. You kind of hit a nerve. I don't want to be a dog walker forever." I grimaced. "Though if I keep bombing interviews like I did this morning, I may have to."

"Ah, an interview. That explains the shoes."

"Not my usual dog walking uniform," I admitted, blushing a little that he'd noticed my power heels. "I'm Jenny, by the way."

He glanced over my shoulder at the black-clad joggers who were still stretching and watching us from the opposite side of the path. A frown flickered over his brow, as if he was debating whether he trusted me enough to give me his name. His posture stiffened and for a moment I thought he wouldn't reply, but then he offered, "Dom."

I smiled, shaking the hand he extended. "It's nice to meet you, Dom. And I'm sorry about the football tackle earlier. I swear to you I'm not in the habit of knocking men off their feet."

He shook his head, his attention still on the men behind me. "It's fine," he muttered, his tone distant and impersonal, the walls that had started to come down as we chatted clearly back up now. "I should..."

He was clearly gearing up to leave—which made sense. I couldn't exactly expect him to stand around forever talking to me. He seemed like the kind of guy with an important life to get back to—a life surrounded by supermodels and CEOs, not off-duty dog walkers and catering servers. But Prince Harry clearly hadn't gotten the message that our jogger was done with us. He picked up the ball, dropping it on top of Dom's feet.

I tugged gently on the leash. "Come on, Prince Harry, he doesn't want to play."

Dom looked at me sharply. "You named the dog Prince Harry?"

I felt myself blushing again as I explained. "He didn't have a name when he arrived at the shelter—and it's perfect, don't you think? He's smart, charming... a redhead."

Dom's lips twitched. "I'm not sure how the real Prince Harry would feel about his namesake."

"I promise not to tell him if you won't," I said with

mock sincerity and Dom studied me with a little frown on his face, as if he couldn't quite figure out if I was joking. "I'm kidding," I assured him, rolling my eyes. "As if I would ever meet a real prince."

Dom studied me for another moment before his shoulders relaxed and something about his expression eased, as if he had decided to like me after all. He bent to pick up the ball. "Real princes are highly overrated."

"You mean they aren't all slaying dragons and climbing towers to rescue fair maidens like in the fairy tales? How will I ever control my disappointment?" He laughed and I nodded at the ball in his hands which Prince Harry gazed at hopefully. "You can't throw that here."

"No?"

I pointed over my shoulder. "There's an off-leash area—"

"I see." He glanced over at the stretching joggers. "After you."

Something that felt suspiciously like zing zipped through my heart as he bowed, like an actual prince, and I laughed, curtsying awkwardly. "By all means."

Chapter Three

W E WANDERED BACK TOWARD THE dog park, across the jogging path and up the hill, out of sight of the black-clad group who were still stretching and watching us like we were an episode of their favorite show.

"So you have a thing for princes, huh?" Dom teased, shifting Harry's ball from hand to hand as we walked and Prince Harry zigzagged to sniff everything in sight.

"Not exactly. I do love fairy tales, but it seems like the princesses do most of the work. The princes are just hanging out in the background being boringly charming while the ladies are off getting cursed and imprisoned and suffering before they get their happily-ever-afters."

My ankle wobbled in my less-than-ideal-for-playing-in-the-park heels and Dom cupped my elbow, gently steadying me and sending another little whisper of zing shimmering through my bloodstream. A bubble of happiness rose up in my chest and curved my lips, and I ducked my head to hide my smile as we crossed into the dog area, me holding Prince Harry's leash and Dom holding my arm.

"You saying the princes have it easy?" he challenged, his tone light.

"I don't know what I'm saying," I admitted. The exact words didn't seem to matter as much as this flirty, fizzing feeling that seemed to be swirling around us and sizzling through my chest. "It does sound like a pretty good gig, though," I said as Dom dropped my elbow and I knelt to unclip Prince Harry's leash. "Royalty."

"In my experience, people dreaming about Prince Charming have no idea what being a prince is really like."

I tilted my head up at him, arching a brow at his tone. "You have a lot of experience with princes, do you?"

"Oh, *tons*." Dom smiled and I found myself returning it. The entire world seeming to fade away for a moment until it was only us and that shared smile—until Prince Harry whined and I averted my eyes and stood up.

"You planning to throw that?" I asked, nodding to the ball. "You've gotten his hopes up now. You wouldn't want to disappoint the prince."

"Heaven forbid."

Dom threw the ball and Prince Harry gave a little yip of joy before scrambling after it, romping into the snow.

"Oh, now you've done it," I said when Dom laughed. "He owns you now."

"I can think of worse fates," he said with a smile— and a little fantasy flickered to life in my mind's eye.

Dom adopting Prince Harry, the two of us playing with him in the park, walking home hand-in-hand—

Harry galumphed back to us, snow flying around him, and flung the ball back down at our feet, going into a wagging crouch. I bent to pick up the ball and toss it, trying to toss away the silly fantasy, too, and keeping my focus on Prince Harry so the man at my side wouldn't realize how acutely aware of him I was. *Play it cool for once, Jenny.*

"So you had a rough morning?" Dom asked, and when I glanced at him in question as Harry trotted back to us he explained, "You mentioned messing up an interview."

"I'm not even sure I wanted the job," I admitted, picking up Harry's ball and rolling it between my hands. "I just wanted to find my thing, you know?"

"How so?" Dom took the ball from my hands and tossed it for Harry.

"I'm the youngest of three and my sisters have always known what they want. What job they wanted to have when they grew up, who they wanted to marry, how many kids they wanted—even which house on the street we grew up on they wanted to live in. And they're good at *everything*—it all worked out for them, just like they planned. And I'm just Jenny, the queen of odd jobs, bumbling my way through life, trying to figure out what I want to do."

I glanced at him, suddenly self-conscious, but far from looking like I was talking too much, he looked genuinely curious. Enough so that I found myself going on.

"I came to New York because I thought if I took this one big adventurous step then I would be that person, you know? Adventurous and confident and capable of achieving my dreams—and of course, a person who knows what the dream is. But I still don't. I want to do something big. Bigger than I could do in Potter's Ferry, Iowa. But I don't know what. Do you ever have that feeling? Like you're meant for something? And if you can just get there, then everything will make sense?"

"Honestly?" He grimaced. "I've known what I was going to do with my life pretty much since birth and it's not all it's cracked up to be." At my questioning look, he elaborated. "Family business."

"Ah." I nodded. "My roommate's family is like that—all lawyers. They do *not* understand her desire to be an actress. But you don't *have* to go into the family business. You can always buck tradition."

"I could," he agreed slowly, his eyes going distant— and I saw something in the hesitation.

"But you love it too much."

He glanced at me, as if startled by the comment, then nodded slowly. "I do. When I was younger it felt more like a curse than a blessing, the responsibility and everything that came with it, but in the last few years I guess I've started realizing how much good we can do."

"That's all you can ask for, right? To have the chance to put more good into the world?"

He studied me, as if puzzled, but then he smiled slowly. "Yes. I suppose so."

The moment seemed to hold, stretching between us. A little ache started in my chest until I realized I'd forgotten to breathe and didn't want to take a breath now because I didn't want to risk breaking the moment.

There was something about him, the way he looked at me, his eyes holding mine, and my fingertips began to tingle as possibility whispered along my spine.

Was this why I'd moved to New York? For this moment? I'd started to wonder over the last few months if I'd made the right call. If I was wasting my time trying to prove I was good enough to make it here. If I should just move back home and accept that my place was in Iowa, doing my own little part. Moving to New York had been a way to take a leap, to find myself, but lately I'd felt more lost than ever.

But now...

Now Dom was looking at me with that unnamable thing stretching between us and everything that had happened over the last two years felt like it had purpose and possibility again. I almost looked up, just in case mistletoe was growing wild in Central Park these days.

He held my eyes, the moment lingering, and I didn't know what was about to happen but there was an inescapable sense of *something*—

Until something caught his attention over my shoulder and the smile slid off his face. "I should go."

No.

I looked over my shoulder, but all I saw was the same group of men in matching black workout gear stretching along another bend in the path and a woman holding up her phone to take a picture of the park. A flutter of disappointment rose up in my throat and I turned back to him, wishing reality didn't have to intrude.

But he wasn't looking at me and the moment was gone.

"I should get going, too." I did have to be at work soon, and I still needed to drop Prince Harry off, but I'd been hoping...

I didn't know what I'd been hoping. For him to ask for my number?

"Sorry to spill all that on you," I babbled. "I promise I don't normally tell my entire life story to every random guy I meet in the park."

"So I'm random, am I?"

"No, I, that's not what I—"

"Jenny. It's okay. Everyone in my life is so polished and controlled, I never know what they're really thinking or feeling. It's nice to meet someone so *real*."

"If by 'real' you mean 'catastrophically klutzy and directionless,' I'm your girl."

Dom laughed. He met my eyes again and I bit my lower lip to keep inside the tongue-tied babble that wanted to erupt from my throat. "It was really nice," he murmured. "Meeting you."

"You too," I said softly around the sudden pressure in my chest. "Though I'm sorry about the whole tackling you into the snow thing."

"It was certainly a unique way to start my morning." A half-grin quirked one side of his mouth, but it faded too soon. "Merry Christmas, Jenny."

"Merry Christmas, Dom," I whispered, my toes curling in my fancy high-heeled boots as he nodded to me one last time before walking away.

Prince Harry whined softly at the departure of his new friend and I crouched down to ruffle the dog's silky ears, the two of us watching as Dom turned the corner out of sight. When he was gone, I sighed and

Prince Harry put his paws on my knees, his little face in my face.

"I kind of chickened out, huh?" I asked the dog, who huffed out a soft sigh. "I know. I definitely should have asked for his number. Not that I would've had the guts to call it. For all I know, he has a girlfriend. Or a wife. Though I didn't see a ring, did you?" He gazed at me, his eyes liquid with adoration, as if I could do anything.

"I think he liked us," I assured Prince Harry. "And maybe if we come back here at the same time tomorrow, we'll run into him again. I bet he's the kind of guy who runs every morning on a schedule. What do you think? You like that plan?"

Prince Harry licked my chin—which I took as wholehearted approval of my new strategy.

"Me too," I murmured, ruffling his ears.

It had to work. I had to see Dom again. I couldn't imagine the universe would drop such a zing-inducing man in my path and then whisk him away just like that.

"Come on," I murmured, clipping on Prince Harry's leash and straightening. "Let's get you home."

The sound of a street musician playing "The Christmas Song" floated through the air as we walked back to the shelter. I'd always loved Christmas—a time of year when everything seemed a little more magical and when mistletoe kisses were always possible—but lately it had become a time to take stock and realize that as another year came to an end, I was no closer to achieving my dreams, and still didn't have a special someone to share the season with. The holiday season had started to feel heavier, and enjoying the old traditions had taken more effort, but now...

I found myself humming as we walked, my steps lighter as I daydreamed about a certain jogger.

Funny how a few minutes in the park could make everything seem a little more possible. A little more magical.

I would see Dom again. I was certain of it.

I just had no idea then how soon.

Chapter Four

THE ELF COSTUME ITCHED.

I tried not to think of the possibility of lice or fleas or bedbugs or any number of other unsavory creepy crawlies making their home in the fabric of the outfit I'd been loaned by the catering company. Instead, I tried to Jedi-mind-trick myself into believing the tickling sensation was just scratchy wool. Either way, I was fantasizing about a full-body bath in calamine lotion as I took my place in the line of servers queueing up in the crowded kitchen to collect our first trays for the party.

"Jenny!" Margo squeezed into the line at my side, her natural grace somehow making her elf costume look like couture as she linked her arm through mine. "Did you hear?"

Margo had done my make-up, painting glitter on my cheekbones and eyelids, but while she managed to look like a celebrity in Christmas gear, I just felt silly with my pointy ears as we lined up with our fellow elves. "Does your outfit itch?"

"Jenny. Focus. This is major," she insisted, leaning

closer and lowering her voice. "The guest of honor. It's a *prince*. An actual, bona fide prince." She craned her neck as if trying to catch a glimpse through the swinging door that led into the posh penthouse apartment that was the venue for tonight's bash. "I know you only have eyes for your mystery jogger, but we're talking actual royalty."

"He isn't my jogger," I protested, blushing. Earlier, I hadn't been able to wait to tell Margo about my moment of zing in the park, but as reality had begun to set in, I'd started to regret it. Somehow, telling her about Dom had added an extra layer of pressure to my plan for bumping into him tomorrow, raising the stakes.

What if I never saw him again? What if a few minutes of banter in the park was the sum total of our relationship? What if—worst of all—I saw him again and it turned out I'd been imagining the zing? The story had distracted Margo from asking me about the interview debacle—which was helpful, since the last thing I needed was another person groaning with disappointment when I explained the *Wuthering Heights* fiasco. But now, I almost wished I'd just confessed and gotten it over with.

"A real prince?" I asked. What were the odds that I'd be joking about princes in the morning with Dom and catering the Christmas party of a real-life prince that same night?

"Prince Alexander of San-Something-or-Other," Margo said with dramatic flourish. "Apparently he's the crown prince of some tiny little country somewhere in the Alps which does business with the company throwing this fiesta. And he's *single*. Europe's Most

Eligible Royal now that Harry and Wills are off the market."

"You considering jilting Harish to be the crown princess of San-Something-or-Other?"

"I would make a good princess, wouldn't I?" she asked with a grin that reminded me not to take anything she said too seriously. "Alas, I am far too madly in love with my darling fiancé to consider Prince Eligible Hottie." Her gaze settled on me and her eyes glittered. "Now *you,* on the other hand..."

"Right." I snorted. "Can you see me with a prince?"

Margo arched a brow. "Honey, if anyone deserves a prince, it's you. You just need to have more faith in yourself."

"I have faith," I countered defensively. "Sort of."

She rolled her eyes as we collected our first trays of the night—freshly poured champagne, fizzing with bubbles—and headed into the sprawling glamour of the posh Central Park East penthouse. "Just promise me that if you see a regal man in a purple sash, you'll flirt your heart out," Margo urged. "Somebody has to land him. Why shouldn't it be you? And then Harish and I can summer with you at the palace. Doesn't that sound glamorous? Summering at the palace."

"How do you know he'll be in a purple sash?"

She shrugged blithely. "People tell me things."

Men told her things. When you were gorgeous and confident, that was simply the way the world worked.

We passed through the doors into the penthouse's two-story great room and Margo only had time to mouth, *"Flirt,"* one more time before we were forced to separate and circulate through the sophisticated throng. I shook my head, fighting a smile.

Considering how catastrophically the day had begun, it wasn't looking half bad right now. I had a best friend who never failed to make me laugh, a sweetheart of a dog I got to pretend was mine a few times a week, the hope of meeting Dom again in the park later this week—*please, please, please, let us meet again*—and now a prince at the party I was working to add a little excitement to the evening.

Things were definitely looking up. As long as I didn't think too hard about the gaping void that was my future.

The sprawling penthouse was already crowded, even though the party had just begun. The two-story room with vaulted ceilings had been transformed into a winter wonderland, the interior balconies sparkling with twinkling white lights. A plush red carpet ran down the center of the wide, curving staircase—either in a nod to Christmas or in honor of their regal guest—and every surface dripped with Christmas luxury.

I navigated carefully through the crowds. So far, I'd managed to avoid any klutz incidents at work, and I wanted to keep it that way. At least it wasn't a banquet. I'd much rather stroll through a crowd in a ridiculous elf costume than work one of the elaborate five-course dinners where it felt like the staff was constantly serving and clearing. Tonight was much more relaxing. I threaded past women in gowns and men in tuxedoes, invisible in the crowd as I passed out champagne.

The decorators really had done a wonderful job. Based on the cheesy elf costumes, I'd expected an over-the-top explosion of Christmas cheer, but the sparkly costumes added a touch of whimsy to the formal surroundings and the overall effect was the perfect blend of festivity and elegance.

Mistletoe had been scattered around the room and I couldn't help noticing a tall, dark-haired man standing beneath one of the boughs, seemingly oblivious to the merry mischief-maker above his head. There was something familiar about him, and I found myself walking closer as he turned. He almost looked like...

My jaw dropped. *"Dom?"*

It was my jogger. Here. In this penthouse with these fancy people—wearing a purple sash with all sorts of medals pinned to his chest.

A purple sash.

No. No no no, please, no.

He hadn't spotted me, standing a few feet away with my Spock ears and tray of glasses, but he was scanning the room. Any second he would see me—

"Your Highness?" A voice spoke from his other side and my relief that his attention was drawn away was matched only by my disappointment that he answered to *Your Highness.*

He wasn't just some random guy who'd decided to wear a purple sash to a Christmas party.

He really was the prince.

And completely out of my league.

I shrank down, half-hiding behind my tray, hoping to make a quick escape before he turned back again— when a slender hand with a delicate snowflake-pendant bracelet plucked a glass off my tray. Distracted, I wasn't prepared for the sudden change in weight distribution and the tray tilted sharply, the four remaining champagne flutes all sloshing their contents toward the elegant silver-haired woman with the snowflake bracelet.

"Oh!" I reached for the glasses with my free hand while simultaneously angling my tray hand to correct the tilt, trying to avert disaster—and the glasses which had been veering precariously toward the silver-haired woman tipped back in the opposite direction. And abruptly spilled their chilled bubbly contents all over me, dousing the front of my elf costume.

"Oh, dear, I'm so sorry." The woman with bracelet put her free hand on my arm. "Are you all right?" Her perfume—which smelled like peppermint—wafted over me as my face flamed and champagne dribbled down my front.

"I'm fine. It was my fault," I insisted, shrinking in on myself and trying to be as invisible as possible. "I just need to clean this up," I said, hoping to escape before anyone noticed the spill, but when I dared a glance toward Dom, I found him watching.

My mortified gaze collided with his and my face heated again. I couldn't seem to stop making the wrong kind of impression on the prince.

The *prince*.

My jogger was a prince.

I turned and fled back to the kitchen—and I still couldn't wrap my head around it as I burst through the swinging door. I handed the empty tray and dripping glasses to the dishwasher and darted back to the laundry room that served as our breakroom to find a towel to dry my costume.

This morning, I'd been so hopeful. I'd thought... well, I'd thought everything in my life that didn't make sense was about to fall into place. He'd seemed so perfect. Almost too good to be true.

And he was. He was a *prince*. And princes didn't fall for girls like me.

"Jenny?" Margo appeared suddenly in the laundry room doorway, her brow wrinkled with concern. "Are you all right? You ran back here like your hair was on fire."

I sniffed, trying hard to cling to my composure. "Did you see that?"

"The spill? It's no big deal. Everyone spills." She reached for a hand towel. "We'll get you dried off—"

"It's *him*, Margo. The jogger I was telling you about."

Margo's eyes widened. "He's here?"

"Oh, he's here. He's the *prince*."

Her jaw fell open as if it was on a hinge. "The prince." She grabbed a magazine out of her purse where she'd hung it on a hook and flipped through it until she found the right page. "*This* prince?"

My stomach curdled as I stared at the headline "Europe's Most Eligible Royal" emblazoned above a picture of Prince Alexander Dominic. Dom himself.

I slumped back against the wall. "I can't believe I argued with him about fairy tales. He must think I'm such an idiot! We actually talked about princes! I didn't know he was a royal!"

"He probably thought you were charming," Margo soothed. "It must be exhausting to have everyone recognize you all the time."

"I knocked him into the snow! And the next time I saw him, I poured champagne all over myself."

"Better than pouring champagne all over him," Margo commented helpfully. I groaned and she handed me the towel to dry my costume. "He probably didn't even see the champagne thing."

"Oh, he saw. He was looking right at me."

"He couldn't take his eyes off you! That's a good thing."

"He's a *prince*, Margo!"

"And you're a saint," Margo insisted loyally. "Who takes all the leftovers from the catering events to a local women's shelter? Who volunteers all her free time at Paws for Love? If you ask me, you're the one who's too good for him."

"You might be a little biased." I stared at her over the terrycloth. "I'm a dog walker and a catering server, not Cinderella."

"Why not? You're about to be the next big thing in publishing—"

"I botched the interview," I blurted out. Margo's mouth snapped shut and I added, "I made a fool of myself trying to describe what I liked about *Wuthering Heights*—and before you ask, no, I haven't actually read it. So I don't think I'm about to be the next big thing." I sank down onto the bench, defeated. "I don't know what I thought I was doing. I know next to nothing about books and publishing—"

"You don't have to be an expert right of out the gate—"

"But shouldn't I know something? I talked to Rachel, and she and Chloe think I have unrealistic expectations—"

Margo held up a hand in a stop sign. "Okay, stop freaking out because your sisters came out of the womb knowing who they wanted to be. You'll find your thing. You'll figure it out. Don't worry! And maybe your thing is being a princess."

"Be serious."

"I am being serious," Margo insisted. "Who better than you? At least promise me you'll talk to him. He could fall madly in love with you and whisk you away to his castle—and of course I would visit you every summer and be the best Royal Best Friend in the world."

I knew I should laugh, but all the lightness had drained out of me.

Me, as a princess? I had even less idea what being a princess entailed than I did a job in publishing—though I was reasonably certain it involved confidence and social poise I simply didn't possess. I may admire real-life princesses and enjoy a good fairy tale, but I'd liked the Dom I met in the park because I'd been myself with him—every clumsy, awkward inch. Everything had been so easy, so natural. Even when I had been babbling, he'd seemed to like me more for it. I'd felt that bubble of happiness that was tied to the possibility that he didn't see someone ridiculous when he looked at me, that he might actually like me exactly the way I was—and then he'd shown up tonight as Prince Alexander Dominic, so completely unattainable that all that lovely sense of possibility had popped like an over-inflated balloon.

"Why did it have to be him?" I asked, disappointment turning the words into a whisper. "I liked him so much when he was just Dom, but if he's a prince—"

"He's still just Dom." Margo squeezed my shoulder. I knew she was trying to comfort me, but we both knew the truth. He had never been Just Dom. There had never been a chance. "Come on. Let's get back out there. It's Christmas. Anything can happen at Christmas."

I couldn't share Margo's confidence, but we did still have a job to do. We slipped back into the kitchen and I ducked to avoid the watchful eye of Stewart, a more senior server who wasn't a manager but seemed to think he had the right to tattle on anyone who dared to take an unauthorized break. Margo, on the other hand, stood up straighter and tipped her chin back, staring him down.

"What?" she snapped when he gave a little smirk as he collected a tray of canapes. "Some guest spilled champagne on Jenny and I helped her get cleaned up. File a complaint with HR, why don't you?"

I expected him to back down instantly—few could withstand Margo's withering glare—but Stewart sniffed haughtily. "It makes more work for all of us when you two slack off."

"When have we ever slacked off?" Margo challenged, clearly ready to go toe to toe. I slipped in front of her, grabbing another tray and meeting Stewart's eyes with apology in mine.

"You're right. I'm sorry. Now why don't we all get back out there?"

Stewart flashed Margo a smug, triumphant grin which had her rolling her eyes at me as he disappeared back into the party. "Why do you always apologize when you know you didn't do anything wrong?"

I adjusted my grip on my tray. "Not everything has to be a battle. It doesn't cost me anything to be diplomatic."

"See?" Margo said as we stepped back into the

winter wonderland. "You'd make an amazing princess. Diplomatic to a fault."

"To a fault?" A deep, slightly-accented voice spoke from our left and my stomach pitched.

Chapter Five

I KNEW EVEN BEFORE I LOOKED who would be standing beneath the archway to my left.

Margo caught my eye, an eager expression on her face, before I turned toward the sound of Dom' voice, mortification swamping me.

"I'll just go, um, serve these," she mumbled and scurried off like the traitor she was, leaving me alone to face the embarrassment—and the prince.

If anything, he was more handsome than I'd remembered.

He wore a slight smile and a dazzling dress uniform, medals gleaming on his chest like a paragon of princeliness while I stood there wearing glitter, fake ears, and a champagne-doused elf costume which was now sticky as well as itchy—and he'd just heard Margo talking about my supposed princess credentials.

Perfect. He probably thought I was some obsessive prince stalker.

"I..." Should I curtsy? Was that what you were supposed to do when you realized the man you'd accidentally assaulted earlier in the day was royalty?

"Your Highness," I mumbled, sinking into a sort of bob that I really hoped looked more graceful than it felt. The last thing I wanted was for him to realize how flustered I was, but right now I felt about as cool and collected as Prince Harry.

Prince Harry. As I straightened, the realization hit. "You probably know the real Prince Harry, don't you?"

Dom's mouth twitched. "Distant cousin," he admitted. "Ninety percent of the royals in Europe are descended from Queen Victoria."

I cringed. "Of course you are."

"Don't worry," he assured me. "He would probably love the dog."

"That's not what you said earlier."

"At the time, I believe I was still trying to recover from being tackled."

I groaned. "I can't believe I tackled a prince. And then I argued with you about princes!" Though I could barely remember what I'd said past the mortification, couldn't think about anything beyond the fool I'd made of myself.

"You did seem very passionate on the subject." His smile was soft and forgiving—the man really was a prince. "And I liked getting your take. I was never much for fairy tales."

"Of course not." He was busy *living* one. "I'm so sorry. I had no idea who you were—"

"I figured that much out."

The doors to the kitchen swung open again and I moved out the path. Dom gently caught my arm and tugged me with him into the shadows beneath one of the room's balconies. He released my arm almost instantly, but my breath still went short at the touch and I could feel the lingering imprint of his fingers. I couldn't meet his gaze, scared he would see my inappropriate awareness of him written all over my face.

"I will admit at first I thought it was a pretty impressive scheme to meet a prince—I've never had someone try to knock me over with a dog before—but then I realized you really had no idea who I was."

"I'm so sor—"

"You apologize too much, you know that?" His mouth curled up slightly.

"I do actually know that," I admitted. "But I also have a tendency to do way too many things that need apologizing for."

He ducked his head slightly, meeting my eyes. "I meant it when I said it was nice. Meeting you. I don't get a lot of that—people treating me like I'm just another guy."

"I didn't think you were just another guy," I blurted—then felt my face explode with heat. "I mean, not that I, that is, I..." I sighed. "Why can I never turn invisible when I want to?"

Dom laughed, his eyes crinkling—and I realized he was standing under mistletoe again. Seriously, how much mistletoe had they put up at this party? My gaze locked on the stuff and my mouth went dry.

"I would think invisibility would come in handy for one of Santa's elves," he said, and it took me a moment to catch the reference—my embarrassment intensifying at the reminder that I was standing there talking to a prince in a freaking *elf* costume.

"I'm not a full-time elf. This is just a side gig."

"That's right. The queen of odd jobs."

I couldn't believe he'd remembered. "Or maybe just duchess of them."

He grinned, inclining his head in a *touché* gesture—and for a moment, it felt like it had that morning. Like we were just two people enjoying a moment together.

But he was still a prince and I still had no idea how I was supposed to behave, standing there in my elf costume with a tray of brie puffs.

"I didn't know this was your party," I said. "I didn't even know the guest of honor was a prince until I got here."

"Jenny, I know." His voice was soft, but it was the fact that he remembered my name that made my ability to form sentences evaporate. "And it isn't really *my* party," he went on. "The company does extensive business in my country and every year, a member of the royal family is invited to attend the December board meeting and the Christmas party afterward. This year, it was my turn, but now that our business is concluded I'll be heading back home to San Noelle tomorrow."

"Oh," I murmured softly, the word *tomorrow* slicing unexpectedly deep. I wouldn't be seeing him in the park again. Not that anything could've happened if I had. He was a *prince*. I swallowed down the lingering traces of disappointment and put on a game smile. "Is it horrible to admit I've never heard of your country? And I'm usually pretty good at geography."

"Not many Americans have. It's a small kingdom tucked into the French Alps, near Switzerland."

The doors to the kitchen opened again, reminding me that I really ought to get back out to the party, circulating my puffs, but I was never going to have the chance to speak to a prince again, he was leaving *tomorrow*, and I simply had to make this moment last.

I sidled a little deeper into the shadows. "What's it like? Your country?"

"The entire kingdom could fit inside the island of Manhattan." He smiled fondly as he described his home. "But we have some of the most beautiful mountain views in the entire world. There's a lake in front of the palace so clear that it looks like a mirror, reflecting the mountains so perfectly you feel like you could dive in to climb them. It freezes over in the winter and my family used to ice skate on it when I was child, though I can't remember the last time we did. I haven't thought of that in years."

I smiled at his enthusiasm. "You must have wicked sledding hills. Iowa isn't much for mountains, but my parents used to take my sisters and me to this sledding hill every Christmas Eve and the only way they could drag me off it was by telling me we were going to upset Santa's delivery schedule if we didn't get home."

"Oh, we're much too busy at Christmastime for sledding."

"Bite your tongue."

He laughed. "It's true. San *Noelle*. My country is obsessed with Christmas and our Christmas festival is legendary. It starts with the tree-lighting ceremony two weeks before Christmas. That's what I have to fly back for. Then there's some new holiday obligation every day until Christmas."

"You make it sound like work."

He shrugged. "It's tradition. And my father hates anything that upsets tradition. I know the festival is special to a lot of my people, so I don't mind it, but when you *have* to do any task, it becomes something to get through, rather than something to enjoy. The next few weeks will be an endless parade of ceremonies and appearances, all leading up to the Christmas Ball."

"You have a ball." I sighed, closing my eyes in wistful Cinderella bliss. "Of course you do."

When I opened my eyes, he was smiling, his eyes crinkling at my reaction. "It's the event we build up to the entire year. The public rooms in the palace are filled to capacity. Dancing, music, more food than anyone could ever eat..."

"Is it all champagne and caviar?"

He cocked his head. "Why do I get the sense you aren't much for champagne and caviar?"

"Other than the fact that I'm wearing one of them right now?" I grinned, shrugging. "I don't know. I guess I've always felt like hot chocolate and warm cookies are more festive."

"Ah. We aren't so much about festive as formal. Tradition, you know."

"So no mistletoe?"

His eyes crinkled again, in that way I was *really* starting to like. "What would a Christmas Ball be without mistletoe?"

I felt my mouth curling into a smile and forced it into somber lines, feigning seriousness—and fighting the urge to look up at the mistletoe above our heads. "Tell me truthfully, has anyone ever lost a shoe at one of your balls?"

He laughed. "No. We insist on very secure footwear."

"Probably a wise policy when you have eligible princes roaming around."

He smiled, crystal-blue eyes glinting—

Until a light, feminine voice with Dom's accent spoke from the edge of the shadows. "Dominic. There you are."

The light in his eyes dimmed as I stepped back quickly, lifting the tray of Brie puffs as if they could explain why I was lurking in the shadows with the prince of San Noelle, leaning entirely too close to him and sharing entirely too many smiles.

Dom—or rather Prince Dominic, since the new arrival curling her arm through his forcibly reminded me that he wasn't *just* Dom—turned his head toward the woman. "Andrea."

The woman was exquisite. Elegant and poised, in a glittering silver gown that hugged her sleek lines. Her dark hair matched Dom's and was coiled into some elaborate updo that I would never have been able to replicate.

"Everyone's been wondering where you snuck off to," she asked softly, her gaze flicking between Dom and me. "Is everything all right here?"

I was trying to skulk back toward my job—which I really should have been doing the entire time—when Dom turned to me with a wry lift of one eyebrow. "May I present Her Grace, Grand Duchess Andrea Korlova? Dray, this is..."

He paused. Was I supposed to supply titles? "Just Jenny."

His lips quirked up. "Just Jenny." The introductions complete, his eyes gleamed at me as if sharing some inside joke, but the magic of our easy rapport had been lost and I felt awkwardness tangling my tongue again. "Dray and I have been friends since we were in diapers, and we always try to look out for one another at these social events. I'm sure she came over here to make sure I didn't need rescuing from you."

Because that was his life. Being accosted by random women everywhere he went because he was a *prince*.

"Good—good to have a friend like that," I stammered.

"Essential," Andrea added, still eyeing me cautiously before turning her attention back to Dom. "But that wasn't why I came over. People really are looking for you, *Your Highness*."

Dom grimaced at the way she emphasized his honorific. "Duty calls." He looked back at me and the ease that had softened his expression slowly left his face. He was still handsome, but seemed to be pulling further and farther away from me with each second. Something almost sad entered his eyes. "Jenny." He nodded.

I knew what he must be thinking. It wasn't like we were ever going to see one another again. We'd had our moment in the park today and had managed to steal a little more time tonight, and it had all been lovely— but he was a prince and I was a cocktail elf. There wasn't exactly a future there. I could dream about going to his Christmas Ball and waltzing beneath the mistletoe, but we both knew I wasn't princess material. I was Just Jenny. And he was leaving.

I bobbed another awkward sort of curtsy—as if to remind us both how completely incapable I was of blending into his world. His eyes crinkled in a slight smile—then he was gone into the crowd with elegant Andrea.

And it was time for me to let go of the pretty fairy tale and get back to reality.

Chapter Six

T HE PARTY FLEW BY, TIME passing impossibly fast considering how badly I wanted the minutes to stretch. I kept trying to sneak glances at Dom without looking like I was stalking him, while simultaneously trying not to spill canapes or champagne on myself or any of the guests in my distraction.

It was not my best night.

Luckily, Margo was running interference for me—when she wasn't pumping me for information about what *exactly* the prince had said to me and why I hadn't leapt on him the second I saw the mistletoe.

"I still can't believe you didn't kiss him," she muttered later as we were taking our turn changing out of our elf gear in the breakroom. "The mistletoe was *right there.*"

"I try not to run around kissing unwilling men." I tugged off my prop ears and dropped them into their container before tugging my ponytail loose and finger-combing my hair.

"Honey, I saw the way that man—excuse me, that

prince—was looking at you. There would have been nothing unwilling about it."

I rolled my eyes at Margo's exaggeration. Dom was nice, and yes, we'd had a little moment, but I'd had a lot of time to think about it over the last couple hours as I'd watched him be all princely and schmooze the execs at the party, and I was now thoroughly convinced it hadn't been a kiss moment.

Some girls are born to be fairy-tale princesses and some, well, some just aren't.

I've always fallen into the latter category.

I'm the kind of girl people think of as cute, not regal. There are women who marry princes—actresses and polished socialites, women with status and poise, women like *Andrea*—and then there's me. Unsure, directionless, Midwestern, boring Jenny James.

I may have watched the royal weddings with Margo, waking up early so we could squeal delightedly when Will kissed Kate on that balcony and sigh over the way Harry looked at Meghan, but I didn't expect that kind of fairy tale for myself.

That wasn't real life.

Real life was the canine version of Prince Harry, and Margo, and struggling to make rent. "You wanna get shawarma on the way home?" I asked Margo. "After we drop off the leftovers?"

"I shouldn't let you change the subject." Margo frowned at me in the mirror someone had hung on the door, where she was bending to redo her makeup. "But I'm meeting Harish for a late dinner. Do you mind doing the shelter run alone?"

"Of course not," I said, grateful to be talking about anything but Dom. "Have fun with Harish."

"Well, he's no prince, but he is pretty dreamy." She fluttered her lashes. "How do I look?"

"Amazing," I assured her. "He won't know what hit him."

"He never does." Margo's smile was all confidence as we gathered up our things and headed for the door, leaving our elf suits on the rack with those the other servers had already shed.

Margo would've definitely kissed the prince when she had the chance.

I sighed, trailing her into the kitchen to collect the leftovers the cooks were boxing up. Shortly after I'd started with the catering company, the girl who'd been doing the shelter run before me had landed a role in the touring company of *Book of Mormon*. The owners liked having the excess food go to local charities and I'd volunteered to be the courier on the nights I worked—it had seemed like the least I could do. Some nights there was more than others, but tonight, there were several bulging bags. Apparently, the guests had been too distracted by the prince to eat much—not that I could blame them.

"Are you sure you can get all this yourself?" Margo asked, taking one of the bags as I thanked the cooks and picked up the other.

"I'll manage," I assured her, heading toward the service exit as Margo fell into step beside me.

The penthouse was one of those luxury types where the help could be whisked out a separate exit so the posh people who lived there never had to see them in the elevators. The catering and cleaning staff should've been the only ones using this hallway, but as we grew closer to the service elevator, I heard a voice speak in that now-familiar accent and whatever I'd been about to say to Margo stuck in my throat.

"Your car should be arriving any moment, Your Highness."

My heart skipped a beat at the *Your Highness* and I froze in place, grabbing Margo's arm to halt her as well. From her wide eyes, she'd heard the voice too. She opened her mouth and I shook my head frantically in an attempt to shush whatever she might have been about to say. If we could hear them, they could hear us—

And then I heard *him*.

"Thank you, Franz."

He was right there. Right around the corner in front of the elevator. I wasn't sure whether to turn the corner or run the other direction. Should I talk to him? What would I say? He was still a prince and still leaving tomorrow—

Margo shoved me forward and the momentum almost carried me into sight. I caught myself just in time and whirled around, gesturing silently at her to knock it off—and then an accented female voice spoke around the corner. "Looking for someone?"

"Hm? What do you mean?" That was Dom again. My heart stupidly fluttered.

"Just Jenny, perhaps?" Andrea asked archly—and Margo's eyes looked ready to pop out of her head as she frantically mimed me forward.

"And if I am?"

My heart stuttered at that. Should I step forward? Say hello? I strained my ears, holding my breath.

"Dom," Andrea said gently. "You know the pressures of our world. Do you really think 'Just Jenny' would be capable of navigating that? In your position, you can't have a harmless flirtation. All it will take is one photo of the two of you leaking and her world will be thrown into chaos. Are you sure you want to do that to her? She seems very sweet—but does she have any idea what she'd be getting into with you?"

My chest ached at the words, my ears straining for his response, but it was Andrea who spoke again. "What do you think, Countess? You saw her."

"Oh, I saw her," another female voice joined the conversation, and I tried not to drown in the mortification of all these fancy people discussing the commoner.

The elevator dinged on arrival and Margo shoved me forward again, I spun toward her, hissing softly for her to stop it—and missed the next part of the conversation in the shuffle.

When I heard them again, it was Andrea who commented, "At least we're going home tomorrow."

"Margo! Jenny! Wait up! We've got one more!"

Margo and I squeaked and whirled toward the shout from the kitchen. Dante, one of the cooks, emerged from the kitchen holding another box of leftovers. I cringed, wondering if Dom had heard Dante yell my name, but there were no more voices from around the corner.

The elevator was gone.

"Thanks, Dante," I mumbled, accepting the box.

"G'night, kiddo." Dante gave a nod and returned to the kitchen—and I turned back to find Margo had rounded the corner and was standing in front of the elevator frowning.

"Why didn't you say anything?" She stabbed the button with one long finger. "He was right there."

"He's a prince, Margo."

"I know!" she exclaimed. "You're good enough for a prince. What's more, you're good enough for a man who treats you like a princess. You liked him. I know you did, I saw you talking to him. So why not just step around the corner and say hi?"

"He's leaving tomorrow."

"That doesn't mean he's never coming back. Or that you can't go to San Whatever."

"San Noelle." The elevator arrived—empty of princes—and we stepped inside. I silently hoped Margo would drop the subject, but I should have known my friend wasn't done.

"He likes you. You like him—"

"And what that duchess said isn't wrong. My life would turn upside down."

"So? You'd be with *him*. And you'd be an amazing princess. Honestly, Jenny, if I could just give you some of my confidence—"

It was a familiar refrain. From Margo, my parents, my sisters, even my academic advisors back in school—to have faith in myself. To not be afraid to go after my dreams. To not be so scared of failing that I never picked a path or took a risk. But it was easy to say and hard to do. How did you ignore that little voice in your head that said big dreams were for other people?

Something bright sparkled on the floor of the elevator and I frowned, crouching toward the flash of light. "What on earth..."

Margo broke off her speech as I picked up the

delicate silver bracelet with the same sparkling snowflake charm I'd noticed on the wrist of the silver-haired woman earlier. Looking at it closely, I saw that the snowflake was encrusted with dozens of tiny diamonds.

"It must be worth a fortune," I murmured as I stood, showing it to Margo, the dazzling snowflake resting on the palm of my hand.

"It's a sign!" she squeaked. "Your prince must know who it belongs to. Now you have an excuse to contact him to return it."

"We have a procedure for returning items lost by the guests."

Margo groaned as the elevator doors opened on the bottom floor and we stepped out. "Jenny. Promise me you won't turn it in to lost and found. This is your chance—*take it*. The universe is throwing you at this guy. Listen to it!"

We stepped out into the December night—and I looked down at the bracelet in my palm, glittering like a captive star. Was the universe trying to tell me something? Could I really be that brave? Could I really be Cinderella, only with a bracelet rather than a shoe?

I closed my fist around the bracelet and Margo squealed delightedly, jumping to the conclusion that I'd decided to go after Dom. She hugged me, gushing, "He's staying at the Plaza. Give me those bags. Harish and I will take the leftovers. Anything in the name of love. Promise me you'll text me all the details."

"Margo."

"Promise!"

I shook my head, feeling like I'd been strapped to

the unstoppable freight train of her enthusiasm. "How do you even know where he's staying?"

Margo just looked at me. "Honey. Did you really think I wouldn't know all the good gossip? Please. A little respect."

My lips twitched. It was tempting. Incredibly tempting...

Now that the idea was in my head, I was starting to get excited by the thought of seeing him again. One last chance to see him before this was just a memory. Obviously, nothing would come of it, but I couldn't stop remembering the way his eyes had crinkled before he smiled.

"Jenny?"

"I promise," I murmured, hugging her back and trying to absorb some of her confidence by osmosis.

Margo squeaked delightedly. "Text me as soon as you get home, okay?" she reiterated, grabbing the bag of leftovers I'd been carrying. Harish came around the corner, his hands thrust into his pockets, and Margo rushed toward him, calling out, "We're doing the shelter run for Jenny and wait until you hear why!"

I watched my best friend fling herself against her fiancé, rocking him on his heels. His laugh echoed down the street before the two of them set off together. I kept my hand closed tight around the bracelet. The Plaza was only a half a dozen blocks away. I could do this.

I turned in that direction, mentally rehearsing what I would say to him—it wasn't every day you got a chance to talk to a prince. Again. I smiled to myself, excitement building—

And a flash of silver hair beneath a streetlight caught my attention.

My breath caught.

She was halfway down the block and I told myself it couldn't be the same silver-haired woman from the party, but as she stepped toward a waiting black town car she turned toward me, and I saw her face clearly.

And my heart fell.

The universe didn't want me to see Dom. It had dropped the rightful owner of the snowflake bracelet right in front of me.

The car door opened, seemingly on its own, and the silver-haired woman stepped toward it. I could have let her disappear inside, could have pretended I didn't see her, but instead I ran down the street, her bracelet clutched tight in my fist. "Ma'am? Ma'am!"

The woman turned toward me with a questioning look that cleared as soon as she saw me—as if she recognized me even without the elf ears and covered in winter gear. "Oh, hello, dear."

"I think you dropped something." I held out my hand, opening it to reveal the sparkling snowflake bracelet on my palm.

"Oh!" The silver-haired woman gasped when she saw it, smiling brilliantly. "Mischievous thing. It does have a tendency to escape on me."

It was an odd way of saying the clasp was finicky, but I figured that must be what she meant. She gently lifted the snowflake off my palm, trailing the delicate silver chain, and I squashed the little surge of disappointment that wanted to rise as I released my excuse for seeing Dom again.

"I would have hated to lose it." She held the bracelet

by the chain, cocking her head at me as the diamond-encrusted snowflake twirled, catching the light. "It's very kind of you to return it. You could have used it yourself." She smiled conspiratorially. "It's magic, you know."

Was she joking? She seemed completely serious. Through my volunteer work, I'd met a few people who had a very loose relationship with reality—though you didn't usually see them dripping in diamonds. But she seemed harmless enough, a sweet, friendly old lady—though her face looked much younger than her silver hair implied.

"It's very pretty," I said.

"Oh, it's not about how it looks. It's about what it does." She tapped my nose and I blinked, startled. "You're very pretty too, but that's not why I'm going to grant you a wish."

"A wish?"

"Haven't you ever made a Christmas wish?" She moved her wrist and the snowflake dangling from her fingers began to spin, the light flashing off the diamonds hypnotically. Something about it seemed to snag my attention and make it impossible for me to look away as she spoke in a smooth, lilting voice. "I saw you tonight and I wondered if the magic would pick you—and here you are. So honest, returning something so valuable. So kind. I certainly think you've earned your reward. What is your wish?"

"I don't need a reward." I shook my head, inexplicably dazed. The sugary scent of peppermint seemed suddenly overpowering around us. "Do you smell candy canes?"

"I insist," the woman said, the snowflake twirling

faster now as lights seemed to flicker at the edge of my vision. "One wish. And no wishing for world peace. Something for yourself. Something you need."

"Who are you?" I asked, trying to shake off the daze.

"Does it matter? Though I will say your costume tonight was very inaccurate."

"You're an elf?" I asked, bewildered.

"Elves, Christmas spirits, *La Tante Arie*, fairy godmothers—who needs labels?" The pendant spun faster, making me feel dizzier the longer I stared at it, but I couldn't look away. "Make a wish," she whispered. "What do you wish for, Jenny? What do you truly want?"

Had I told her my name? Had Dom? His face rose up in my mind. His genuine smiles. His incredible blue eyes and the way they seemed to look right into my heart.

"Just one wish..." The scent of peppermint and evergreen grew stronger, my eyelids becoming heavy. A wish... One Christmas wish... One little Christmas miracle...

My lashes fluttered and I could see it. The vision of exactly what I would want, if I were brave enough to wish for it. If I let myself dare, I could be that girl. It could be my turn...

"I want a fairy-tale Christmas," I heard myself say, captivated by the light of the spinning snowflake, my voice seeming to come from a great distance. "The whole Cinderella deal. That's my Christmas wish. To be the princess and go to the Christmas Ball in a beautiful kingdom and dance with the prince who falls madly in love with me and kisses me beneath the mistletoe. I wish for that."

The light shooting off the spinning pendant coalesced into a blinding flash. The streetlights flared like candles in a storm, and a peppermint-scented wind gusted down the street, bowing the tree branches and sending my hair whipping across my eyes as a rich voice said a single word that seemed to reverberate down my bones.

"*Granted.*"

The hair on my arms stood up and I gasped, closing my eyes as the peppermint wind whirled around me in a cyclone.

I clutched my coat tight around me, bracing myself—

And the wind suddenly died, leaving an eerie stillness in its place. When I opened my eyes, the street was empty.

The silver-haired woman and her snowflake bracelet were gone.

Chapter Seven

"Hello?" I spun in place, searching for some trace of her, but it was as if the silver-haired woman with the peppermint perfume had never been there at all. Even the town car had vanished. "Ma'am?"

Goosebumps covered my arms and I shook my head, my thoughts strangely fuzzy. What had just happened? Had she hypnotized me?

I stepped out of the street as a car passed, shaking off the surreal moment and the memory of the candy cane-scented hurricane.

I still felt off-balance as I made my way to the train back to the apartment Margo and I shared. In a stroke of luck, the subway car was nearly empty, and I claimed a seat tucked against the window. I sank down and stared out at the darkened subway tunnels, trying not to think about Dom. Determined to distract myself, I opened my bag to fish out my phone—and right there, sitting on top, was the magazine Margo had been reading, folded open to the page about Dom.

"Europe's Most Eligible Royal."

I almost shoved the magazine aside, until I saw the

subheading I hadn't noticed before. *"Is San Noelle's prince about to tie the knot?"* My heart stuttered and I found myself frantically scanning the article for details—and studying the full page spread of photos of Dom with the duchess I'd met tonight. The one he'd called a childhood friend.

The one he was apparently going to propose to at the San Noelle Christmas Ball.

I hadn't gotten a romantic vibe from the two of them, and Andrea hadn't seemed even remotely jealous when she was noting Dom's interest in me by the elevator. But then again, why should she be jealous? I wasn't really competition. She was precisely the kind of woman who married a prince. And me? Just Jenny. Not exactly palace material.

The article gleefully speculated that it was obviously only a matter of time before Dom and Andrea tied the knot, and wouldn't it be romantic if the proposal happened at the very Christmas Ball where his father had famously proposed to his mother?

My stomach tightened and I sank down lower on the subway seat. At least I hadn't gone to the Plaza. At least I hadn't embarrassed myself any further.

I shoved the magazine to the bottom of my bag, trying to bury my tangled feelings just as effectively. I didn't know Dom. He'd just been a possibility, nothing more. A lovely dream. A Christmas wish.

The train came aboveground in Queens and my phone buzzed with a text notification. I ignored it, staring out the window at the passing lights. By the time I got off the train, Margo had texted me three times, asking how things were going with the prince. Not known for her patience, my roommate. I waited until I was letting myself into our building to text back that I was home safe. I confessed that I'd run into the bracelet's owner and given it back to her directly instead of going to the Plaza, but I left out the bizarre thing about the wish. It felt silly to even think about it—more dream than reality.

I ignored the flurry of responses from Margo as I climbed the three floors of our walk-up. I didn't need her to tell me that I'd chickened out again.

I unlocked our apartment and let myself in, flipping the switch we'd connected to the Christmas tree's twinkle lights though I left the overhead lights off. Two weeks until Christmas. I tried to find comfort in the Christmas cheer, but all I felt was a sudden swamping sense of exhaustion as the weight of the day caught up with me.

I'd flubbed an interview, met a prince, discovered he was a prince, discovered same prince was practically engaged to someone else, and made a ridiculous, impossible wish all in one day. I stumbled, nearly running into Margo's poofy princess wedding gown, and corrected my course.

It would've been nice if the wish could've possibly come true, I thought wistfully, my legs growing unnaturally heavier with each step toward my bedroom. A Christmas Ball, a handsome prince... They wouldn't have solved any of my problems, but they could have been a lovely break from reality.

A fairy-tale Christmas.

With Dom, of course. The only prince I could imagine dancing with at a Christmas Ball.

He'd made his nation's holiday celebrations sound like work. Like an obligation. But I couldn't help thinking it would be magical. If only... If only I really were a princess. If only I really was the kind of girl who could belong in his world. The kind of girl Perfect Andrea would never question as belonging there. The kind of girl who could end up with the prince.

I barely made it to my room, staggering with exhaustion, and dropped my bag on the floor with a thunk before falling face down on top of my comforter, crashing into sleep so hard it felt like I was falling down a well.

A well that smelled like peppermint and seemed to carry the echoes of distant sleigh bells.

I hoped to dream of Dom, but instead flashing snowflakes and peppermint gusts blew through my dreams, spinning me around and jumbling everything up. I could still smell candy canes when I pried my eyes open the next morning. The light was unusually bright in my room and I groaned, rolling away from it—

And frowned as I encountered fluffy down softness. Not the lumpy mattress of my secondhand bed. This was indulgence in tactile form. Lavish and cozy. My eyes flew open.

I wasn't in my bed. I wasn't in my apartment at all.

Sheer opulence greeted me on all sides, and I twisted to take it all in. How had I gotten into the world's silkiest pajamas on thousand-thread-count sheets? Was this some sort of bizarre kidnapping scheme where the kidnappers whisked you out of your own life and dropped you into the lap of luxury?

Because the room was definitely luxurious.

I sat up in a tangle of sumptuous bedding, twisting to try to stare everywhere at once.

My entire apartment could fit between the elegantly wallpapered walls, which were punctuated by multiple sets of tall, hand-carved French doors. High, coffered ceilings arched above me and massive furniture pieces that would have dwarfed any other space looked right at home in the expansive bedroom—including the king-size bed I was currently swimming in.

"I'm still dreaming," I whispered, just to hear my voice in the room. "I'm totally dreaming."

But it didn't feel like a dream.

Then one of the room's doors opened and I *knew* I was dreaming. Prince Harry scampered in, his tail furiously wagging his greeting—

—followed by Prince Alexander Dominic of San Noelle in head-to-toe princely regalia with a lazy smile on his face. "Good morning, darling."

Darling?

Nobody had better pinch me. I didn't want to wake up.

Was this what my subconscious thought the Plaza looked like? Had my dreams whisked me away to the hotel I hadn't visited last night, straight to Dom's suite?

"Sleeping in?" Dom asked as he crossed to a mirror and straightened a medal that was pinned to his chest. Prince Harry padded over to prop his front feet on the edge of the bed and beg for attention. "You'd better get moving. The reception starts in half an hour. Would you like me to call your lady's maid?"

"My what?" I reached down to ruffle Prince Harry's ears—and froze when I saw the gargantuan rock on my left ring finger. "*Whoa.*"

I'd never seen a diamond that big in real life. It

75

was *gorgeous*. Impossibly gorgeous. The kind of extravagance you see on movie stars...

And royals.

Oh, this was a *good* dream.

"Do you have to let him up on the bed, Jenny? We've discussed this."

I looked over at the *prince* of freaking *San Noelle*, who was scolding me like we were an old married couple, and I nearly giggled. "Down, Harry," I told the dog, who dropped to the floor with a canine sigh— apparently in my dream, the Plaza hotel allowed pets, though they probably did in reality also, if you were engaged to a prince. I wiggled my fingers, admiring the epic ring.

"My father wants you to butter up the French ambassador," Dom said as another door opened and a young woman in a crisp uniform entered the room.

"Good morning, Your Highnesses," she called cheerfully. She crossed to the heavy drapes and whisked them open to reveal not the New York skyline, but a panorama of the breathtaking mountain vistas.

"Holy monkeys." My eyes popped and my jaw dropped as I tried not to gawk—but that was some seriously impressive work my subconscious was doing. Apparently, the setting for this dream wasn't the Plaza, but the mountain kingdom of San Noelle.

The woman bustled around the room, setting a tray with something that smelled temptingly like coffee on an ornate little table while Dom crossed to the bed. "I'll see you down there," he murmured, dropping a kiss on my cheek.

I lifted my hand to my cheek, startled by the warm, real feeling of the casual kiss. "Down...?"

"Come on, Prince Harry," Dom said to the dog, patting him on the head. "Let's let your mistress get ready."

Dom strode out of the room with Prince Harry at his heels, and I gaped after them for a moment before scrambling out of bed and going straight for the window. Gorgeous mountain vistas stretched in every direction. A cute little town was nestled below next to an ice-covered lake. It looked *exactly* like Dom had described the capital of San Noelle. And it looked *real*.

Impossible.

But this didn't feel like any dream I'd ever had.

I threw open the window and cold mountain air hit my skin. Sounds rose up from the courtyard below and the scent of pine wafted up to me on the breeze.

My knees went weak. No way.

"Your Highness? Did you decide which dress you'd like to wear for the reception and which for the tree-lighting ceremony tonight?"

I looked over my shoulder, trying to figure out who she was talking to, but the maid was watching me expectantly.

"Princess?" she prodded gently—and the other shoe dropped. I lifted my left hand. A second ring nestled beside the rock on my finger, a slim, diamond-studded wedding band.

Not engaged to the prince. *Married.*

"Oh wow," I whispered, making a beeline for the coffee—which tasted like *real coffee* and even seemed to be waking me up. That shouldn't be possible in a dream, right? But what other explanation was there?

I gripped my coffee cup, my gaze skipping

everywhere around the room as I considered the options.

One: amnesia. I'd hit my head or something and somehow completely forgotten that I'd *eloped with a freaking prince* and run away to his winter kingdom. If that was true, then it raised the question of how exactly I was going to explain *that* to my parents—but that kind of selective amnesia didn't seem particularly likely.

It was much more probable that I was dreaming.

Unless...

"The wish," I whispered.

I'd wished for a fairy-tale Christmas. Could I really have woken up *married to a prince*?

No dream had ever felt this real.

But that was impossible. Wasn't it?

So not amnesia, not the impossible wish, too real to be a dream...

A prank, maybe? Though it would have to be an incredibly elaborate one. Something Dom was in on. Was he really a prince? Or perhaps an actor friend of Margo's? Could this whole experience be a ridiculously over-the-top Christmas present? Or some kind of hidden camera thing?

I scanned the room for hidden cameras. Not that I knew what they looked like, or where they might be hidden. If this was a film set, it was an impressively realistic one. They'd certainly spared no expense— which raised the question of *why*?

What possible reason would anyone have for pulling something like this?

As crazy as it sounded, the idea that all of this was

the result of the wish actually made the most sense. Which made *no* sense.

"Your Highness? The dress?" the maid prompted gently, and I realized I'd been standing there muttering to myself over my coffee and probably looked like I'd lost it.

Okay. What would a princess do?

Apparently, there was some kind of reception I was supposed to go to. Dream, wish, prank—whatever this was, I should probably play along. Hopefully, I'd either wake up or figure out the rules of the game soon.

Which meant I needed a dress. "I want to look at the options again," I announced in what I hoped was a princessly way.

The maid nodded, seemingly relieved by my declaration, and opened one of the sets of French doors beside the bed. Still cradling my coffee, I followed her into what appeared to be a dressing room where she pushed open another set of double doors—and my breath whooshed out on a gasp.

It was heaven.

I walked to the center of the room and turned slowly in a circle, trying to take it all in. It wasn't just a walk-in closet. It was a suite for clothes. A walk-in paradise. There was an entire nook just for shoes. One wall was lined with evening gowns, another with cocktail dresses. A hat-rack overflowed with hats. I'd never thought of myself as much of a clothes person— my barely-scraping-by state hadn't allowed for a lot of shopping sprees since I moved to New York—but I could get used to this.

I looked around the room, my smile growing. Talk

about Cinderella. I set my coffee on a delicate little table so I wouldn't spill on anything that cost more than my first car and wandered over to run my hand along a row of gowns, shaking my head in awe as the silky fabrics whispered over my fingers. "Hel-lo, Fairy Godmother."

Two cocktail dresses had been plucked out of the couture feast and were displayed to one side. They were both exactly my style—but my style on an unlimited budget. One was a gorgeous rich green and the other a bright, festive red. "They're both so beautiful."

"If I may, Your Highness?" the maid murmured. "The red would look incredible with your white coat with the faux fur cuffs and you'll want a coat for the ceremony tonight."

"Sold." I grinned. "The green today, the red tonight."

My maid suppressed a small smile—and I wondered exactly how strange it would sound if I asked her what her name was. But before I could reveal my ignorance, she launched into action, gathering accessories, refilling my coffee cup from the tray she'd brought into the room while I was gawking at the clothes, and ushering me into the bathroom where an array of toiletries plentiful enough to make a spa proud had been laid out for my use.

She seemed to know exactly how to pamper me. I *felt* like a princess, and before long I looked like one too, twirling in front of the full-length mirror when Andrea, the duchess from last night—if it had been last night—walked into the dressing room.

I froze, feeling suddenly awkward in the face of the woman who was *supposed* to be marrying Dom, but Andrea was smiling like we were old friends. Maybe in this dream, we were. It wouldn't be the craziest thing that had happened this morning.

"Oh good, you're ready," Andrea said as she crossed to drop an air-kiss near my cheek. "Dom sent me to check on you. Apparently, the French ambassador is restless and until the new trade agreement is signed, *he* might as well be king."

I grimaced sympathetically—as if I had the first clue what she was talking about—and went along as she linked arms with me and began heading toward the door. At least that saved me the necessity of asking my maid for directions to the reception, which I had a feeling wouldn't have gone over so well.

"Franz was in a dither when you didn't make your entrance with Dominic," Andrea went on, bending her head toward mine with a wry grin as we walked. "You know how he is about his schedules."

Since I had no idea who Franz was, I made what I hoped was a vaguely affirmative noise.

"Don't worry," Andrea soothed. "I know everyone is making a big deal about the French trade agreement, but you have nothing to worry about."

I resisted the urge to laugh—having a feeling if I started, I might tip over into hysteria. What she said might be true, in a weird way, because none of this was real, it was just a wish or a dream or a fantasy, but it *felt* real, and that was starting to freak me out. Were they really expecting me to be a princess? What would the consequences be if I failed?

Before I could consider running for the hills, we arrived in an antechamber of some kind where a man who looked vaguely familiar was frowning at the tablet in his hands.

"Here she is," Andrea called cheerfully. "Ready for duty."

Tablet Guy looked up, visibly annoyed. "Are you unwell, Your Highness? Because I don't need to express to you how important this event is and punctuality—"

"—is the height of courtesy," Andrea broke in. "Yes, Franz. We know. Now are you going to have the princess announced or are you going to delay us even further?"

Franz gave Andrea an impatient look, but he spoke something into the Bluetooth device I hadn't noticed attached to his ear and then the double doors beside him swung open as a loud voice announced, "*Her Royal Highness, Princess Jennifer of San Noelle.*"

Chapter Eight

I REALIZED I WAS IN TROUBLE the second I stepped into the reception hall.

You know that moment in pretty much every fairy-tale movie where the princess or princess-to-be glides majestically down a staircase while everyone in the room gazes on admiringly and the prince is drawn to her by the sheer force of her beauty and grace?

This was not that moment.

This was more like that nightmare where you realize you have to give a speech and you've lost your notes.

And you're totally naked.

As Princess Jennifer, I was undoubtedly supposed to know the several dozen people filling the formal reception chamber, but all I saw was a mass of strangers. Every eye in the room turned toward me as I stepped inside. I tried to project regalness, but what did I know about being a princess?

My stomach churned as people bowed and nodded. Was I supposed to bow and nod back? I'd seen enough movies to know there was court etiquette that needed to be observed, but I had no idea where I fell in the ranking—or where anyone else fell, for that matter. My time as a caterer may have taught me which fork to use at a formal meal, but it wasn't going to help me in that sea of faces. Was I offending people? Creating an international incident by *walking into a freaking room*? Royals had training for this stuff for a reason.

At this rate, I'd probably end up bowing to the butler and high-fiving the king.

I didn't know what to do, but before I could give in to the impulse to run screaming from the room, Andrea linked her arm with mine.

I clutched her arm with an enthusiasm born of desperation as the buzz of conversation returned to normal levels—or perhaps it hadn't actually gone silent when I was announced and it had only been the ringing in my ears that had made it seem that way. "Help me," I whispered urgently. "I don't know who any of these people are."

I could tell myself it didn't matter—that it was just a wish or a dream and obviously not real—but it *felt* so real and I didn't know a single person. I couldn't see even see Dom.

Andrea smiled sympathetically, squeezing my arm. "I know. These things are always a mass of people you see once a year and yet you're supposed to remember every little detail about everyone. Come on," she murmured. "We'll get through it together."

I was so grateful to have an ally I didn't bother explaining that I *literally* had no idea who any of these people were. "Just don't let me high-five the king."

Andrea laughed. "Now *that* I would pay to see.

Though I suspect King Reynauld would be so startled that he wouldn't know what you were trying to do."

King Reynauld. I filed the name away. Was that Dom's father? Brother? Uncle? I needed a family tree at the very least. Or Google.

Google.

I hadn't seen a cell phone in my bedroom, but even royals had Google, right? "Do you know where my phone is?" I asked Andrea in what I hoped was a subtle way as she navigated us through a variety of dignitaries, greeting each one by name and with a courteous smile. No wonder Dom was going to marry her in the real world. She was perfect.

I tried to mimic her as Andrea slanted me a glance. "Did you misplace it?"

"I must've dropped it on my way to this alternate reality."

Andrea laughed and called one of the footmen over with a gesture so graceful and understated I couldn't have replicated it with a lifetime of practice. "Could you please locate Princess Jennifer's phone and have it brought here, Jacques?"

"Certainly, Your Grace. Right away." He bowed smartly and spun on his heel, darting out of the room in search of my salvation.

"I could get used to that," I muttered. "Imagine never having to find your own lost keys again."

Andrea laughed, gently squeezing my elbow where our arms were linked. "It does spoil you. Come on. I see the countess waving us over."

I plastered on a fake smile and braced for another awkward social encounter as Andrea guided me up a short flight of steps—and a flash of silver caught my gaze. My eyes widened, locking on a delicate wrist—and the glittering snowflake bracelet that flashed on it.

"You!"

The silver-haired woman smiled benignly at me as if she hadn't just thrown my life into a blender and hit puree.

At my side, Andrea ducked a little curtsy. "Countess."

"Countess?"

The silver-haired woman smiled. "Andrea, darling, I'm parched. Could you find me a glass of champagne while I speak with our Jenny?"

"Certainly, Countess." Andrea smiled serenely and slipped into the crowd on her mission. The silver-haired woman smiled at me.

"Technically, she outranks me," she explained as Andrea moved away, "but I was Dom's late mother's best friend and that comes with some perks."

I couldn't concentrate on rank and etiquette—I was too busy concentrating on the fact that the woman with the snowflake bracelet was *here*. My subconscious could have summoned her, since she'd been at the party last night with Dom and Andrea, but it was feeling more and more likely that this wasn't a dream. That I really had gotten my wish.

"I thought you were an elf, not a countess," I blurted, then felt ridiculous for saying it out loud.

She brushed away the question with an elegant wave. "I told you I don't care for labels."

She had said that. Right before she'd said my wish was granted.

"You did this, didn't you?" I waved around the ballroom with all its fancy people.

"You could say *you* did this," the countess corrected with a smile. "It was your wish."

"I didn't think I'd wake up married! Christmas wishes aren't real. You don't just magically become a princess overnight."

"Well, no. I don't. But you did."

"That's impossible," I insisted. "*This* is impossible."

The countess sighed. "I find people are entirely too reluctant to believe in impossible things."

"That's because they're impossible!"

Her brow pinched. "Really, Jenny. I'd thought you'd be a little more grateful. This is some of my best work and all you can focus on is what's supposed to be possible. I don't have to be here, you know." The countess turned away in a huff—and my panic spiked at the thought of losing the one person who could explain what was happening.

"Wait! Please. You have to tell me what to do." I caught her arm before she could escape, but she looked down at my grip on her with an arched brow, making me realize we weren't alone and I was supposed to be acting like a princess, not grabbing the guests. I blushed, releasing her with a hasty apology, and she sniffed.

"I don't have to do anything. *I* didn't make the wish."

"But you granted it, didn't you? I don't know how to be a princess."

"Then you really should have been more careful what you wished for, my dear." She patted my arm. "Don't worry. I'm sure you'll figure it out."

"Figure it out? Isn't there a rule book for wishes? You can't expect me to figure all this stuff out on my own. What if I cause an international incident?" I glanced around the room at all the dignitaries I didn't know. "None of this is going to have lasting effects, is it? It isn't *really* happening, right?"

She shrugged. "That depends how you define real. And lasting effects."

"What's that supposed to mean?" My stomach dropped. "Will there be consequences?"

"Of course there will. That's just physics. Cause and effect."

I blanched. "But this isn't real!"

The countess frowned. "You're very hung up on reality. Honestly, Jenny, I expected a little more gratitude."

"I am grateful!" I insisted, lest I offend the magical woman who seemed to be in control of my destiny right now. "I just don't know what I'm doing."

"Of course you don't," the countess said blithely, looking over my shoulder with a smile. "There you are, Jacques."

I turned, startled, and saw the footman Andrea had sent in search of my phone standing behind me, trying to be as invisible as possible. I knew that feeling—trying to provide some service for a guest at a fancy catered dinner without making them think you were intruding on their privacy.

That I could do. Princess stuff? Not so much.

"Your Highness," he murmured, extending a phone to me.

"Thank you, Jacques," I said, taking it automatically. I looked down and realized this wasn't my phone with the broken case held together with duct tape. This was the latest model iPhone. The phone of a princess, not my five-year-old beat-up cell. I wasn't even sure I knew how to *use* this model.

"I'm sorry. This isn't mine," I started to protest, but when I looked up from the phone Jacques had already melted back into the crowd. I turned back to the countess—and she was gone. Of course. Vanished again, leaving only the scent of peppermint in the air to convince me she'd been there at all.

I groaned. "I really wish she'd stop doing that."

At least she'd confirmed that this wasn't a dream, but rather my wish come to life. If I could make myself believe that.

I frowned down at the phone. Maybe I could Google *how to tame your Christmas elf fairy godmother.*

Or at least figure out what my new family tree looked like.

I pressed my thumb on the phone and it unlocked. I Googled the royal family of San Noelle—and the first picture that popped up was of *me.*

Well. Me and Dom. In full wedding gear.

Apparently, the royal wedding had been international news.

"Holy monkeys," I whispered, flipping through pictures and articles.

I'd married a prince.

My heart began to beat faster as I found myself starting to believe that this was truly real. That I had somehow made a wish and woken up in an alternate reality in which Dom and I had actually made it to happily-ever-after-ville.

If it was a dream, my subconscious would have

had to come up with all of these details all on its own, which didn't seem likely. And it *really* didn't feel like a dream.

"You'd better not let my father see you on that phone."

I looked up, and my knees almost melted. *"Dom."*

I lowered my phone, hiding it against my side and trying to lock the screen so he wouldn't see that I'd been Googling us, but he wasn't looking at the phone, or at me. His attention was on a passing dignitary as he nodded and smiled.

"We're needed for the toast," he said, resting his hand on the small of my back in a familiar way that made me jump. He arched a brow. "Is everything all right?"

"Of course!" I gushed, then realized I was overselling it and dialed my enthusiasm down to normal levels.

I'm a princess, apparently, and we had a splashy international wedding I don't even remember, but sure, I'm fine.

Was I allowed to tell Dom about the wish? He'd probably think I was having a breakdown, so I might not have told him even if I knew it was permissible, but I wished I knew what the rules were. Would telling someone the truth break the spell? How long would it last? Was there some sort of mission I needed to accomplish or was this really all about my Cinderella experience? Because since I'd walked into the reception hall I didn't feel so much like Cinderella at the ball as I did a deer in headlights.

Waking up in the lap of luxury and playing princess sounded fun, but what if I couldn't get home again?

What if I was stuck here and there were repercussions for my actions?

Dom guided me through the crowd toward an elevated stage at the front of the room flanked by marble pedestals topped with beautiful poinsettias. My feeling of being on display multiplied with every step. Everyone watched us, nodding to us. Nerves roiled in my gut. I was so much better at being invisible than I was at being the center of attention. Luckily, it didn't seem like I was supposed to do anything but walk at Dom's side as he led me up on the stage.

An older man whose attire matched Dom's—and whom I assumed must be his father, King Reynauld— already stood on the stage, speaking to another man with a neatly trimmed white goatee. Dom accepted two glasses of champagne from one of the silent, somber footmen and absently passed one to me.

As my hand closed around the cool glass, I remembered our conversation about not being a champagne-and-caviar girl and almost mentioned it to him, but would he even remember that? Had it happened in this alternate world?

I searched his face for some sense of connection, some sign of the crinkly-eyed wry smile that had made my heart squeeze yesterday, but all I saw was the prince, regal and distant. He stood, his posture perfectly straight, and placed his hand on the small of my back again, so lightly that I wasn't sure if I was imagining the touch. He was facing the room and I took my cue from him, turning to do the same, and found myself confronted by a sea of faces.

My stomach pitched again and I placed a hand over

it, trying to stand still and look dignified as Dom's father began his speech.

"Since the foundation of our nation, the Christmas season has been a time of festive celebration and joy in San Noelle." He went on, extolling the virtues of community and tradition, but though he spoke about the joyous celebration of the season, his tone was about as merry and festive as a eulogist at a state funeral.

I glanced around, realizing for the first time that this was a *Christmas* celebration. The room was beautifully decorated for the holiday, yes, but everyone seemed so stiff. So formal. None more so than the men up on the stage with me.

Looking at the king, I could definitely see where Dom had gotten his somber prince mode. Had the crinkly-eyed laugh come from his mother? The countess elf had mentioned the late queen. Was the royal family still grieving her loss? Was that why everyone was so stiff and reserved? It wasn't exactly the kind of question I could ask.

I waited anxiously for the end of the king's speech. Not just so I could stop being part of the royal tableau that everyone was staring at, but because I was desperate for a chance to talk to Dom.

I'd wished for this because I'd thought... Well, I don't know what I'd thought. That we were soulmates? I certainly hadn't meant to wake up married. I'd wanted the fairy tale, yes—for Dom to whisk me off to his kingdom and dance with me at the ball and fall madly in love with me, but I hadn't expected any of that to actually happen. And now, I seemed to be stuck in a world where I was married to a near stranger and everyone expected me to know how to be a princess.

King Reynauld raised his glass and I automatically followed suit, hoping my smile didn't look as numb and dazed as I felt. Cameras flashed and I tried not to flinch, stapling my smile in place with sheer willpower. Just a few more minutes and I could talk to Dom. I had this feeling that if I could just talk to Dom, I could finally get my bearings. Somehow, we would figure this out.

But as soon as the photo op was over, he turned to me and murmured, "My father would like you to meet the French ambassador," and nodded toward the man with the white goatee.

Terror surged. I hadn't spoken to many people so far, but from the snatches of conversation I'd overheard it was clear how important the French ambassador was—and the countess elf hadn't exactly assured me that my actions inside the wish would be consequence-free. What if I said the wrong thing, ruined the trade deal and somehow that carried over into the real world?

"*Votre Excellence...*" Dom started toward the ambassador, and I grabbed his arm, panic making me feel lightheaded. I couldn't do this. I had to get out of here. My stomach roiled and I blurted the first thing that popped into my head.

"I don't feel well," I said, a little too loudly. "My stomach." Which wasn't even entirely a lie with nerves making my stomach do cartwheels.

On the other side of the stage, the king frowned and the ambassador looked startled by my sudden declaration, but Dom immediately turned to me with concern darkening his eyes. "You do look pale. Should we call the doctor?"

"I'm fine. I think I just need to lie down."

"Of course." His arm went around me and I leaned into him, taking comfort in his warmth even as guilt rose up over the way that I was lying to get out of the reception.

Dom guided me off the stage and I became aware of the commotion I had caused. Every eye in the room seemed to be watching us—and a few had even lifted their cell phones and were recording my exit. Apparently, when you were royal, even an upset stomach was newsworthy. I flushed, looking down, acutely embarrassed by the attention.

A knot of security personnel I hadn't even been aware of closed around us as soon as we reached the foot of the steps and I was suddenly grateful for the way their presence shielded me from prying eyes. And prying cell phones.

Tablet Guy—Franz, I remembered—appeared at Dom's other side, frowning over his ubiquitous tablet as we were all hustled out of the room. "I've notified the palace doctor. She's on her way."

I groaned internally. "That really isn't necessary. I don't need all this fuss."

"It's just a precaution," Dom assured me as Andrea burst out of the reception hall behind him.

"Is she all right? What happened?" the duchess demanded.

"Nothing happened," I insisted as we were ushered from one antechamber into the next. Dom said at the same moment, "It's her stomach."

"What did you eat, Your Highness?" Franz asked,

his stylus poised like he was going to make a note on his tablet. "We'll need to rule out poison."

"*Poison?* I just feel a little queasy. My stomach has been off all morning. I'm sure it's nothing."

"Just in the morning?" Dom asked

"Are you allergic to anything?" Andrea added, while Franz mumbled, "We'll need to screen for biological weapons. Anthrax."

"Don't overreact. I'm sure it's not anthrax. E. coli, maybe?" This from Andrea.

"It's just a tiny stomach bug!" I insisted.

But they weren't listening. Andrea and Franz spoke over one another as Dom gently squeezed my hand. "Humor us. Better safe than sorry. Do you have any other symptoms?"

I didn't have *any* symptoms, if you didn't count hallucinating that I was royalty, but I couldn't tell him that. Luckily, the doctor entered the room then—a no-nonsense woman carrying a small medical bag who instantly took charge of the situation, shooing the others away from me and guiding me to a chair.

"How are you feeling, Your Highness?" the doctor asked, businesslike and brisk as she took out a blood pressure cuff.

"Ridiculous?" I quipped, earning a small, wry smile from her.

"If only there was a pill for that."

I grimaced. *If only.*

Chapter Nine

IF YOU'VE EVER CONSIDERED FAKING an illness while royal, let me tell you, it's not nearly as fun as it sounds. Especially if you aren't a fan of being the center of attention.

This certainly wasn't what I'd hoped for when I wished for a fairy-tale Christmas.

The doctor checked my vitals while Dom, Andrea, Franz, and what felt like half the palace security staff looked on.

"I'm fine," I insisted. "I don't need all this."

"Better safe than sorry," the doctor said lightly as she shined a flashlight in my eyes, checking my pupils. "Any dizziness? Fatigue?"

"I guess I'm a little tired." Being a princess was mentally exhausting.

"You can skip the tree lighting tonight," Dom offered, his gaze never leaving me, though he'd moved back so the doctor could work.

Franz frowned over his tablet. "Sir, I must insist— if at all possible, the princess really should make an appearance at the ceremony. It's her first Christmas in

San Noelle and her absence will only generate gossip that she's seriously ill. We need to be defusing any speculation and refocusing attention on the holiday celebrations."

"I'm more worried about whether she is seriously ill than controlling the gossip about it," Dom said before returning his attention to me. "It's your decision. You don't have to attend. Only if you're feeling up to it."

"Can you lean forward for me?" the doctor requested.

"I'm sure I'll be able to come," I assured Franz as I leaned forward so the doctor could press her stethoscope to my back.

"You can skip the afternoon engagements, of course," Dom said—shooting Franz a look when he made a little sound of protest. "I'll have Franz look at your schedule and see what else we can remove."

"I'm sure I just need to rest."

"Your health comes first," Dom insisted, and I met his eyes, seeing for the first time the layers of worry, concern and something else in his gaze. My heart jumped up into my throat and my breath went short at the look in his eyes. Like I mattered. Like I was his world.

"Deep breath," the doctor commanded, her stethoscope to my back, and I reminded myself to breathe.

"I'll be fine," I whispered to Dom, the private words made awkward by the lack of privacy. It felt so strange to be having this conversation while a doctor took my vitals and a team of security guards surrounded us as if I'd been attacked rather than faked a tummy ache.

"You'd better be. I don't know where I'd find another

date to the Christmas Ball at this late date," he said in an attempt to lighten the mood.

"Luckily, I don't think you'll have to," the doctor interjected. "The princess's vitals all seem normal."

See? I wanted to say. *No need for all this fuss.* But the doctor was already turning to me and continuing, "I'll want to run a few tests, just to be safe, and I'd like you to rest this afternoon, but as long as you feel up to it, I see no reason you can't resume your usual activities after that."

"Thank goodness," Franz muttered, nodding to the security detail as if giving instructions, and I finally realized why he seemed so familiar. He'd been in the park yesterday, or whenever it was that I'd met Dom. One of the black-clad joggers. They must have been some kind of security detail. Of course the crown prince wouldn't be running around the park unprotected, even if he wasn't very well known in America.

The doctor stepped back and Dom helped me to my feet. I started to argue, "Are the tests really necessary—"

"For me," Dom said. "For my piece of mind."

"All right," I whispered, caught once again by the look in his eyes. It wasn't the crinkly-eyed connection, but there was something intent and serious that forced me to lock my knees so they didn't buckle. There'd undoubtedly be no end to the tests if *that* happened.

"Your Highness, we really should get you to your next engagement," Franz interrupted—he was so good at that. "Now that we've confirmed the princess is all right."

Dom hesitated, and I touched his arm. "I'm fine. Go. I'll see you later."

"Update me if anything changes," Dom insisted of the doctor before turning those soft eyes back on me. "Get some rest. You don't need to do anything until the tree lighting."

He squeezed my hand one last time, brushed a kiss on my cheek, and then he was moving out of the room, taking Franz and half the security detail with him. Andrea had slipped away at some point, but there was no lack of spectators, footmen and guards all watching me. I nodded awkwardly to my security team and allowed the doctor to guide me out of the room and through the halls to the palace infirmary.

I wanted to quiz her about everything from the palace's layout to whether there could be a possible medical explanation for hallucinating that you were a royal figure, but I was trying to avoid spending my entire day being prodded and tested. So I kept my mouth shut and played the part of the obedient princess, going where she told me and doing what she wanted me to, until I was released from the informatory an hour later—and I realized I had no idea how to get back to my room.

I needed a map, but even if I could find a palace schematic online, I couldn't exactly bring it up on my phone while under the watchful eyes of the pair of guards who'd been left with me. The last thing I needed was to spend my wish under the supervision of a psychiatrist because everyone thought I'd scrambled my brains.

I glanced at the guards and smiled. "I think I'll just, ah, walk a bit to settle my stomach."

That was natural, right? That way they wouldn't

think it was weird if I wandered aimlessly through the palace until something looked familiar.

I started off through the halls, thinking over everything that had happened since I'd woken up in the palace. At first it had been fun—the posh room, seeing Prince Harry and Dom, the crazy closet, being treated like a princess—but walking into that reception and having everyone watching me had felt entirely too real and I'd been off balance ever since.

I needed to see the countess elf again. I needed to figure out the rules of this place, and what she'd meant by "lasting effects."

And I needed to Google everything I could find about San Noelle, my new history, and how to be a princess. Everyone was calling me Princess Jennifer, so I had the same name, but was I still from Iowa? Had I met the prince in the park? Was this some possible future? Or a completely separate alternate reality?

After wandering for entirely too long, I finally spotted my maid exiting a room into the hallway. She stopped when she saw me, bobbing a curtsy and murmuring, "Your Highness," as the footman beside the door held it open for me.

Palatial apartment, sweet palatial apartment.

I really wished there was some way of learning the maid and footman's names without asking them who they were because I had a feeling everyone was already starting to wonder if I'd lost my mind. Since I couldn't think of a stealthy way to get that information, I just thanked them and slipped into the room.

Prince Harry scrambled up from the plush dog bed in the corner and scampered over to greet me. I knelt to cuddle him, overwhelmed with relief to be able to let my guard down.

"Can I get you anything, Your Highness?" the maid spoke from behind me and I jumped, not having realized she'd followed me into the room.

"No, thank you." I glanced up at her without standing from my crouch. "I'm just going to, um, rest."

She bobbed a curtsy and slipped out of the room. I wondered if Cinderella ever felt this way during her happily-ever-after: like she knew more about being a maid than being a princess.

The door clicked shut behind her and I realized I was finally, blissfully alone for the first time since those initial moments when I'd woken up in this alternate reality.

"I don't think we're in Kansas anymore, Prince Harry."

Prince Harry looked at me and flung himself onto his back for a belly rub, thrusting all four legs into the air. I obligingly rubbed his tummy, unspeakably grateful that he was here. "What do you think? Good wish?" He made a little noise I decided to take as affirmative and I smiled, sinking down onto the floor beside him. "Yeah, it could definitely be worse, though I have a confession. I don't have the first clue what I'm doing." He licked my hand, wriggling cheerfully. Prince Harry always had been a good listener.

I felt a little guilty for the lie about being sick, but I was also incredibly grateful for the chance to be alone. The weight of being a princess lightened now that I was in my incredibly gorgeous suite and no one was watching me or expecting anything from me. I'd been in stressed-out fight-or-flight mode since the second I fell out of bed this morning, trying to mentally catch up to everything around me, but now I finally had a moment to let everything sink in, and I felt... surreal.

"I'm a princess," I whispered, just to say it out loud—and it sounded just as crazy as I thought it would. "Princess Jennifer, charmed, I'm sure," I said haughtily, ruffling Prince Harry's ears.

He cocked his head at me and I laughed, shaking my head and flopped onto my back on the plush carpet to stare up at the coffered ceiling. I knew I should get up and change clothes, but the posh dress was already hopelessly wrinkled. How much worse could it get from lying on the spotless carpets of the royal suite? Prince Harry went into overdrive, leaping up and circling around me and trying to lick every inch of my face. "This can't be happening."

But here I was.

Maybe the countess or Christmas elf or whoever she was had been right. Maybe I wasn't being grateful enough. Yes, I didn't have a clue what I was doing, but I was in the lap of luxury. How many people woke up married to a gorgeous prince? With the world's most perfect dog, no less?

Prince Harry circled three times before flopping against my side with a puppy sigh.

"What do you think, Prince Harry? Should we find out who we are?"

First stop: Google.

I picked up my phone, unlocking it with my thumb, and pulled up the articles I'd been reading earlier. I needed a crash course in etiquette, and palace staff, and European dignitaries, but my first stop was trying to learn what my own history was.

It was surprisingly easy to find. Our wedding hadn't quite been the circus Meghan and Harry's was—San Noelle was a much smaller country and I wasn't a gorgeous actress—but there had been numerous articles on the Cinderella story of the American girl and the European prince.

Apparently, in this version of reality, my parents—my normal, no-frills, schoolteachers-from-Iowa parents—had unexpectedly inherited a title and a massive estate in France during my freshman year of college. When they'd moved to Europe to take over their responsibilities, I'd changed my major to political science and communications—and learned French.

"I speak *French*?"

Prince Harry twisted to look up at me from his back.

I clicked on a link and watched a video of myself giving a speech—in fluent French, though the words might as well have been gibberish for all I understood. It was, quite possibly, the most surreal moment in an intensely surreal day, watching myself speak a language I had never learned.

So far, everything at court had been English. Fortunately, that was one of the official languages of San Noelle, but what was I supposed to do if someone started speaking French at me?

"Oh, no, the French ambassador." Everyone kept saying I needed to charm him. They didn't mean *in French,* did they?

I read through the rest of my bio quickly. After graduating college, I'd attended a charity gala in Paris—*Paris!*—where everyone said Prince Dominic had taken one look at me and fallen head over heels.

He'd proposed only months after we met. We'd married the following summer and had been living in royal wedded bliss ever since.

At least I wouldn't be expected to know all the San Noelle traditions if this was my first Christmas, but even so, I wasn't that girl with that past. I was Just Jenny, not an heiress who spoke fluent French. Who did they expect me to be? What *were* the consequences the elf had mentioned?

Maybe it was a wasted effort trying to find the logic in a Christmas wish. I was actually believing this was *real*, because it was getting hard to believe anything else.

I bookmarked a few articles on our courtship to read later and opened a link to the Wikipedia page for the royal family, which—thank goodness—included a family tree complete with pictures.

Dom's father, King Reynauld, looked stern and unsmiling in all his pictures—except those taken when he was as young as Dom. In those, he wore a crinkly-eyed smile that looked just like Dom's. The queen was in those pictures as well. Queen Amilia, a gorgeous young woman who always seemed to have a secret smile waiting to appear in even her most serious photos—and then photos of a somber young Dom, at that gawky age between childhood and adolescence, walking beside the casket at her state funeral.

My heart clutched at the sight. She'd passed away when Dom was barely a teen—and it seemed, from the photos, like she'd taken all the laughter in the palace with her. Had Christmas been a time of laughter and joy when she was alive? Before it became so stiff and formal?

I filed the stories I found about her along with the courtship stuff under *things to read about later* and continued trying to memorize names and faces, but reading more about how Dom and I had met was irresistible and before long, I'd fallen down the rabbit hole of articles on our relationship.

"Your Highness? Are you all right?"

I jolted, sitting up suddenly—and realizing how it must look to my maid to find me lying on the floor, especially after my supposed illness. "I'm fine!" I said too brightly. "Is everything all right?"

The maid frowned but didn't push me on the bizarre behavior. Maybe that was one of the perks of royalty: no one pointed out when you were eccentric. "I came to see if you needed assistance getting changed before the tree lighting."

Changed. I glanced down at the lovely green cocktail dress I'd been wrinkling on the floor. "Right."

I scrambled to my feet, swaying a little at the head rush, and the maid rushed forward to pick up my phone and hand it to me before Prince Harry could trample it as he jumped up to see what we were doing.

She glanced at the screen of my phone, which was open on my Wikipedia page, and frowned. "Did someone edit your page?" she asked. "It's supposed to be locked. Do we need to have the PR team contact them to correct any errors?"

"No." As far as I knew the information was accurate. Unless that was just the public story and we really had met in the park. I searched my brain for some way to ask without sounding like I'd lost my mind. "I, ah, I had a dream last night that Dom and I met for the first time in New York, in Central Park. I was playing with Prince Harry and he was jogging and I knocked him over..."

My maid giggled. "The crown prince of San Noelle jogging in Central Park like a commoner?"

But he had. Hadn't he? That had been real life, hadn't it?

"Besides, you adopted Prince Harry together when you went to New York earlier this year. How could you have already had Prince Harry when you met? And what would you have been doing in New York?"

"Right," I mumbled, inexplicably sad that those playful moments in the park and at the Christmas party where I was dressed as an elf were no longer part of our history. "Crazy dream."

Who were we if we weren't those people who had clicked in the park? Who was *I*, if I'd never lived there? Was I even friends with Margo? I hadn't seen her in any of the Princess Jenny pictures. The pictures where we looked so serious and posed.

"Are we happy?" I blurted, somehow needing that one question answered more than any other. "The prince and I?"

My maid laughed, before realizing I wasn't laughing with her. "Of course you are. You're crazy about each other. That must have been some dream for you to question that. The prince loves you. That's one thing I know for sure."

"Of course he does," I whispered as my maid headed into the capacious closet. "I wished for him to."

But was it real?

"Your Highness?" she called from the closet.

"Coming."

Apparently, I had a tree lighting to get ready for.

Chapter Ten

IT HAD NEVER OCCURRED TO me how much thought and preparation went into princessly attire, but I was definitely getting an education now.

My lady's maid—whom I had finally figured out was named Amilia after the late queen—completely redid my hair and makeup, which was somewhat the worse for wear after my medical examination and sprawling on the floor being licked by a dog for half the afternoon. She curled and restyled my hair to perfectly accent the jaunty little hat I would be wearing for the tree lighting—though there had apparently been a flurry of emails between my maid and the palace's etiquette guru to ensure it wasn't traditional for a princess to wear a tiara for the ceremony.

A *tiara.* Because that wasn't surreal at *all.*

I was seated at my vanity, marveling at Amilia's skill with a curling iron, when a deep voice behind me asked, "How are you feeling?" and I jumped so high I nearly burned both Amilia and myself.

"Careful," my maid tsked, her concentration unwavering on my hair while I couldn't help gawking in the mirror at the man who was strolling up behind me, casually unpinning medals from his chest.

"Any other symptoms?" he asked as he lifted my hand and kissed my knuckles in a way that was sweet, but so formal it made me miss the crinkly smiles from the park. Amilia continued to work on my hair, both of them acting as if there was nothing at all unusual about the prince wandering into my dressing room while I was getting ready. And maybe there wasn't, just the normal, domestic routine with a prince, but I had a feeling it was going to take more than a few hours for the idea that I was *married to Dom* to sink in.

"I'm fine," I assured him. "It was nothing."

Dom nodded, studying my face as if trying to reassure himself that I really was okay, his fingertips gently cradling my chin.

"Do you always worry this much?" I asked, curious about this formal prince who seemed at once so similar and so unlike the man I'd met in the park.

He laughed, as if startled by the question. "Yes. I do." He dropped my chin, straightening and returning to the medal removal he'd been doing as he came in, absently setting them in a neat little row on the vanity, as if he'd done it a thousand times. "I think I drove Franz crazy this afternoon, badgering him for updates from the doctor on how you were doing. If I'd had my phone on me, I probably would have been texting you every five minutes—and you know how my father is about texting at state functions. He probably would have disinherited me and then where would we be? Not much work out there for former princes."

"Somehow, I think we'd get by." Though I made

a mental note to hide my phone whenever I saw the king. "I could always support us as a dog walker and catering server." I tossed the words out casually, testing to see if he would react to the reference to my real past. Would it ring any bells for him? Could that life have sent echoes into this one?

But Dom merely smiled without a trace of recognition, absently unfastening his cuffs.

"Luckily, I don't think it will come to that. At least, not as long as everything goes smoothly with the French ambassador."

Right. "Anything I should know before I meet him?" I asked, since I couldn't very well feign illness forever—at least not without ending up being poked and prodded by a team of medical specialists.

"Just be your charming self and he'll adore you," Dom assured me with a smile, gathering up the medals he'd set on the vanity. "You're our secret weapon."

He strolled out of the room, doubtless off to change into whatever a prince wore for a tree-lighting ceremony, leaving me staring after his reflection in the mirror. "Oh, good," I mumbled, as dread knotted in my throat. "No pressure."

Why had I spent so much time Googling myself this afternoon? I should have been taking emergency French lessons.

"*Voilà.*" Amilia declared, stepping back to admire her handiwork, and I nearly groaned at the French word. I was going to cause an international incident. I could just feel it.

But at least I looked amazing.

My hair was twisted into a sleek chignon. My eyes looked larger, my lips fuller, but I didn't just feel beautiful. I felt regal. "Amilia, you're a miracle worker," I informed her, gazing at the princess in the mirror. "Thank you."

My maid beamed, reaching for the hanger to her left. "And now, the dress."

The red tea-length dress fit as if it had been made for me—and for all I knew, it had been. The rich color did, indeed, look stunning with the brilliant white coat with the faux fur cuffs, and I stood in front of the mirror, looking like a princess and trying not to feel like a fraud.

"You look magnificent," Dom said as he appeared in the dressing room door, carrying his own elegant winter coat. The dress uniform he'd been wearing earlier had been replaced by a sleek designer suit, but even without the purple sash and the medals, he still radiated princeliness.

"Thank you. So do you." I just hoped I didn't trip over my heels and ruin the entire effect.

As he approached, his gaze searched my face. "Are you sure you're up to this?"

It was so tempting to say no. To take the coward's route, plead a mild case of plague and hide in the palace all night. But I'd wished for this. I'd wished for *him*. And part of me really wanted to know what that entailed.

I wanted to see this through. So I gave him my best smile and tried to forget my nerves. "Absolutely."

"In that case, shall we?"

He extended his arm and I placed my hand on it, trying to build up my courage. "Let's do this."

His smile had a cynical twist as he guided me

through the suite toward the palace corridors. "The sooner we go, the sooner we get it over with."

I scrunched my brow in confusion. "I thought you liked the tree-lighting ceremony."

"I do," he said, though the words sounded more automatic than heartfelt. "But it doesn't really matter whether I enjoy it or not. The ceremony isn't for me. It's for our people."

"That doesn't mean we can't enjoy it too. I'm actually kind of excited. And nervous." I grimaced. "Definitely nervous."

He smiled down at me, bemused. "You sound like we don't do these things every day."

"*Every* day?"

I'd thought all the ceremonial stuff must have been amplified for the holiday season. Was this really what every day was like? Meetings and ceremonies and constantly dressing for this and redressing for that? I had to admit I hadn't really thought about what the royal life must actually be like.

Luckily, Dom laughed as if I'd made a joke as we stepped out into the courtyard—and I tried to channel every princess in every movie I'd ever seen. I could do this. I just had to play the part. I may not be an actress like Margo, but I could do this.

Margo...were we still friends in this reality? We'd been freshman roommates in college—that had still happened, hadn't it? I desperately wanted to call her to get a dose of perspective like only she could give, but I seemed to have missed my window.

Distracted by trying to figure out where my real world ended and this new one began, Dom was handing me into the first of two black town cars with flags on the hood before I knew it. I caught a glimpse of his father climbing into the following car and thought perhaps Dom and I would get a moment alone together to continue our conversation and build on the fragile sense of reality I seemed to feel when I was with him. But Franz was already waiting in our car, in the seat facing ours. He began rattling off instructions for the evening as Dom climbed in and we pulled away from the curb.

Words like *schedule* and *precision* rolled over me as I gazed out the window. It was only five o'clock, but dusk had already fallen and faux gas lampposts along the side of the curved driveway came on as we wended our way down toward the park at the center of the capital where the national Christmas tree stood.

We passed through a set of gates, and all at once it wasn't just lanterns lining the streets—crowds of people pressed against barricades, waving as we cruised slowly past. Parents lifted their children on their shoulders to see and a thousand flags seemed to be waving everywhere I looked.

Dom smiled and waved—though the people we were passing must have had a hard time seeing us inside the car, in the darkness—and I took my cue from him, waving out the opposite window.

"Good crowd this year," Franz commented.

Dom nodded, still smiling and waving. "It's always a special time."

But it didn't feel special inside the car. It felt rehearsed and stilted and organized to within an inch of its life. Outside, the people might be laughing and passing cocoa and pressing together for warmth, but the mood inside the royal cavalcade was far from celebratory. I found myself remembering what Dom had said when we'd talked at the party the previous night about the Christmas season being something to get through. An endless run of obligations. My chest tightened with sadness at the thought.

Everyone deserved some holiday magic. Especially the man who'd grinned at me back in Central Park.

Though nothing felt like it had back in New York.

We arrived at the area security had cordoned off for the royal family and the two town cars rolled to a stop, met by a jubilant cheer from the crowd. *They,* at least, were in the holiday spirit.

Bodyguards approached the car in a well-rehearsed move, opening the door, and Dom got out first. A cheer rushed through the crowd as he extended his hand for me. I placed my gloved fingers onto his and held them there even after I exited the car, hoping for some sign that we were in this circus together, some squeeze or wink or something, but he simply placed my hand on his arm and turned back to the crowd with a wave.

I forced a smile, following his lead. Then we turned, continuing to wave, facing the other direction, and my breath whooshed out on a gasp. "*Whoa.*"

The palace loomed above us on the hill, illuminated from the ground by spotlights that seemed to make it shimmer like a fairy castle. The snow-capped mountains curved around it as if they had been created for the palace, rather than the other way around.

"What is it?" Dom asked, following my gaze. "You act like you've never seen it before."

"I—" I barely stopped myself from saying I'd only seen pictures and they hadn't done it justice. The photos I'd seen online hadn't managed to convey the majesty of the palace. "How can you ever get used to a view like that?"

Dom smiled—and then it happened. His eyes crinkled and he squeezed my hand where it rested on his arm. Just that, but it seemed to make the entire world go away until it was just us. Suddenly, all the insanity of the wish seemed to make sense. *This.* That promise of zing. *This* was what I'd wished for.

Franz appeared, frowning, and the spell was broken. "Your Highness, after the choir performs, you'll introduce your father and the ceremony will begin. Princess Jennifer, you'll press the button along with Prince Dominic to officially light the tree and open the festival. If you'll take your places..."

We were quickly ushered up onto the stage in front of the towering Christmas tree that dominated the square. Dom nodded stiffly to his father, murmuring, "Sir," and then we took our places beside him.

I'd been to tree lightings in my hometown, but nothing on this scale—or nearly this formal. Margo and I had always talked about going to see them light the tree at Rockefeller Center, but something had always seemed to come up. And now, here I was, about to light a tree that could give the one at 30 Rock a run for its money.

Dom and his father stood rigidly side-by-side, a matched set of stiff, regal posture as a children's choir began to sing. The poor kids looked more terrified that they were going to mess up and be thrown in the dungeon than they did filled with the joy of the season. I couldn't really blame them, given the way the royal family was watching them so sternly.

Where was the man from the park? My chest ached for him as the high, sweet voices hung on the last note of "O Tannenbaum." Dom stepped to the podium and began his speech, sounding eerily like a replica of his father from earlier in the day—more funereal than festive.

My stomach growled and I blushed, putting my hand over it and hoping none of the microphones had picked up *that*. I'd only had a couple of frou-frou little canapes at the reception earlier, and though my lady's maid had kept asking me if I needed anything as she was helping me get ready, it hadn't occurred to me to order a tray of snacks. Maybe not all of my stomach rumblings earlier had been nerves like I'd thought.

Scents from the festival square traveled to me, seeming to taunt me now that I'd realized how *hungry* I was. Roasted chestnuts. Fruit pies and savory pies. Cinnamon-dusted soft pretzels and sausages of every variety. Pastries and cookies and cakes, each scent more luscious than the last, and here I was, stuck on stage, wondering why I hadn't eaten all day.

It all smelled wonderful, but smelling chestnuts made me homesick for New York. Suddenly, I wanted nothing more than chicken shawarma from the little hole-in-the-wall place on my block.

Dom finished introducing his father and stepped back to my side behind a large red button. The king came to the podium amid cheers, and I half-expected some sort of dramatic New Year's Eve-style countdown, but instead, he simply spoke about the tradition of opening the festival and then turned to Dom and me with a nod. Dom took my hand, placing both of our hands together over the button. We pressed down and the massive tree erupted with light. The assembled crowd cheered, and the king gave a slight smile and a stiff nod to his people before moving toward the back of the elevated area.

"That's it?" I whispered, as Dom raised a hand to wave to the crowd and then turned us toward the stairs off the stage. I'm not sure what I had expected, but I was strangely disappointed by the anticlimactic ceremony.

"That's it," he murmured. "Now we just smile for the cameras and admire the crafts at the Christmas market, and we're done."

I wondered if admiring the crafts could include sampling the food. My stomach growled again and I pressed my hand over it as if I could contain the sound as we made our way down the steps that were so close to the tree that pine boughs snagged the skirt of my dress.

The scent of chestnuts hit me again and I looked toward the smell—right as a cameraman rushed forward and a flash erupted in my face. Startled, I swayed away from the light—and toward the tree—missing a step.

My breath caught and I could see it all playing out in horrifying slow motion—me tumbling into the tree, the entire massive thing toppling over, crashing down on top of the stalls at the Christmas market and ruining Christmas for all of San Noelle.

Then a firm arm wrapped around my waist, catching me in midair, inches from the tree. "Careful there," a deep voice murmured—and I looked up into the most gorgeous crinkly eyes.

"My hero," I whispered, only half joking.

Dom held me there as if I weighed nothing, as if it were only the two of us. The rest of the world seemed to fade away until it was just us in this moment. The lights of the tree flickered on the edge of my vision and he leaned an inch closer—only an inch, but it was enough that all of a sudden, I was *sure* he was going to kiss me. And why wouldn't he? We were married, weren't we?

As many times as Wish Dom may have thought he'd kissed me, I'd never been kissed by him—and all of a sudden, I couldn't imagine anything more perfect. My lashes fluttered closed—

"Your Highness. The French ambassador is leaving."

My eyes popped open. Dom grimaced, releasing me after steadying me back on my feet. That dang French ambassador.

"Are you all right?" Dom asked softly, offering me his arm again. "Is it your stomach?"

"I'm fine. Just hungry. I barely ate today," I admitted as we descended toward the crowds and our entourage of guards. "I'd kill for some shawarma right now."

He smiled. "Don't worry," he assured me. "We're almost done. We'll walk through the booths, then just tell the French ambassador how much you love his tie and we'll get out of here and get something to eat."

"Can't we stay and eat here, enjoy the festival?"

"We'd only disrupt it," he said softly. "This is for the people, not for us."

I smothered my disappointment—not even *one* little cinnamon-covered pretzel?—and smiled for the cameras as we began our ceremonial tour, two steps behind his father, flanked on all sides by a security detail.

The townspeople smiled, bowing and curtsying as we passed, and I had never felt more like a princess— which wasn't quite the feeling I'd been expecting. We were so separate from our citizens. So isolated in our security bubble.

"The ambassador is just ahead," Dom murmured into my ear, and we made our way to a tent filled with elaborate ice sculptures.

"*Votre Excellence*," Dom said, calling to the ambassador. He was an attractive older man with a neatly trimmed white goatee and when Dom spoke he turned toward us, pulling his attention away from the towering ice carving of a nutcracker he'd been admiring. Dom smiled, drawing me forward with a hand on the small of my back. "*Je vous présente ma femme, la belle Jennifer.*"

The lyrical French coming out of Dom's mouth reminded me why I'd faked an illness to avoid this meeting. Panic buzzed in my ears. Why hadn't I said my stomach was still upset and begged to go back to the palace right away? Or at least told Dom that my stomach flu had wiped all my knowledge of the French language out of my head? That was believable, right?

"*Bien sûr. Enchanté, votre Altesse Royale.*" The ambassador smiled, his arms extended welcomingly as he stepped toward me. Were we supposed to know each other? I'd had the impression I was meeting him for the first time, but maybe the French were really friendly because he definitely seemed to be going in for a hug.

I responded automatically, putting my arms

around him, and it wasn't until I felt his body stiffen in my grasp that I realized he wasn't hugging me back and had, in fact, been moving forward for an air kiss. I released him quickly, trying to cover my gaffe with an air kiss of my own, but the ambassador looked startled and uncomfortable as I stepped back to Dom's side. Dom, who was watching me as if I'd just groped the Queen of England. Thank goodness the king wasn't here to see this.

The ambassador cleared his throat awkwardly. *"Appréciez-vous le festival?"* he said—and they both looked at me expectantly.

French. A language I was supposedly fluent in. And a language I'd never studied. Though how different could it possibly be from Spanish? I knew a couple words...*yes, no.* I went with, *"Oui?"*

Dom and the ambassador both smiled and relief melted in my gut. Okay. I could salvage this. *Fake it till you make it, Jenny.*

The ambassador was talking again. *"Quelle belle tradition. Quel est votre tradition de noël préféré?"*

Another pause. Another expectant look.

"Ah..." Why had I taken Spanish? Why had I thought it would be a more useful language? I'd caught one word. *Tra-dee-cee-ow.* Tradition, right? He had to be referring to the festival or the tree lighting. I took a step back and waved one hand, meaning to encompass the entire experience and hopefully get away without a verbal response.

My hand smacked into a tall, spindly ice sculpture of a candy cane. It looked solid. It looked like no mere wave of the hand could knock it over.

Looks could be deceiving.

The candy cane lurched and I spun to grab it, yelping with horror. "Oh!" My security detail moved at the same time, circling around the candy cane and saving it from the forces of gravity. I backpedaled quickly, to give them space to save the day—

And backed right into the nutcracker.

It was larger. Heavier. But I'd hit it much harder than the candy cane, with my whole body instead of just my hand—and the bodyguards were all distracted. The nutcracker swayed ponderously. I reached for it as it seemed to tilt in slow motion—directly toward the French ambassador.

Adrenaline flooded my brain and I shouted, "*Attention!*" in a flawless French accent—which meant this had to be a dream, right? Speaking perfectly in languages you'd never learned *only* happened in dreams. Right? I had to be dreaming.

But as the nutcracker descended toward the ambassador, I realized my mistake.

This wasn't a dream.

It was a nightmare.

Chapter Eleven

IT'S AMAZING HOW QUICKLY YOU find yourself whisked back to the palace after you nearly crush the French ambassador with a giant ice nutcracker.

The security team swarmed around Dom and me. Everyone seemed to be speaking at once, and I was hustled into a town car before I knew what was happening. The ambassador was rushed away in an ambulance. Everyone assured me he hadn't been badly injured and had only sprained his wrist when he'd fallen while dodging the Nutcracker of Doom.

Dom's father had already shaken the obligatory hands and returned to the palace before I inadvertently attacked the French ambassador, but the news of the incident preceded us. We'd barely made it inside the palace walls before Franz was somberly touching the Bluetooth device at his ear and intoning, "His majesty the king would like to speak with you immediately. He's waiting in the council chamber."

"I'm so sorry," I said again—for the twelve-thousandth time, and this time no one told me that I apologized too much. Even Dom seemed nervous.

I didn't know what exactly the French ambassador was doing in San Noelle. I only knew that it was important, and I'd just managed to cause a major international incident with an *ice sculpture* at the national tree-lighting ceremony.

I tried to tell myself that it didn't matter. That I was inside the wish and this wasn't real—but the countess elf's words about "lasting effects" had my stomach tied in knots as Dom and I moved quickly through the maze of palace hallways.

He was still holding my hand. That had to be good, right? If he'd decided to divorce me on the spot, he probably wouldn't still be gripping my hand in his a little too tightly.

He'd asked me repeatedly if I was all right as we'd rushed to the car and driven the short distance back to the palace, but now that it was time to face his father, he wasn't looking at me anymore.

There had been cell phones, I knew. Lots of cell phones recording every second of the Princess of San Noelle committing Ice Sculpture Assault on a major political figure. It would be on the internet by now. And to think I'd been so happy *not* to have knocked over the national Christmas tree. Though, to be fair, that would've *much* worse. Maybe I should be thankful I'd only wounded the ambassador.

We reached what must have been the council chamber and Franz opened the door to reveal Dom's father and half a dozen somber-faced men and women. I started to follow Dom inside, but the king froze me with a look and a hard, "Just the prince."

Dom gave my hand a little squeeze before releasing

it. "It's all right," he assured me, but I could see the worry in his eyes, and I doubted even he believed that.

I bobbed an awkward curtsy—which I had a feeling didn't help my cause—and stepped out of the room. As soon as I exited, Franz snapped the door shut, positioning himself in front of it as if I was threatening to burst inside and start throwing around some more ice sculptures.

What was I supposed to do now? Go to my room and wait for my punishment like a child? What would a princess do?

But see, that was the problem. I wasn't a princess. And maybe *that* was why my wish had been granted. Not so I could experience a fairy-tale Christmas, but so I could realize I didn't belong here. To figure out that even fairytale lives were more complicated than they seemed—so I could learn to wish for things within my reach.

I'd watched the royal weddings. I knew how to be fancy and formal, thanks to watching dozens of attendees at the banquets I'd catered over the last couple years. I knew which fork to use and how to sit straight and smile serenely—but I wasn't a princess inside. I was just playing a part.

And the look Franz was giving me right now said he knew it.

"You don't like me very much, do you?" I asked him, too disheartened to be diplomatic.

Franz didn't even blink at the question. "It doesn't matter what I think."

"But you think I'm bad for him." I'd picked up on that much. Franz was a dictator with his tablet, but he was protective of the prince, and he saw me as detrimental to the royal family.

Another door to the council chamber opened around the corner, some late arrival slipping into the war council—and we both heard King Reynauld's raised voice. "This is *exactly* what we worried about when you married an American. Her connections in France were her *one* advantage, but it's obvious Andrea would have been much more suitable—"

The door closed again, cutting off the voices, and I tried not to flinch. To my surprise, Franz's stern expression softened.

"It isn't your fault," he said sympathetically— but then he went on. "You weren't raised for this. Inheriting a title as a young woman and marrying into the royal family isn't the same thing as being born and bred to this life. I know it can seem frivolous—the ceremonies and receptions—but your role is important. Performing it well is important. You represent something. San Noelle's economy, the very continuation of the country, relies on our international reputation and our diplomatic ties. We aren't rich in natural resources nor are we powerful on the international stage. We have to do what we can to foster a positive image—for tourism, for business ties. Everything you do reflects on this family and this nation."

I swallowed, feeling more than a little sick.

"Stop scaring her, Franz. She knows she messed up." Andrea appeared, moving down the hallway toward us. When she arrived at my side, she took my hands, squeezing them comfortingly. "Are you all right?"

I shook my head. "The French ambassador—"

"Is fine. And he'll have a great story to tell." She glanced past me to the door. "Did they tell you to wait here?" When I shook my head, she tugged at my hands. "Come on. Let's get you something to eat. Dom texted me and told me you were hungry."

I'd completely forgotten how famished I was—nerves had taken over my stomach—but my eyes pricked with moisture at her kindness as she guided me down the hall. Andrea was so perfect. So poised and kind. She'd grown up with Dom, which mean she'd been born to this. She was the woman he was about to propose to in the real world—the one he *should* propose to.

"I can't believe how badly I screwed up," I whispered as she pulled me into the massive, darkened kitchen. "You're the one he should be with. It's so obvious."

"Dom and me? Oh, sweetie, no." She opened the fridge, pulling out a platter of meats and grabbing a loaf of bread. "We never would have worked out. We're too alike. And besides, he doesn't love me. He loves you."

"Does he?" I echoed weakly. And if he did, was it only because I'd wished him that way?

He didn't seem like the same man who'd given me that zing in the park. He'd kissed me half a dozen times today—always on the cheek, always absent, never with intent. And that moment at the tree, when he'd caught me when I was falling and it had seemed like there might be something real—was it all just an illusion? Wishful thinking?

"That's hunger talking. Eat." Andrea dropped her finds on the counter and began whipping together sandwiches. *And she cooks, ladies and gentlemen.* "I know it's not shawarma, but I make a mean sandwich."

She slid one across to me and sank down opposite me, nibbling on a bit of bread. "Dom is crazy about you," she insisted. "This time of year is chaotic in San Noelle. It's a gauntlet of responsibilities. Once the Christmas Ball is over, I'm sure things will go back to normal."

But what was our normal? And if it went back to "normal," would I even be here?

"Is it always like this?" I asked Andrea softly. "So stiff and formal?"

"Oh yes," Andrea said. "Well. For the last decade anyway. I remember when we were young, when the queen was alive, she could light up a room by walking into it. The palace was a different place then, and she was always out in the town, talking to her people. Now it's all tradition and ceremony."

Dom had talked about tradition, about how his father loved nothing more. And here I was messing it all up.

I'd wanted to be here to be with Dom, but he was busy putting out the fires I'd started with my minor international assault on the French ambassador. I'd dreamt of being a princess, but the fact was I simply wasn't. And I was ruining everything for him by pretending to be.

After our sandwiches, Andrea offered to spy for me to see if she could find anything out and I retreated back to the bedroom—but I felt no better pacing in the luxurious confines than I had anywhere else. Prince Harry thumped his tail sleepily from his dog bed but didn't get up as I shrugged off my fancy coat and toed off my heels. I strode to the window, but the sight of the Christmas tree lit up in the town square below only reminded me of my shame.

This wasn't at all the fairy tale I'd expected. Cinderella had it rough in the beginning, but getting married and living in the palace was supposed to be the happily-ever-after, wasn't it?

My phone was resting on the bedside table and I made the unbearably stupid choice of checking to see what social media was saying. Note to self: checking social media is *never* a good idea when you nearly bludgeon someone with an ice sculpture.

They were calling me Princess Graceless. Which would have been funny if it hadn't been so true.

And apparently, the ice sculpture incident hadn't even been my only faux pas. There was a lively debate online over which was worse—hugging the French ambassador or trying to take him out with an ice carving. How was I to know French people didn't hug to say hello?

I sank down to the floor with my back to the bed and flopped my head back against the mattress, closing my eyes. What was I doing here? Could I undo the wish as easily as I'd made it? Would I want to if I could?

I just wanted Dom to walk in the door and tell me it wasn't a big deal. That everything was okay. But as the seconds stretched and he didn't appear, I began to feel more and more like I'd made a huge mistake by wishing for this at all.

I'd had this fantasy of how perfect life would be if I was his princess, living the fairy-tale life, but the reality was much harder to deal with. People expected me to be someone knowledgeable. Someone sophisticated. To know what I was doing. But I just wasn't good at being perfect and poised. I wasn't good at being what Dom needed.

Soft steps padded across the floor and then warm puppy breath huffed in my face as Prince Harry licked my chin. I smiled and opened my eyes, stroking his head, but even his furry face couldn't make me feel better. I needed someone to talk to who had two legs, not four.

Still stroking Prince Harry's ears with one hand, I opened my contacts list and right there at the top of the favorites was Margo. Thank goodness we were still friends, because I *needed* my bestie tonight.

I dialed her number, almost melting with relief when she picked up on the third ring. "Princess J!" she cried as she answered. "How are you this fine evening? It's evening there, isn't it?"

"I just caused an international incident by nearly crushing the ambassador from France with an ice sculpture."

Margo barely missed a beat. "Okay. So not your finest hour?"

I laughed, but only because it was either that or cry. "Oh Margo. I don't know what I'm doing here. What do I know about being a princess?" Once the words started, they just kept pouring out. "I'd be a better fit as a maid. At least then I'd be able to disappear in the background when I make a mistake instead of being a media sensation."

"I'm watching the video now," Margo admitted. "You know, it's really not that bad."

"You're lying, but I love you." I groaned, flopping

my head forward to thunk against my knees. "Why did I think I could be a princess?"

"Honey. You're an amazing princess."

"You're biased," I reminded her, the familiarity of the words vaguely comforting.

"All it is is a title. So you married a prince. Labels are overrated."

I blinked at the echo of the countess elf's words. The wish, my disastrous day—all of it piled on top of me and suddenly I needed to tell her. I needed to tell *someone* and Margo seemed like a bridge between this crazy world and my reality. If anyone would understand, she would.

"I have to tell you something."

"Are you pregnant?"

"What?" I yelped and Prince Harry, who had thumped down to lie against me, lifted his head in alarm. I petted him to soothe him. "Why would you ask that?"

"I don't know. You've been married a while. That website that does the royal baby watch has a whole page dedicated to you and Dom."

"That is so disturbing."

"So you're not?" Margo confirmed.

"I can't be pregnant. I've only been married for twelve hours."

A long pause met that declaration. "I'm sorry, what?"

"I know it sounds impossible, but last night I fell asleep in the New York apartment I've shared with you for the last two years and this morning, instead of waking up in Queens, I woke up married to a prince."

I could almost hear Margo's frown. "You lost me."

"I'm not a princess," I insisted. "My parents never inherited a title. I never studied political science or French. I *don't* speak French. You and I moved to New York after graduation because you wanted to and I was piggybacking on your ambition. For the last two years, I've been working as a catering server and a dog walker and applying for jobs that don't suit me at all because I don't know what I want to do with my life. And then yesterday, I was walking in Central Park with Prince Harry—who is one of the dogs at the shelter where I volunteer—and I physically ran over Dom. I had no idea he was a prince until later that day when you and I were serving champagne at the Christmas party where he was guest of honor. I met this strange countess lady who said she was a magical Christmas elf or something and told me to make a wish and because I liked Dom I wished for a fairy-tale Christmas and this morning I woke up *married to him.*"

I took a breath. "This isn't my life. I'm not a princess. I don't have the first idea what I'm doing and I'm screwing everything up for him."

"Right..." Margo murmured slowly. "Are you feeling okay?"

"I'm not making this up," I said so emphatically I knew I sounded like I was mid-nervous breakdown. "This is all part of my Christmas wish. It isn't real."

"Well," Margo mused, "If it isn't real, does it matter that you nearly brained the ambassador from France with a giant block of ice?"

"I don't know! I tried to ask the countess—or elf or whoever she is—and she said it could have lasting effects, whatever that means."

Margo clucked her tongue. "It's all fun and games until someone starts messing around in international politics."

"This isn't a joke, Margo!" I yelped.

"I know, I know, sorry. I'm just not used to my best friend calling me and informing me that she isn't actually married when I was a bridesmaid at the wedding. It was a really nice wedding, by the way, since apparently you missed it."

"I did miss it," I insisted. "I woke up this morning with clear memories of the last few years of my life which do not include a ring on my finger or a prince wandering around apparently in love with me."

"And you're complaining?"

"Margo! I need your help!"

"Right. Sorry. What am I helping with? Saving you from this horrible wish where you're a princess married to a man who thinks the sun rises and sets in you?"

"Does he really? Or does he only think he does because I wished for him to?" I asked, hating the insecurity in my voice, but I had no secrets from Margo. "He doesn't really know me. Whatever he thinks he feels isn't real. He's all sweet and caring and acting like we're married, but this is only the second day I've known him, and I've barely seen him all day. And when I do see him, it's not like we can really connect. It's all ceremonies and receptions and throwing around ice sculptures."

Margo snorted. "At least you can laugh about it."

"I don't know what else I can do. I don't know what I'm doing, Margo. How am I supposed to avoid more international incidents when I don't have the first idea how to be a princess?"

"Learn?"

She always made everything sound so easy. "How am I supposed to do that?" I pleaded.

"That palace is full of people who know all the rules, isn't it?" Margo said. "Ask one of them."

"They'll think I've lost it. I'm supposed to know all this already and there's only so much Google can do."

I could almost hear Margo shrug. "Sounds like you have two options. Let a few people think you're a little off because you need princess lessons, or let everyone think you are because you're not acting like you should."

"Well, when you put it like that."

Margo laughed and I smiled, letting the relief of talking to someone who felt like she knew *me*, not Princess Jennifer, roll over me. But my throat was still tight with nerves. "Do you really think I can do this?" I whispered.

"Oh honey. I've watched you do it. I know you can."

Chapter Twelve

I FELT BETTER AFTER TALKING TO Margo, but as soon as I hung up the phone my nerves still jangled. Dom still wasn't back and Prince Harry was curled against my legs, fast asleep. I considered going down to the council chamber to see if there was anything I could do to help, but one glance at my phone and the internet storm in progress had me chickening out.

I changed into the royal pajamas—which felt much more luxurious than I deserved—and climbed into bed, wondering again if this was all a dream and if I would wake up in my own bed in the morning, my wish complete. Part of me wanted to escape the scandal, but a much bigger part hated the idea of leaving this world—even if it was just a fantasy—when things were so uncertain.

And I really wanted to see Dom again.

I'd been supposed to fall in love with the prince, right? Hadn't that been part of the wish? The actual details of what I'd wished for were fuzzy, caught up in that peppermint cloud that had seemed to fog my senses when I'd made the wish, but I was certain I would have asked for that.

I sat up in bed, waiting for my supposed husband, fiddling with my wedding ring and trying to think of what I would say when he came in. I thought I was too anxious to sleep, but I must have dozed off because I jerked away at the sound of the door shutting softly.

Dom moved stealthily across the room, obviously trying not to wake me as he crossed to his dressing room, unbuttoning the collar of his shirt.

"How bad is it?" I asked, sitting up in bed.

"Don't worry." He glanced absently in my direction before he slipped into the dressing room. "Go back to sleep."

"Saying that doesn't make me worry any less," I called through the door. I waited a moment, but when he didn't respond, I climbed out of bed and padded across the floor. I didn't quite have the guts to walk into his dressing room—we weren't *that* married—but I leaned my back against the wall beside the door and spoke through the opening. "Does your father hate me?"

"My father hates unpleasantness and anything that upsets tradition," Dom said, after a slight pause. "It has nothing to do with you."

So basically *Yes, but I'm too polite to say that.* I cringed. "I'm sorry."

"Everyone knows that. No one thinks you did it on purpose."

"They just think I'm Princess Graceless."

A grunt came from the room. "I saw that one. Twitter always thinks it's so clever."

"I'm so sorry—"

"Jenny. Stop. You're fine. You weren't feeling well. You never should've had to go." He stepped out of the dressing room in pajamas and I wanted him to put his arms around me and say everything would be okay, but he moved past me toward the bed. "You know how my father is. All that matters is tradition and the prestige of the royal family. What we represent."

I walked slowly back to my side of the bed, Franz's words from earlier echoing in my head. "Those things are important," I murmured.

Image *mattered* when you were royal. It wasn't like being some catering server who spilled a glass. It wasn't my job at risk because of my clumsiness—it was the reputation of an entire country. Diplomatic relationships. International politics. And potentially the livelihood of tens of thousands of people.

"But they aren't the only things that are important." Dom sighed, the fight seeming to drain out of him as he met my eyes. "My father doesn't mean to be harsh. He has a frustrating tendency to cling to tradition, but you have to understand. The tree-lighting ceremony tonight... Some of these traditions were started by my mother. He doesn't talk about it—we never talk about it—but my father is very sensitive to things that touch on the memory of her."

I hadn't thought it was possible for me to feel worse. I was wrong. "I'm so sorry."

"Jenny. I know. It's okay. I'm just exhausted," he said, climbing into bed. "Can we talk about this tomorrow?"

"Of course," I murmured.

He was exhausted because he'd spent all day covering for me when I was "sick" and all night trying to clean up after *me*. I'd been in this wish one day and so far, all I'd managed to do was make things harder for him.

I didn't know how long this wish would last, but I didn't feel much like a princess. Maybe I should be wishing to wake up back in New York, back in the real world where I may not know what I was doing, but at least I wasn't ruining anyone's life but my own.

I woke up on my second day in the posh princess bed determined to do better.

I wouldn't cause international incidents by attacking foreign dignitaries with ice sculptures. No doctor would be called to assess whether or not I'd been poisoned by anthrax. And at no point would I risk knocking over Christmas trees that were the symbol of the entire freaking nation.

I would do better, dang it.

Dom was already gone when I woke up—probably off continuing to fix my messes.

I didn't know what my second day as a princess would hold—I just knew that I'd woken up as a princess again, rather than back in my New York apartment, so the wish wasn't over yet.

I needed to find that countess elf again, I decided with the clear head gained by a full night of sleep. I needed to figure out exactly what the rules of this world were and what exactly my wish entailed.

Then I needed to talk to Andrea about some princess lessons.

I'd decided last night that she was the logical

choice of instructor, along with my maid, who I was unlikely to be able to fool anyway. Today's resolution was to be a better princess. I was determined not to embarrass Dom again.

Which also meant I needed to find some way to make things right with the French ambassador.

I climbed out of bed with a game plan. Prince Harry bounded off his dog bed to greet me and I cuddled him for a moment before I rang for Amilia. While I waited for her, I brushed my teeth and gave myself a mental pep talk. There were certain ingredients to every fairy tale, and facing your fears was one of them. So I needed to step up and start facing my fears. Starting now.

"Today is a new day, Prince Harry. Today we pretend to be a princess and figure out this freaking wish."

"Your Highness?"

I jumped at the voice behind me and spun to face Amilia, flinching at the reminder that maybe I shouldn't share secrets with my dog since there were now people everywhere paying attention to every little thing I did.

Amilia stood watching me, radiating efficiency and sweetness.

"Right. Amilia. I need the Duchess Andrea and an amazing outfit that will make me look properly princessly at all the events on my schedule today. Help?"

Amilia was a marvel. Within minutes, she'd helped me select an appropriate outfit for the day's responsibilities and had slipped out to send a message to Andrea while I showered and dressed. I might not know what I was doing yet, but at least I looked the part of a princess by the time Andrea arrived a few minutes later.

I turned to face my Two A's, as I'd begun mentally calling them, and I almost lost my nerve, but I forced myself to stand up straight and met them head-on.

"Ladies, I need your help."

Amilia and Andrea exchanged a look and I spoke quickly. "I need a crash course in being a princess. I need you to teach me as if I know nothing. As if I just woke up as a princess yesterday with no warning." When Andrea frowned and Amilia blinked at me, I pushed on. "I need to know all the etiquette and how to dance and how to bow and who to bow to. All of it."

Andrea shook her head. "I don't understand."

"You want us to teach you to be a princess?" Amilia asked hesitantly

"Exactly," I confirmed. "As if I have amnesia and know none of it."

"Okay..." Amilia said slowly. She sounded more like she was appeasing me than agreeing.

"And I also need to speak with the countess..." I trailed off, realizing I still didn't know her name and I couldn't exactly call her an elf. "The countess?" I asked Andrea, who shook her head with a frown. "Um... silver hair? Beautiful, always smells of peppermint? She called herself, ah, *La Tante* Something?"

Amilia shook her head, baffled. "There isn't anyone like that at court."

"No, there is. I saw her yesterday at the reception. *You* talked to her with me," I said to Andrea. "The countess." Andrea just shook her head, as if she had no idea what I was talking about, and I searched my brain for another way of describing my errant fairy godmother. *Godmother.* "The one who used to be friends with the queen." At their blank looks, I tried to remember what she had called herself when she was talking about labels. *"La Tante Arie?"*

Both women blinked, broad grins spreading across their faces.

"What? Do you know her?"

Amilia shook her head, barely restraining her giggles. "She's a legend. A myth. It's like you asked us to find Santa Claus for you."

"So you *do* know her?"

"La Tante Arie?" Andrea laughed. "She's not real."

"But if she were real. If the legend were real—who would she be?"

"She's a good fairy," Amilia explained. "A children's story. A beautiful fairy who disguises herself as a peasant and wanders the countryside with her donkey, granting wishes to the charitable and virtuous at Christmastime."

"Okay, except for the donkey and the peasant disguise that sounds pretty spot on. So how do I find her?" When Andrea and Amilia exchanged another quick glance, I realized how I sounded and backpedaled. "Okay, never mind that. I'll figure it out. You'll help with the princess lessons though, won't you?" When they continued to look dubious, I stepped forward, pleading. "Please? I don't want to be an embarrassment to Dom."

"You never could be," Amilia insisted loyally.

"I appreciate the vote of confidence, but I'm sure you've both seen the video. Yesterday was a disaster. Please. I can't be Princess Graceless." They both winced, proving they'd definitely heard the nickname. "I'll do anything—"

Andrea stepped forward, catching my hand and stopping my words. "Of course we'll help you."

"Oh, thank goodness." Relief poured through me, nearly buckling my knees. "Now I just have one last favor to ask." I swallowed and forced myself to do the hardest part of all. "About the French ambassador..." I trailed off as Andrea visibly cringed. "What?"

"He left."

"Oh no. Because of me?"

"Apparently, it was already on his agenda," Andrea explained, "but it doesn't look good, from an optics standpoint."

I sighed. "What can I do to make it better?"

"Nothing right now, but he'll be back, and in the meantime, you can prove to everyone that you're no Princess Graceless," Andrea said briskly.

"Great. How do I do that?"

The women exchanged a look and Andrea held up a finger. "Lesson one: grace is all about control and confidence."

Control and confidence weren't exactly my strong suits, but I was determined to figure this out. I would act like the perfect princess if it killed me. "Right. Control and confidence. Easy."

Chapter Thirteen

FOR THE NEXT SEVERAL DAYS, whenever I wasn't playing the princess in public, I was taking princess lessons in private. I practiced how to sit, how to stand, and how to walk. How to curtsy and who to curtsy to—and most importantly, who was who at the royal court and what I needed to do butter them up in the name of diplomacy.

My two coaches were determined to turn me into the perfect princess, but they were no more determined than I was. I was going to be better for Dom, even if I rarely got to see him apart from public functions. We were both busy running the gauntlet of ceremonies and appearances leading up to Christmas.

To say princessing didn't come naturally to me would be an understatement. Luckily, Andrea had been able to rearrange her schedule so she was often available to join me for my events, keeping me on the straight and narrow. And it did feel narrow. Like a tightrope I could plummet from the second I stopped being vigilant.

My instincts seemed to be all wrong. When we

toured an elder care home, passing out gifts to the residents, Andrea had coached me that I needed to remain elegantly reserved, but it all felt so stiff and non-festive—until one man shook his head when I tried to hand him a neatly wrapped present.

"Thank you, Your Highness," he said gruffly. "But the only gift I need this year is my release papers so I can get out of this dour place and back home."

It was a beautiful facility, but I could definitely empathize with the desire to be home for the holidays and feel that warmth that no care facility, no matter how homey, could match. So I squeezed his hand and said, "Then I hope you get your Christmas wish, but maybe take this as well?"

He accepted the present with a slight smile, but one of the nurses sighed as we exited the room. "Poor Philip can't go home. He can't manage on his own anymore and there's no one to care for him there."

"I'm sorry. Did I say the wrong thing?" I knew I was supposed to avoid promises and getting too personal, but it had seemed so harmless to say that I hoped he'd get his wish.

"Oh, no, Your Highness, you were perfect," the nurse assured me.

But I was still second-guessing myself when we stepped out of the care home and a puppy rushed out of the crowds being kept back by my security team, a bell jingling on its collar. It slipped through the legs of my guards and scampered straight to my feet, as if it knew I was a dog person.

I crouched down, ruffling silky ears. "Hello, baby. Where did you come from?" I crooned—until I heard a discreet throat clearing and looked up to see Andrea gently shake her head.

Right. Dignity. Grace. Not puppies.

I gave the dog what I hoped looked like a dignified pat and straightened, smoothing my skirt and proceeding toward the car.

Elegance. Restraint.

I was trying to be more like Andrea, but it wasn't working. In the evenings, when our separate responsibilities for the day were complete, Dom and I would attend various receptions and Christmas concerts together, sitting side by side watching those who had been selected for the honor of performing for royalty. We would applaud reservedly, with controlled smiles—grace, I was learning, was all about being controlled and contained.

But that wasn't me.

I found myself thinking more and more of the saying *If the shoe fits.* Because it didn't. Cinderella's slipper was chafing.

Between the constant fear of saying the wrong thing all day and the stress of keeping the perfect smile on my face each night, my favorite part of the day quickly became the moments Dom and I spent together in between, when we would meet in our suite as we were both getting ready for our duties. Sometimes we would only have a few minutes, those little stolen moments when I would toss a ball for Prince Harry while Amilia fixed my hair, and Dom would tell me about each of the San Noelle Christmas traditions as he pinned the medals to his dress uniform. It was the one time of the day when I felt like I could be myself for a few minutes—but it still felt like I was living someone else's life. And not doing a very good job of it.

One evening, I was sitting on the floor, rolling Prince Harry's ball for him to chase while Amilia searched for an earring that had gone missing, when Dom entered our suite, looking as flawless and princely as ever.

"Hello, love. How did your appearances go today?" he asked as he bent to pat Prince Harry.

"Great." I scrambled to my feet, reminding myself that princesses didn't sit on the floor. "I mean, I probably said the wrong thing at least a dozen times, but overall, really good." I hadn't attacked anyone with an ice sculpture, so I was calling it a win.

He leaned down to kiss my cheek. "I thought I was supposed to be the one who worried too much."

"Are you worried?" I studied his face, seeing the strain etched there.

"Not about anything you need to fret about," he assured me—which undoubtedly meant it had to do with the French trade deal I'd ruined.

I wished I could do something to make his life easier rather than constantly complicating it with my ignorance of royal ways. "You should take a minute to unwind." I held up Prince Harry's toy. "You wanna toss the ball? It's surprisingly cathartic."

Prince Harry whined softly at our ankles and I wagged the ball temptingly, earning a grin from the prince. He took the ball from me and gently tossed it across the room, laughing as Prince Harry raced after it. "You're right. That is surprisingly fun."

"See? Canine therapy."

"Very effective. Unfortunately, I can't stay. His majesty the king requires my presence before the concert this evening, apparently. I need to get changed."

"Right. Of course."

Prince Harry scampered back with his ball and I took it from him to throw while Dom turned and headed for his dressing room. Of course he didn't have time for playing with the dog. He had responsibilities. Things a real princess would be able to help him with.

"Are you sure I can't help?" I called.

"You do help. You keep me sane." Dom voice filtered out of his dressing room, but the words were absent. Automatic. Why had he married me? What did I possibly bring to the table? Beyond my supposed connections to France. "Who else is going to get me to stop and smell the roses? Or throw a ball?" he asked, humor floating with the words out of the dressing room.

"Like that's so helpful."

"It is to me." He emerged from the dressing room, his eyes crinkling. "I'm just glad you're willing to put up with me."

As if we both didn't know that he was the one putting up with me. He was the prince and I was the one bumbling along trying not to cause an international incident. Sitting stiffly through concerts and always somehow saying the wrong thing. He made it sound like I was the one who was the catch. Like he'd gotten the better end of the deal when we married.

I couldn't imagine that. But then, I also couldn't imagine Dom getting down on one knee and proposing to me, either. Who was I in this reality? Beyond a French-speaking pseudo-noble. What had I done to make him look at me like he was now? Like I mattered. Like I was his world.

Because I was having a hard time trusting that it was real. The look in his eyes. The way he seemed to feel. Wasn't it all just ordained by the wish?

Dom crossed to take my hand, raising it to his lips. He brushed a kiss on my knuckles and murmured, "I'll see you at the concert," before turning and leaving the suite.

I was still thinking about Dom and the worry lines on his face the next day as Andrea and I rode through the mountains to a nearby town famous for its gingerbread.

"Remember," she reminded me, "you're just there to award the prizes to the winners of the gingerbread competition."

"So no building a gingerbread house to bring home to Dom?" He needed to smile more. To remember he didn't always have to be the prince.

"No," Andrea said firmly. "If you do, all the attention will be on you and what you build. The focus should be on the town, to promote their famous gingerbread and honor the winners. You're there to be a spotlight, shining attention on their accomplishments, not your own."

"Right," I murmured. "A spotlight."

But that was harder than it sounded. I strolled through the hall where all the gingerbread displays had been set up, admiring them—I wasn't officially judging, just there to pass out the prizes to the winners who had already been determined.

There were gingerbread palaces—exact replicas of the palace where I lived—and gingerbread towns, complete with towering trees and ice-skating ponds. The displays were art in edible form—though there were some, made by those in the younger age groups, which were more like the gingerbread houses I'd made as a kid, weighed down with gumdrops until the roofs sagged.

As the judges announced each winner, I handed out the ribbons and posed for a photo with each recipient, but I couldn't help noticing a little girl about seven years old with a particularly lopsided gingerbread house. She was beginning to sniffle next to her creation as it listed more and more to one side.

As I watched, standing at the podium, shaking hands and smiling serenely, the leaning tower of gingerbread gave up the fight, collapsing in on itself, and the little girl seemed to shrink in on herself in solidarity. A woman knelt beside her, murmuring something, and the little girl nodded, though her eyes stayed downcast and tears trembled on her lashes.

My heart went out to her. I knew exactly what it was like to be the one whose gingerbread house looked more like something out of a Dr. Seuss book than edible art photo-ready for *Food & Wine* magazine. My sisters were always good at everything, but me... well, I knocked things over so often I could probably be in the Guinness Book of World Records.

"Your Highness?"

I snapped to attention, turning to award the appropriate ribbon, my smile in place, but I couldn't stop thinking about that little girl with her downturned head. Couldn't stop thinking about how I would feel if I'd tried my hardest to make something beautiful and a princess had witnessed its collapse.

Even if I couldn't make her a winner, I couldn't let her leave today upset. Not at Christmas.

When the final prizes had been awarded, after we'd golf-clapped our appreciation for all the participants and they'd applauded me for my prize-distribution prowess, my security team guided me toward the exit—and I slipped down the aisle instead, pretending to take one more admiring stroll through the displays when I really had one destination in mind.

She didn't look up when I stopped in front of her collapsed display, not even when I knelt down to her level.

"Your Highness," said the woman behind her, whom I assumed was her mother, bobbing a curtsey. She bent down as well. "Say hello to the princess, Cora," she prompted gently.

The girl mumbled something that could almost have been hello.

"Cora," I marveled. "That's a beautiful name. Do you want to know a secret, Cora?"

The girl's lashes flickered at the temptation of a secret, but she just shrugged one shoulder, still looking down.

"I was always the absolute *worst* one in my family at building gingerbread houses."

The girl's gaze lifted an inch. "Really?"

"Oh yeah. Ask anyone. My sisters, Rachel and Chloe? They would build castles and cathedrals. One time, Rachel even built the Eiffel Tower. To scale. While my gingerbread houses *always* fell over. But you know what?"

"What?" Cora asked, meeting my eyes now.

I leaned forward, as if this was the most secret

part, and whispered conspiratorially. "Mine always tasted the best." Cora giggled and my heart lifted at the sound. I nodded to the pile of gingerbread debris beside her. "Do you think I could steal a gumdrop? The gumdrops were always my favorite."

The little girl nodded eagerly and I grinned, snagging a gumdrop and popping it into my mouth. I gave an exaggerated sigh of happiness and Cora giggled again.

"You'll keep trying, won't you?" I asked her. "We can't let the professional gingerbread architects have *all* the fun." Cora nodded and I smiled. "Good."

I straightened and her mother did as well, moving straight into a curtsy. "Thank you, Your Highness."

I nodded, becoming aware of our audience for the first time—and the slight frown on Andrea's face. She hadn't wanted me to make a scene, to make it about me, but how could I have ignored Cora's tears?

I smiled serenely at everyone—and waited until we were back in the town car with the flags on the hood, wending our way through the mountains back to the palace, before I asked, "Did I do something wrong?"

"No," Andrea murmured, but I could hear the hesitation in her voice. I hadn't been supposed to talk to Cora. I knew I was meant to be the spotlight for the event and not make the story about me and a little girl, but what could the harm possibly be? And I didn't know how to ignore an upset child when I was sure I could do something to help.

I'd tried not to pay attention to my press clippings since the Princess Graceless incident, but this time, as we rode back to the palace, I pulled out my cell phone and looked.

There were already articles posting at the speed of the internet. Some were about the winners of the contest, about the little town famous for its gingerbread—but the majority featured photos of me with Cora. Photos I hadn't even realized were being taken. Including one attached to a story that claimed "Princess Graceless" had knocked down the little girl's gingerbread house and made her cry.

I groaned, closing my eyes. Should I have ignored her? Walked away so the focus would stay where it was supposed to be? That didn't seem right, either.

"The French ambassador should get back this afternoon," Andrea said—and I latched onto the chance to redeem myself for one of my biggest mistakes.

"Can I meet with him?" I knew my schedule was packed with events, but hopefully, we could find a few minutes so I could apologize.

I'd learned what the French trade agreement was all about. Despite its small size, San Noelle had been forward-thinking in the areas of technology and financial services. One of their primary tech exports depended on a mineral that had historically been imported from nearby France. The agreements governing trade between the two countries were up for renegotiation and San Noelle needed to ensure a positive relationship continued.

I may be struggling to figure out all the details of this princess gig, but I was determined to fix things with the French ambassador.

Andrea looked uncertain—and I couldn't exactly blame her because I didn't have the best track record. "Please," I begged. "I need to make this right."

My princess tutor nodded. "Let me talk to Franz."

Franz thought it was a terrible idea, which shouldn't have surprised any of us, but his arguments apparently annoyed Andrea enough that she became determined to help me get around him.

Amilia used the servants' grapevine to get the ambassador's schedule—and so I found myself hiding behind a garland-wrapped column, lying in wait outside the council chamber as the French ambassador and his entourage approached for a meeting.

I stepped into his path, cringing when I saw that his arm was still in a sling. "*Votre Excellence?*" The French flowed easily off my tongue, surprising me.

The ambassador paused when he saw me, smiled, and bowed. "*Votre Altesse Royale.* How are you?"

Grateful for the switch to English, even though I seemed to inexplicably be able to speak French when I didn't think about it, I met his kind eyes. "Do you think I could have a moment of your time?"

"Of course," he murmured in accented English, waving his entourage ahead of him into the council chamber. "What can I do for you?" he asked when we were alone.

"I wanted to apologize for the other night. The nutcracker. *Je suis désolée.* I never intended..."

"My dear child. Don't you think I know that? It was an accident. And a rather amusing one, once I saw the video."

I groaned. "How can you laugh? I feel horrible."

"We can't have that," he said with a smile. "Come

now. All is forgiven. Though there was nothing to forgive. Women in your condition have done far worse."

Condition? He seemed to have a good command of English, but perhaps he meant position. Or maybe he was referring to my supposed illness from earlier that day. Either way, I wasn't about to reject his forgiveness when it was offered.

"Thank you for understanding."

He squeezed my hand and gave me a wink, then turned toward the council chamber. "Now for the boring part."

I smiled, marveling that he was so extremely understanding. Almost ridiculously understanding. But maybe that was a function of the wish? I was still mulling over the conversation when I returned to my suite—

And then I saw the papers.

Chapter Fourteen

ROYAL BABY!

THE HEADLINE WAS MASSIVE, GIANT block letters taking up half the page over a photo of me at the tree lighting with my hand over my stomach.

"What the—" I took a step forward as Amilia, who had been reading the newspaper, hastily lowered it.

"I'm sorry, Your Highness," she said, hurriedly trying to hide the paper.

"What is that?"

"It's just a tabloid," she said. "One of the guards had it and I—"

"What are they saying?" I rushed over and Amilia reluctantly handed over the paper.

"It's just silliness," she insisted, but I was already opening the paper to the full-page article inside which was complete with more pictures, including one in which my coat had billowed in a gust of wind and I looked like I was eight months pregnant with twins.

"'Lately, the antics of Princess Jennifer of San Noelle, dubbed Princess Graceless by social media, have been raising eyebrows around the globe, but could there be a simple explanation for her behavior?'" I read aloud. "'Sources close to the palace say a doctor was called to see the princess on the morning before the San Noelle tree-lighting ceremony with the now-infamous ice nutcracker incident, and no less than two sources overheard the princess discussing her cravings for unusual foods at that same event. Numerous palace sources report the princess has been particularly forgetful lately—and one source even reported witnessing her asking for directions in her own home. Could that be baby brain? Princess Graceless has us all on bump-watch.'" I lowered the paper. "My 'condition.' The French ambassador saw this! No wonder he was so nice."

"There are always rumors like this," Amilia assured me, taking back the paper.

"So it's just this one?" I pulled out my phone and quickly typed in my name—and the first five hits were all pregnancy conspiracy theories. I groaned. "Oh, no. It's Baby-Gate."

I'd been so good, too! Trying so hard not to cause a scandal or do anything to embarrass Dom or make my father-in-law frown at me.

"Do we need to refute it?" I asked, and Amilia gave me a deer in headlights look. "Never mind. I'll ask Dom. Or Franz. This seems like his kind of thing."

Amilia quickly folded the paper and tucked it into her pocket. "I'll get rid of this. I was just going to walk Prince Harry anyway," she said, producing a leash from the same pocket.

"Could I?"

She blinked, and it belatedly occurred to me that

princesses probably do not pick up after their own dogs. I blushed and tried to think of a way of covering the gaffe, but she was already bobbing a curtsy and handing over the leash.

Prince Harry perked up at the sight of the leash and I grabbed my coat, pocketing his ball and my cell phone as well. I needed to escape, just for a second. I just needed to step outside this life and feel like myself for a minute.

I clipped the leash to Harry's collar and we were out of the room and moving quickly down the hallway before I realized I didn't know where he went on his walks. I had learned my way around the palace a little over the last few days, but I hadn't spotted any handy dog parks lying around—and the last thing I wanted to do was fuel the baby brain rumors by asking for directions.

I let Prince Harry take the lead, hoping he would guide me to his usual exit, but instead he tugged me all the way to the ankles of a guard on duty at the throne room doors. The guard, who couldn't have been more than twenty, blushed and pulled a treat from his pocket, offering it to Prince Harry.

"Shall I take the royal leash?" he offered, and I nearly laughed at the somber seriousness of the question.

"No, thank you. I'd like to take him."

I glanced around, trying to figure out where one might walk a royal pooch without asking outright, but then decided I was just going to have to get used to looking like I was suffering from temporary amnesia. "Erm, where do you think is a good place to take him? Where we won't be in the way of the, ah, French delegation?"

The guard nodded to the left. "The south garden should be empty of guests."

I nodded, as if I knew what that meant—and turned to the left. "Thank you," I said, trying for regal and dignified. "Come on, Prince Harry."

The dog reluctantly left his friend, his nails tapping on the fancy floors, and this time he did lead me to a pair of double doors which let out into a small courtyard garden.

The south garden was breathtaking—and cold. My heels sunk into the snow as I let Prince Harry off his leash, watching him cavort through the snow-dusted topiary, sniffing everything. Ivy climbed the stone walls that enclosed the garden, snow and frost clinging to the vines, and there was a gorgeous outdoor fireplace in the center of the garden. It wasn't lit, but I wandered over to it as Prince Harry came bounding back. I could just picture myself here, sipping cocoa in front of a fire with Dom in the winter, or cuddling up next to him with a glass of wine in the summer months.

If I was still here in the summer months.

I perched on the edge of the hearth and ruffled Prince Harry's ears, wondering again what I was doing here. I hadn't seen the countess elf again, I'd barely seen Dom for more than a few minutes at a time, and so far, I seemed to be a complete screw-up as a princess. Prince Harry was the only part of this crazy world that felt right.

"Do you want the ball?" I asked in my high-pitched Prince Harry-only voice, plucking the ball out of my pocket. He immediately went into his crouch, wagging wildly. "This ball?"

My phone rang as I flung the ball and Harry leapt into the snow to give chase—reminding me of another game of fetch, back before I'd had any idea there was such a kingdom as San Noelle. I fished out the phone reluctantly, half-planning to ignore the call until I saw Margo's name on the screen.

"Hello?"

"*So*. I hear you're preggers."

I groaned, thunking my head back against the stone façade of the fireplace as Prince Harry came galumphing back with the ball. "Those awful articles."

"They aren't so bad. You look great in the pictures, and no one actually believes that stuff until the palace makes a statement anyway. How's the wish going?" she asked, though I had a feeling she didn't *really* believe in the wish. More likely, she thought it was my way of coping with doubts about my marriage and my future. Whyever she pretended to believe me, I didn't care. As long as I had someone I could talk to.

"Kind of horrible?" I replied. "I asked Andrea and Amilia for princess lessons, so now I can sit and stand and curtsy properly—but apparently I suck at being a spotlight."

"A what?"

"I'm supposed to be a spotlight, shining my fame on the people of San Noelle rather than focusing the attention on myself, but I keep screwing up and making it about me when I don't mean to. This pregnancy thing is just going to eclipse all the other stuff the palace is trying to focus on—"

"If it's possible for the pregnancy stuff to eclipse

it, then that other stuff must have been too boring to hold the media's attention anyway. That isn't your fault."

"I'm just starting to wonder if this entire situation is designed to show me that I don't belong here and I shouldn't wish for things."

"Hey," Margo began—but snow crunched near the door and when I looked up, there he was. Prince Charming. I didn't hear a word Margo said, my gaze locked on Dom as he closed the door behind him.

"Margo, I've gotta go," I mumbled into the phone, barely hearing her response.

Prince Harry rushed to greet Prince Dominic, and I watched the prince of San Noelle ruffle his fur before throwing the ball and sending Harry into delighted pursuit. Dom continued through the snow to perch on the hearth next to me, his warmth lined up against my side.

"I thought you had meetings all day," I murmured, equal parts nervous and excited that he was here.

"My father released me." He pulled out his cell phone, turning it so I could see the screen. "Something you want to tell me?"

It was a royal baby article. Of course it was. I blushed. "I'm not...there's no baby."

"I know."

"You do?" How did he know?

"I had a hunch you'd tell me before you told the tabloids," he said, his eyes crinkling in that way that never failed to make my stomach flip. "Also, I asked your doctor the other day if that might be why you were sick in the morning and she confirmed that we aren't currently expecting. Are you all right? Amilia texted me that you seemed a little rattled."

"I just wanted to feel like myself for a while." I sighed. "I keep screwing up."

"You do?" He sounded genuinely surprised and I sent a pointed look at the article that was still up on his phone. "The obsession with royal babies is an international phenomenon and not something you invented—or that you can control. We've been on bump-watch since we announced our engagement. How is this new?"

It was new to me. "It's in the tabloids," I said, frowning at his phone. I knew I was supposed to be the princess, but I'd never been in the tabloids before making my wish. "*Everything* I do is in the tabloids. I feel a little queasy and it's in the tabloids. I knock over an ice sculpture and it's international news. A gust of wind makes my coat billow and suddenly I'm six months pregnant overnight. It's just..." It was too much. And worst of all, I felt like I was failing him. "I'm supposed to be a spotlight."

"A what?" Dom's brow wrinkled.

"To make it so it isn't about me. To shine my fame on the causes that need attention."

"Sweetheart, it was always going to be about you," Dom said gently. "We do all we can to bring attention to things that matter to us, but our presence is what does that. The international fascination with royalty is what gives us a platform to help, but it's always us they're staring at and scrutinizing, waiting for us to do something that they can turn into a story, good or bad."

"Princess Graceless has a baby?" I dropped my

head against Dom's shoulder. "Your father is going to love that."

"He probably will if it gets him an heir." I lifted my head, frowning at him, and Dom smiled. "Trust me. The pregnancy rumors will not be something his majesty has a problem with." His grin turned mischievous. "In fact, maybe we shouldn't tell him you aren't really pregnant for a while."

"Lie to the king?"

"Let him wonder. He'd probably tell us not to publicly deny it anyway. You know how it is. Nothing spikes royal approval ratings quite so much as a wedding or a baby." When I sighed, he took my hand, lacing our fingers together. "We always knew this would be part of the deal. Everyone is going to be watching us until we have an heir and a spare. And then they're going to be watching our whole family."

Prince Harry had gotten distracted by something beneath a bush and now came back to us with snow on his nose and ears. I reached out my free hand to dust him off, stroking his silky fur. "I guess I never really thought about that part," I admitted.

"I don't have any siblings," he said softly. "That was always going to add to the pressure. If anything happens to me, the next in line is a second cousin— and there are those who would probably use the opportunity to try to dissolve the monarchy entirely."

"Don't talk about something happening to you," I murmured, squeezing his hand. I knew it wasn't real, this marriage, but my chest still felt tight at the idea of losing him.

"But you understand why everyone is preoccupied with our family."

"I know. And I do want a family. I just never thought I'd be in a position where it would be international news. This isn't... it isn't how I thought it would be."

Dom reached out to casually pet Prince Harry. "Any regrets?" he asked lightly, but I could feel a sudden tension in him, as if he was trying not to let on how much my answer affected him. "I know it isn't easy, living in the fishbowl."

And suddenly he wasn't just Dom the prince. He was also Dom the man. Someone who wanted to be loved and accepted as much as I did. Someone who worried that I would change my mind. That I would decide he wasn't worth the trouble.

It wasn't just about having someone who looked at you like you were their world, like Rachel and Chloe's husbands looked at them. It was also about being that person for someone else. Being the one who made him feel certain that I would always be there for him. That his heart would always be safe.

I lifted our linked hands, wrapping my other hand around them too until he looked at me. "No regrets," I whispered when he met my eyes, and his smile quirked up on one side. "You?" I asked.

"Not for a second. Not since the moment I laid eyes on you."

Something about the words made the zingy, connected feeling retreat. "At a charity gala," I murmured. "What if I hadn't been invited to some fancy fundraiser? What if I was just a dog walker and we ran into one another in the park?"

"In that case, I'm sure I would have chased you through the park until you gave me your number. I never could resist a dog walker."

"I'm serious," I insisted, pulling back my hand to take the ball Prince Harry offered and throw it. "If my parents hadn't inherited a title. If I was just Jenny—"

"It's an academic argument. You don't honestly think I married you for the title, do you?" he teased.

I met his eyes, unsmiling. "I think if my parents didn't have that title, you never would have even asked for my phone number." He hadn't. In real life.

"Ouch."

"I just mean, in the real world, would our lives have matched up?"

"Maybe I wouldn't have asked because I wasn't brave enough." His blue eyes were serious. "Maybe I wouldn't be so sure you'd say yes."

"A *prince* who's afraid of rejection from a dog walker?" I asked skeptically.

"I know there's a lot of baggage that comes with me. It isn't always easy to meet people in the real world. I'm not just a date, I'm a job interview. You never know if people want you or the title—and when you find someone who does seem to want you more than she wants to be a princess, you have to wonder if she would ever be able to love you enough to put up with this circus. The media exposure that's so different from everything she's ever known. The bump-watch and the memes—not to mention how hard it is to find a private moment when we can just be us."

"You're worth the circus," I whispered, linking our hands again.

I thought of the royal weddings I'd seen over the years and how the couples never seemed to be touched by all the insanity that surrounded them, safe together inside a love bubble. It was that connection that could make any moment become a private moment. Being that one person the other person was reaching for and sharing each moment with, even across a crowded room. That was what I had wanted.

"I thought it would be easier for you to accept this life because you were used to it," he went on when I couldn't find the words to explain what I was thinking. "And the title certainly made it easier to convince my father."

I sighed, leaning my head against his shoulder. "Does he hate me?"

"No, he just..." Dom trailed off, rubbing his thumb over the back of my hand. "My mother loved Christmas. She made everything special. She started the festival and the ball—but it wasn't the ceremony or the tradition that was important to her, it was the people. It was the feeling of being together. When she died—I didn't realize it at first, stuck in my own grief—but I think the lightness just went out of my father. Some families get closer after a loss, but it was like he and I became coworkers rather than father and son. He had a job to do as the king. I had duties as a prince. And that became who we were. It's all we ever talk about. But I think he has a hard time at Christmas. I think he misses her, even if he would never say it."

I curled myself around his arm. "I wish there was something I could do to help."

"Are you kidding? Jenny. You are the antidote to everything that was wrong in my life before we met. Do you know why I fell in love with you? It wasn't for the title or the fact that you looked so gorgeous that I couldn't take my eyes off you. It was because you were unlike anyone I'd ever met."

My heart shivered with the reminder of what he'd said in the park and I had to remind myself that he didn't really love me, that it was only the wish. "I'm a terrible princess," I whispered. "I keep messing up."

"I didn't marry you so you could become the perfect princess. I married you for who you already are. The one who lit everything up and made the whole world feel real and alive again."

I shook my head, trying to shake away the feeling as my insides melted down to a puddle of goo. I needed to remind myself that this wasn't real, but I couldn't look away from him. The look in his eyes slayed me. It looked so sincere, so genuine.

"I wished for this," I whispered, as much to remind myself as to tell him. "That's the only reason you're saying this. I made a wish—"

"Jenny... What makes you think I didn't wish for you just as much as you wished for me?"

His hand gently cupped my face and my awareness of the rest of the world faded away. The garden, Prince Harry, that ridiculous tabloid story—all of it simply ceased to exist as Dom inclined his head toward mine, his eyes never leaving mine. Suddenly I didn't feel like a stranger in a strange land, I felt like I was right where I belonged, leaning toward Dom, breath suspended—

"Your Highness—oh. Apologies, sir, madam."

I nearly groaned in disappointment as Franz the Efficient shattered the moment. Dom straightened, dropping his hand from my face. "It's all right, Franz," he said briskly, all business again, though he looked a bit apologetic as he glanced back at me. "I should go."

Should you? I wanted to wail. But he was already moving.

He kissed me—so fast he was walking away before it could occur to me to kiss him back. An absent, placeholder kiss. Which was fine when you would have a million more chances, but what if we didn't? What if the wish ended tonight? What if I had just missed my *one chance*?

"Dom." I was on my feet, moving after him before the conscious thought to do so had time to form. He stopped, turning back, with Franz looking on impatiently, and my courage caught in my throat, clogging there.

What if the kiss was how it ended? What if I was going to wake up like Sleeping Beauty the second he kissed me for real? I wasn't ready for the wish to end.

"I'll see you tonight," I said awkwardly, hoping the words were true.

He flashed a smile—the crinkly one, the one that made me feel like I wasn't alone in this fishbowl after all—and then he was gone. Prince Charming, off to save the world one trade agreement at a time.

I turned back to the garden, a sudden sense of purpose filling me. "Come on, Prince Harry. We have a countess elf to find."

Chapter Fifteen

MY PHONE RANG AGAIN AS I was making my way back to the royal apartments with Prince Harry. I was lost in thought, trying to think of some logical way to track down the very illogical countess elf. So far, all I'd established was that everyone seemed to believe she was part of the royal court when she was there, but no one remembered her when she was gone—which didn't sound like it was going to make finding her any easier.

I fished my phone out of my pocket and answered, still distracted by the problem. "Hello?"

"Are you having fun, dear?"

The scent of peppermint suddenly swamped me, thick in the air. "Countess?" I said into the phone, spinning to look all around me for the source of the scent.

She tsked. "Labels."

"You never told me your name. Is there something else you'd like to be called?"

"You didn't answer my question. Are you enjoying your wish?"

I couldn't think about enjoyment as I realized I finally had her there to answer my questions. "I don't know how any of this works. When does it end? *How* does it end? *Does* it end?"

"Well, it's your wish, dear. How did you wish for it to end?"

"I didn't consciously wish anything." I ducked into an alcove, clasping the phone to my ear. "Do I need to learn something? Is that it? Or will it all vanish the second Dom kisses me, like Sleeping Beauty waking up?"

"What an odd thing to ask."

"This whole thing qualifies as odd, don't you think? I just want to know how it works. Is this forever? Temporary?"

"It's out of my control, dear. I'm not the one who made the wish."

"I don't remember what I wished." I wracked my brain, but I couldn't seem to remember the exact words I'd used. Something about a fairy tale, definitely, but I didn't remember anything about an end. Could it really be forever? Did I want it to be?

I thought about Dom. About how uncertain I'd felt for the last several days, but also about that moment in the garden just now and how perfect it had been. How real it had felt. And suddenly there was one question that was more important than all the others combined.

"Is the wish forcing him to love me?"

"Oh, no, dear. Even wishes can't control the heart. We just give it a little nudge now and then."

I still had a million questions for her, but they all seemed to have been erased from my mind with that single answer. The idea of reality inside the wish was hard to wrap my brain around, but suddenly all I could think was *could he really love me? Could that be real?*

"I'll see if I can find a copy of your wish," the countess elf mumbled. "I must have the contract around here somewhere. Good luck, dear."

"Wait, Countess! There's a contract?"

"Of course there's a contract! As if we just go around granting wishes willy-nilly. Honestly, dear, I don't know where you get these ideas. Such an imagination. Goodbye now!"

"Countess!" But the call had already disconnected, the scent of peppermint rapidly fading from the air. "Dang it!"

"Countess?" a voice spoke behind me. "Not *the* countess."

I spun—and my knees nearly gave out at the surge of relief when I saw the familiar face. Tall. Gorgeous. Perfect. "*Margo.*"

I flung my arms around my best friend and she squeezed back, laughing as Prince Harry danced around our legs. "I'm guessing this is a good surprise."

"What are you doing here?" I asked when we separated. I led her through the maze of corridors to the residential wing.

"I thought my best friend sounded like she could use some moral support—and you know I'll take any excuse to go to a ball and flirt with some courtiers."

I frowned, the pieces not quite adding up. "Where's Harish?"

"Who?"

"Your fiancé..." My voice trailed off as the penny dropped.

I'd introduced them. Or at least, I'd been the catalyst for their first meeting. But if Margo and I had never moved to New York together after graduation, if I'd moved to Europe and become a princess instead...

"Is this a wish thing?" she asked. "Do I have a fiancé in your world? Is he cute? Does he live near here?"

"He lives in New York," I explained, something uneasy shifting in my chest. I hadn't thought about the other things beyond my own life that would be different. The other ripples of my wish.

"Well, if I'm supposed to marry him, maybe I'll just get myself to New York and find him. *After* flirting with all the spare princes at the Christmas Ball," Margo declared with a wink.

"Don't you live in New York?"

"I moved back home, remember? I gave it a shot, but New York is tough on your own. I wasn't making any headway with the acting thing, so law school here I come. Just as soon as I take the LSAT."

"You gave up?" I asked, my heart sinking for my friend and her dreams. She'd always seemed so confident. So sure she could overcome any obstacle. Had she really needed my support as much as I had needed hers when we first moved to the city?

"I like to think of it as a strategic pivot." We entered the royal apartments I shared with Dom, and Margo flung herself down on the chaise lounge with the familiarity of someone who had been in these rooms a thousand times. "Now what's this about a countess? Did you find the wish lady?"

"She called me, but now I'm more confused than ever."

"Wait, she called you? So you have her number." Margo waved a hand. "Call her back."

My heart jumped. "It can't be that easy."

I pulled out my phone again, quickly bringing up the call list and tapping on the last number. I paced as it rang, clinging to the phone with both hands, until a recorded message picked up on the third ring. *"You've reached Santa's workshop. I'm afraid all the elves are busy at this time. Please leave a message and your call will be returned as soon as the busy holiday season is over. If this is an emergency, please hang up and dial Santa directly."*

I rolled my eyes and hung up. "Cute."

"What?" Margo prompted.

"Apparently, I called the North Pole and it's the busy season."

Margo snorted. "I guess that's what happens when you make wishes with elves."

"I'm not sure she's an elf. She might be some kind of San Noellian Christmas fairy godmother." At Margo's look I held up a hand. "I know it sounds crazy. And I know you probably think I'm having some kind of psychotic episode, but I swear, a week ago we were living in New York, you were engaged, and I'd never even *met* Dom." I flopped down beside Margo. "I just wish I knew what I was supposed to do. I tried asking the countess elf lady, but it's all riddles. She says it's my wish."

"Well," Margo said, in her let's-think-logically-tone. "If you wished for this, it's just a fantasy, right? So enjoy the fantasy."

"Easy for you to say. You'd be an amazing princess. You're gorgeous and charming—"

"Jenny James Monteville, I wish you could see how amazing you are," Margo said. "I'm no more attractive than you. And certainly no better. The only difference between us is that I *own* it."

"Own what?"

"Who I am."

I slumped deeper on the couch. "I'm so busy trying to contain my clumsiness and avoid causing another incident I feel like I can't be myself. Or enjoy being a princess."

"Restraint isn't what you need. Too much enthusiasm was never your problem." When I frowned at her, she went on. "Have you ever noticed that every time you knock something over or mess something up, it's always because you're backing away? Second-guessing yourself? Trying to escape, trying to be invisible, panicking that you aren't good enough?"

"I don't..." My protest died on my tongue as I thought back through my history of mishaps both inside the wish and in the real world. The bungled interviews, the spilled champagne, my fake illness that snowballed out of control, and the infamous nutcracker incident. I hadn't been trying to escape when I ran into Dom in the park or when I spoke with Cora at the gingerbread competition, but I also couldn't bring myself to regret those moments. And I genuinely hadn't known any better when it came to hugging the French ambassador. My regrets all seemed to circle around those other times.

"You need to have more confidence in who *you* can be as a princess instead of trying to ram yourself into some ideal of what a princess should be. Your enthusiasm is your superpower, not your kryptonite."

"You're the one who told me to get princess lessons. To learn how to be controlled and graceful," I reminded her.

"And you listened to me? Terrible idea." Margo flashed a smile, then took my hand, squeezing gently. "A princess can do absolutely anything she wants, as long as she does it with confidence. She sets an example. So... who do you want to be?"

Margo's words whispered around in my head for the rest of the night.

Who do you want to be?

It had always been a question I struggled with, because there was always this other little voice in my head that seemed to say *you can't do that* whenever I tried to answer it. Always that voice of doubt and insecurity, telling me that my secret aspirations were just pipe dreams and I shouldn't bother even hoping for them.

But here I was. Inside a dream. A real princess.

So who did I want to be?

If impossible things were really possible, who could I become?

Margo and I hung out until the state dinner, which she attended with me, keeping me company when Dom spent the entire night wrapped up in politics with his father and the various members of parliament I was starting to recognize.

I'd always wanted to be important. To have status.

Something that I could hold up as evidence that I wasn't just Jenny, the youngest and least impressive of the James girls. But now that I had that title— *princess*; now that I was in the room with all the important people and I could actually do something big, actually influence people and effect change; now that I'd gotten my wish, what did I want to do with it?

Dom had late meetings, as usual, and I fell asleep before he got back to the room we shared, as usual, but this time my thoughts as I drifted off weren't filled with insecurities and doubts, but with possibilities.

Who could I be tomorrow?

I woke up with a plan.

Chapter Sixteen

DOM WAS ALREADY GONE WHEN I woke up—again—and part of my new plan was definitely going to involve figuring out a way to see more of my husband and help him erase some of those worry lines. In the meantime, I darted into my closet, energized by a new sense of purpose as I picked out an outfit for the day. I was already showered and dressed by the time Amilia arrived to wake me with Andrea on her heels.

"Please don't be offended, but I'm abandoning the princess lessons." I wasn't going to try to be perfect princess material anymore. Part one of my plan was to follow my own instincts and be the kind of princess I wanted to be, not the one I'd thought I needed to be.

Amilia and Andrea exchanged a small smile—Amilia handing me a cup of coffee before moving to plug in the curling iron, since I hadn't gotten as far as hair and make-up yet.

"What?" I asked, as Andrea perched on the edge of the vanity with her own coffee, observing.

"Neither of us thought you actually needed them,"

she commented. "But when royalty asks you to do something, you humor the hormonal pregnant lady."

"I'm not pregnant."

Andrea and Amilia exchanged another grin as Andrea answered, "We know. Though I admit, I did wonder for a minute when I saw the article. It wouldn't be a bad thing. Everyone would love a royal baby."

"No baby," I insisted. "All I'm focused on right now is Christmas. We are going to turn this palace into Christmas central."

I'd wished for a fairy-tale Christmas and I wasn't going to wait around for the wish to deliver. San Noelle may pride itself on its Christmas celebrations, but the royal family needed an infusion of Christmas cheer and I was just the girl to give it to them.

"I'm going to need your help getting Franz on board," I told Andrea.

"My help?"

"He listens to you."

She blinked, startled. "He does?"

"More than he listens to me." Something I couldn't quite identify shifted across her face and I plowed on before she could object. "I need to find a time when the entire royal family has a few free hours in our schedules—and if there isn't one, I need Franz to help me create one. I was thinking about something Dom said and I have an idea."

"I'm on it," Andrea promised, pulling out her phone and tapping in a note.

"Is Margo around?"

"Still asleep," Amilia explained. "Jet lag."

"Right." She hadn't simply woken up halfway around the world. She'd had to fly. I shook my head, grinning to myself. "Okay. What's on the agenda today? Any princessly duties?"

"You're meeting with the administrators at the local school and observing the children's Christmas concert," Amilia informed me.

I nodded, picturing another stiff ceremonial visit—and what I could do to make it more me. "Perfect," I murmured as an idea began to take shape. "How much wrapping paper do you think the palace can come up with on short notice?" When my maid just blinked at me, I grinned. "We're going to need *a lot* of bows."

Shouts of laughter echoed in the auditorium. The Christmas concert had been a hit—but the impromptu present-making party was what had really made the joy of the season fill the room. Luckily, the administrators had loved the idea when I'd met with them before the concert. I'd been a little nervous, standing on the stage after the concert to explain how we were going to spend the rest of the morning, but since my audience was mostly kids and their parents and only a few members of the press, I'd bucked up my courage and explained my plan.

The kids had latched onto it wholeheartedly—drawing pictures, cutting paper snowflakes, and some of the older ones crafting gorgeous ornaments, each of which got wrapped with care. As soon as the last present was wrapped, we would put on our jackets and boots and walk down the cobbled streets to the elder care home on the opposite side of the town square, where the children would have the chance to give their presents to the residents before performing their concert one more time for them.

And if the administrators and parents seemed a little surprised to see a princess sitting on the floor cutting snowflakes with the third graders and coloring with the kindergartners, they could just chalk it up to the eccentricities of royalty. Or pregnancy hormones. I was finding it hard to care. I felt more myself than I had in days.

Amilia had come along and even dignified Andrea sat with the older kids, crafting the most exquisite ornaments out of glitter and glue. Margo had arrived midmorning, groggy from the seven-hour time change, but she'd quickly overcome the last of her jet lag with the help of the local children. The only thing that could have made it better would have been if Dom were here—but the kindergartners and I had already made a little present to bring back to him.

It felt silly, making him a present out of popsicle sticks and glitter, but what did you give the man who had everything? It was the thought that counted, right?

"Are we about ready?" the school's principal asked, jolting me out of my thoughts. I looked around, seeing that all of the presents did indeed look ready to go and the kids were already clambering into their coats and boots.

I slipped on my own coat and gloves quickly, and before long, I had a swarm of kids bouncing around me, excitedly chattering and showing off their gifts, each convinced that theirs would be the absolute *favorite* of the folks at the care home. Andrea had arranged things with the administrators of the home that morning while I was talking to the school's principal and they would be ready for us.

The kids lined up by class, bouncing with eagerness, and we began the walk through town. I walked with the smallest kids, helping them stay in line. Ahead of me, one of the older kids began to sing one of the songs from their concert, and it was quickly taken up by the others. Before I knew it, we were caroling, picking up more singers among the adults at the Christmas market as we passed it. By the time we reached the care home, our group had nearly doubled in size and everyone came with us into the care home.

The mobile residents had been gathered in the common room and the children led the way through the halls, singing to those who weren't well enough to be moved and eagerly passing out their presents. There was no court photographer following along to document it all, but I saw several of the parents snapping pictures on their cell phones, and I knew I wouldn't forget the expression on a single face.

The same gruff man who had spoken to me on my first visit caught my eye, a wry glint in his. "These presents are much better than the last batch," he told me. "No offense."

I grinned. "None taken, Philip. I happen to agree."

The concert was more hodgepodge than staged, with kids moving around as they sang, spreading into every part of the home as they passed out their presents, but it couldn't have been more perfect. From the looks on the faces of their parents and the home's residents and staff, as well as the other townspeople we'd collected along the way, everyone agreed. *This.*

This was Christmas. The community coming together, sharing the spirit of the season.

One of the care home administrators hugged me on the front step as we were leaving, blushing when she realized what she'd done. "I'm so sorry, Your Highness. I didn't mean to be so informal."

I laughed, catching her hand and squeezing it. "I've never been good at formal anyway."

Out of the corner of my eye I saw a ball of fur dart across the parking area. The same puppy I'd seen the last time I was here, bells jingling on its collar. This time it didn't rush up to be petted, but an idea slipped into my brain as if conjured by the dog. I glanced at the administrator, smiling. "What's your animal policy?"

The San Noelle Animal Shelter was housed in a small building on the outskirts of town. The area wasn't as darling and cobbled as the downtown district, but it still had an undeniable appeal. I found myself smiling as we walked through the front door and I heard the familiar cacophony of dozens of dogs excitedly barking to one another.

Andrea lingered behind me, glancing around uncertainly as my guards took up positions around the room. Margo and Amilia had returned to the palace, but I'd been too eager to put my plan into motion to wait another minute. I didn't know how much time I had in the wish and I wanted to make every second count.

There was no one standing behind the reception

desk, but there was a bell. I stepped forward, but before I could ring it the doors to the back area opened and a woman stepped through.

"Cora's mom!" The woman blinked, startled, and I blushed at my unprincessly outburst before reminding myself that I was being my own kind of princess today. "I'm sorry, I don't think I got your name the other day," I explained.

"It's Eleanor. I can't believe you remembered Cora's name." She belatedly dropped into a curtsy. "Your Highness."

"She was unforgettable. She reminded me of myself, always trying hard and never *quite* having things go the way I'd like them to."

Cora's mom glanced at Andrea uncertainly—and I realized maybe there was a good reason princesses were always supposed to say the prepared, unremarkable thing. It let everyone else know what they were supposed to say back. Since I'd already thrown out the script, I pressed on. "I was hoping I could talk to you about your dogs."

She shook her head, bemused. "What about them?"

"It occurred to me today that this town really needs some good therapy dogs."

I already felt like I had accomplished more in one day than I had the previous week of princessing when I got back to the palace that night. And my plan was only half done.

I'd just changed out of my daytime princess duds and into my evening princess attire and was flicking through photos from the afternoon that were popping up on social media when a pair of arms closed around me from behind.

"What's this I hear about a parade through town?"

My instinctive stiffening instantly relaxed at the sound of Dom's voice and I leaned against him, tipping my head back to grin at him. "You heard about that, huh?"

"I think everyone heard about that. Franz is also complaining—something about upsetting his schedule?" Dom said, but he was smiling and there was no censure in his voice. Good. Because I finally felt like I was doing something to be proud of.

"I'm spreading Christmas cheer," I informed him. "Outside *and* inside the palace walls. Speaking of which." I was reluctant to pull away from him, but I wanted too badly to show him his present. I twisted out of his arms and rushed to pick up the lopsided package I'd set on the edge of the vanity. "From the children of the Mont Noelle Primary School—and me."

I held it out on the palm of my hand, suddenly nervous. He could be so formal. So regal. Would he think this was silly? Juvenile?

Dom frowned at the package in his hands. "You made me a present?"

"It's just a little something—"

It happened so fast, I was being kissed before I knew it. Dom's hand on my face, his lips on mine— then he was smiling down at me and I was too discombobulated to pretend I hadn't been affected by the impulsive kiss.

"Thank you," he murmured and I blushed. Did

no one give him presents? He was the prince. Didn't *everyone* give him presents?

"It's nothing fancy. I..." I squirmed under his gaze, even more nervous now, and my heart still beating entirely too fast from the flustering kiss. "Go on. Open it."

"Before Christmas?"

"Right away." Who knew how much time I had left in the wish?

He grinned like a child and my heart squeezed at the sight. He tore off the paper, revealing a lumpy colored mass of popsicle sticks and glitter glue.

"It's a nutcracker prince ornament—see the crown?" I pointed to the gold glitter at the top of the figure's head, nerves spilling words out of my mouth. "I told the kids I had bad memories of nutcrackers, but they insisted. You're the prince, right? I know it's silly—"

"It's perfect," he interrupted, and I bit my lip, catching his eye, something soft and breathless shifting inside me.

"I thought we could maybe get a Christmas tree in here?" I said, swallowing down the unexpected emotion. "Fill the royal apartments with a little more family cheer?"

"I love that idea," he murmured, reaching for me, and this time I had time to realize he was about to kiss me. Anticipation tingled from my toes to my fingertips to the top of my head, fizzing through me like champagne—

"Jenny? Oh, sorry."

Margo. Our ability to be interrupted was reaching uncanny proportions. I was starting to wonder if that was somehow part of the wish—that we would be interrupted at every turn. Or maybe that was just part of being royal.

We were in the dressing room off my closet; Amilia must have let Margo into the main part of the apartments. Just another reminder that we were never really alone.

Dom leaned away from me with a wry smile and I stopped Margo from retreating. "It's all right, Margo. I was just about to go looking for you."

"I'll see you later." Dom squeezed my hand and bent to kiss my cheek, whispering, "I love my present," against my skin. I shivered and watched him tuck the little nutcracker into his pocket on his way out of the room.

"That looked cozy. Sorry to interrupt, Princess J."

I smiled, floating too high to be bothered by anything. "You're forgiven. Just this once. Next time, off with her head."

Margo laughed. "Noted." She came deeper into the dressing room, as I slipped my feet into the heels Amilia had set out for me. "How did things go at the shelter? Are you changing the world for the better?"

"Maybe someday. Right now, I'm just changing me. I'm meeting with a local women's group tomorrow afternoon. Would you like to come?"

"Is this a fancy formal appearance? I might have to raid the royal wardrobe to borrow something appropriate." Margo winked, clearly not averse to the prospect.

I shook my head. "We're going incognito," I explained. "Sometimes the exposure of having The Princess there helps, but I met someone at the animal shelter today who told me about a group of local women who are active in the community and she arranged for me to talk to them tomorrow afternoon—to actually talk to the people who know where help is needed the most and find out what *they* think will improve life for the people of San Noelle. No publicity. No guards. Just us."

"You're crazy, you know that?" Margo asked, shaking her head. "You got your wish to be a princess. How many people would spend their time in the lap of luxury trying to figure out what kind of community programs would have the most impact for everyone else?"

"That's not all I'm doing. I have big plans for tomorrow tonight—Andrea got Franz to clear the royal schedules—but first, why not see if we can help a little? The countess elf lady said this could have lasting effects. If it does, don't you want to be putting good into the world, making things better?"

Margo smiled, taking my arm. "Of course I do. I happen to like your brand of crazy. But we're still going to the ball, right?"

I laughed. "Absolutely. Cinderella never misses the ball." At least I hoped she didn't. I really wanted to be here for that moment. For my mistletoe kiss.

"Come on." I tugged on Margo's arm, linked with mine. "You can help me make a plan to ditch our guards tomorrow."

Chapter Seventeen

THE WOMEN OF SAN NOELLE were extraordinary. When Eleanor had invited me to a meeting of a group that included the administrator of the care home as well as the school principal and several of the community organizers, I hadn't been able to say yes fast enough. Margo and I had slipped away from my guards and I was wearing the most casual, relaxed clothes I had: a sweater, boots and jeans. It was all designer, thanks to the magic of my closet, but I had tried to look my least princess-like. I didn't want to be intimidating or distant today.

I'd brought Margo with me, hoping that she would help me stay relaxed and put the women of San Noelle at ease, but it turned out no such measures were needed. Everyone had brought cookies and cocoa to share and by the time it was all passed around, we were laughing like we'd been friends for years.

They talked about their struggles and their triumphs. These people were already doing so much for San Noelle—but when I asked them if there was any way the palace could be more supportive of their efforts all eyes turned to the administrator of the care home who set down her mug with a determined thunk.

She leaned forward in her chair, meeting my eyes. "Let me tell you about my residents..."

By the time our meeting finished, we'd lingered so long over our conversations that we were all running late for other holiday obligations. I felt like one of the ladies of San Noelle as we hugged and said our goodbyes. They'd all taken to calling me Princess J, the way Margo did, and I couldn't stop grinning. We'd talked about the issues that mattered to them, but we'd also laughed and chatted about everyday things. It was that feeling of community that had me walking on air. Feeling like I was on the path to becoming exactly who I wanted to be.

After the meeting, Margo and I hurried to meet Andrea to prepare things for my surprise this evening. We got so caught up in our preparations that only when the sun went down did we realize what time it was. I raced back to the palace, not caring who saw the princess of San Noelle running down the hallways with her best friend and the duchess who had become another invaluable friend.

"See you two later!" I called to them, bursting into the royal apartments, rushing into the bedroom—

And coming face to face with a massive Christmas tree.

I skidded to a stop, staring at the evergreen currently occupying the corner of the room.

It was gorgeous. Nine feet tall, crowned with a glittering star, and magnificently, flawlessly decorated. And it had just appeared while I was gone.

I frowned at it, walking closer. Something shifted

strangely in my chest when I recognized some of the ornaments from my childhood. The gaudy glittering ball my grandmother had made. The twirling ballerina my parents had gotten me before we all figured out I didn't have the grace for dance.

Someone had picked out the tree, put it up, and decorated it with my own ornaments while I was out this afternoon.

It wasn't that it wasn't gorgeous. It was just that I'd daydreamed about decorating the tree with Dom, about hanging each ornament together and telling him the story behind them. In my wilder fantasies I'd even pictured us going full Christmas card and tromping through the snow to pick out and cut down our own tree. And now...

"There you are." Dom's voice had me turning away from the tree. He glanced up at it, distractedly. "Oh, good, it's here. Do you like it?"

"I..." I stalled, at a loss, but Dom was already speaking again, the subject of the tree forgotten.

"Your guards said you gave them the slip this afternoon. You know you can't do that, Jenny."

"I was safe," I said, still distracted by the insta-tree. "I went to go see some women in town and I wasn't alone. Margo was with me."

"Margo isn't trained to protect you. Promise me you won't do that again. I know the guards can be a little much, but if there's somewhere you don't feel comfortable bringing them then at least take your maid."

"Amilia's trained?" I asked—right as my maid appeared in the open doorway.

"It's ready, Your Highness," she murmured.

I hadn't had any success in getting her to call me Jenny yet—and now, I had a dozen questions for her. Like whether she was secretly a kung fu master. Or if she'd been decorating trees behind my back. But there was no time for those questions now.

Dom was frowning. "What's ready? Franz said something about you hijacking the plans for the evening—"

"It's a surprise," I said, hoping it would be a good one. I shook off my preoccupation with the tree. "Come on. And dress warmly." Dom hesitated and I flashed a smile, determined to make this night wonderful. "Don't you trust me?"

He smiled. "Always."

The lake had been transformed. Twinkling white lights filled the trees at the shoreline and lanterns had been arranged around the hard-frozen ice, creating an impromptu skating rink. A cocoa stand was set back from the water a little ways, along with fire pits scattered along the shore for those who needed to warm up.

A local vendor was on hand with skates of every size and style, ready to lend them to princes and kings who hadn't been skating in so long that no one had been able to locate the royal skates. And local musicians had set up on a tiny stage, playing holiday tunes.

It was exactly what I'd envisioned when I'd planned this night, remembering the sound of Dom's voice when he'd talked about skating when he was younger—back in New York, before the wish—but now I glanced at the prince at my side nervously.

"Good surprise?"

Dom swallowed, looking out over the ice where courtiers and members of the palace staff were already trying out their skates.

He could be so rigid when he was uncomfortable, using formality as a shield. I'd seen it, especially with his father, and I was worried I would see it again now, but he blinked and murmured, "Great surprise." He tucked me against his side, still looking out over the ice, and I realized he was choked up. "Is this where you were all day?"

"Part of it," I admitted. "I really did go into town with Margo to meet with some of the townspeople, but I wanted to do this for you. I remembered you used to go skating when you were a kid."

"With my mother," he murmured.

"I thought maybe this could be a new twist on an old tradition. I even enlisted help to get your father here."

I nodded over to a bench where Margo was helping the French ambassador with his skates while the king looked on, shaking his head. "Oh, no. The ambassador's going to sprain his other wrist," Dom said. Then his gaze landed on his father's face. "Don't be surprised if my father doesn't skate. He's not much for frivolity."

"Never underestimate the power of Margo. But also, try not to break your royal neck, I'm not sure your father would forgive me." I smiled up at him. "Shall we find some skates of our own, Your Highness?"

He grinned. "By all means, Princess."

I am, unsurprisingly, a terrible skater. Balance has never really been my strong suit and gliding along a hard surface on sharpened blades always sounded to me like a good way to sustain permanent injury. But Dom, unsurprisingly, was an *amazing* skater. Apparently, lessons learned in youth really did stay with you forever, because after a few tentative moves, he was gliding across the ice like a professional.

He skated over to where I was shuffling slowly along the edge of the lake and spun to move backwards in front of me.

"You'd better keep your distance," I warned. "I don't want to take you down with me."

Dom glided closer, catching my elbows when I wobbled. "Come on," he urged, tugging gently. "I'll help you. We're a team, right?"

My left skate slid forward without my permission and I clutched his shoulders to keep from hitting the ice. "This member of the team is too hazardous to skate close to," I cautioned.

"I'll take my chances." He swirled to my side and I leaned away, trying to put some space between us so he wouldn't get hit by my skates when my feet flew over my head. "Whoa." Only his arm around my waist kept me steady on my feet as he tucked me close against his side. "Just hold on. I've got you."

My breath went short at the look in his eyes—and then Dom pushed off, and I discovered how much fun it was to put my hand in his and let him make us soar across the ice, a shriek of startled laughter bursting out of me as the wind we generated ruffled my hair.

A crowd had begun to gather, some of the locals even grabbing their own skates and joining in. The

French ambassador skated past, laughing with Margo, their arms linked together—and a moment later the king himself glided by.

"Lovely idea for an outing, Jennifer," the king said, inclining his head regally as he skated past, elegance in motion.

"Thank you, Your Majesty," I called, before lowering my voice just for Dom. "See? Never underestimate Margo."

"I don't think it's Margo," Dom murmured. "Have you noticed my father is being particularly biddable, lately? I think he might believe those pregnancy rumors."

"I know," I whispered. "And I'm taking shameless advantage." I wagged my eyebrows wickedly and Dom laughed—until Franz and Andrea skated past, hand-in-hand, and Dom's laughter faded as his gaze followed them.

"Is that something I should know about?" he asked.

"I'm sure I don't know what his highness is talking about," I teased.

"You're sure, are you?" He spun gracefully to skate backwards, facing me, but in my infinite grace, I was unprepared for the maneuver. My feet wobbled in my skates—and then all of me wobbled.

I yelped, grabbing at his arms for balance, and Dom moved closer, reaching for me—but all I managed to do was tangle my legs with his and we went down in a laughing heap, grunting as we hit the hard ice.

"*Unh*," I groaned as half a dozen guards rushed over.

"Are you all right, Your Highnesses?"

"Fine, fine. We're fine," Dom assured them, and

then lowered his voice just for me as the guards retreated. "Are we fine?"

"I'm all right. Are you?" I'd landed on him and I untangled myself from him carefully.

"All parts functional," he said, and I blinked at the reminder of our first meeting, memories of Central Park. My gaze caught his, that impossible blue gaze with the crinkly smile.

"We must stop meeting like this," I teased softly. "Princess Graceless strikes again."

"I like Princess Graceless." His smile softened, his gaze lowering to my lips—and suddenly, I was certain he would have kissed me if we hadn't been in public. His smile was almost a kiss in itself.

"Are you injured, Sire?"

Trust Franz to ruin the moment.

"No, Franz. We're fine. But perhaps we should take a break." Dom arched a brow at me. "What do you say? Shall we go warm up?"

I nodded, even though after that look I was feeling plenty warm, and I let him help me awkwardly to my feet. "Maybe next time I plan a big surprise, I'll avoid activities involving balance. Or grace. Or the ability not to knock anyone over."

"Grace is overrated," Dom said as he gently guided me toward the edge of the ice. "This is perfect."

The way he looked at me as he said it made me feel like he was saying I was perfect and my heart thudded loudly in my ears—

And I nearly fell all over again as my skate caught a ridge in the ice. Dom caught me, laughing, and steadied me on my feet until we made it to the shore. Once on stable land, we wobbled our way to an unoccupied fire pit and I sank down onto one of the cozy little benches beside it.

"Don't move," Dom commanded. "I'll get us something warm to drink."

He could have easily sent a servant to fetch us whatever we wanted, but he seemed to sense that this was a night without rank—footmen skating alongside the king—and he went to the drink stand himself, chatting with the vendor while I warmed myself by the fire. He returned moments later, bearing two cups and somehow looking good even walking the awkward walk of skates on land.

"Two hot cocoas," he announced, handing me one of the cups. "I'm afraid they didn't have warm cookies on hand, so we'll have to muddle through without."

I inhaled the decadent chocolatey scent of the drink as Dom reached for one of the blankets that had been strategically scattered around the seating areas and spread it over our legs. It wasn't until I took my first sip, the rich, silky warmth traveling down my throat all the way to my stomach, that I remembered when our conversation about warm cookies and hot cocoa had occurred. At the Christmas party.

Before the wish.

I looked at him sharply, studying his face. "How did you know that? That I like hot cocoa with warm cookies?"

He frowned. "I don't know. Just something I remembered. Didn't you tell me?"

Had Alternate Me told him? Or was he remembering that other world? Somehow, the little echoes of our first meeting made this world feel more real, rather than less. Like it could really happen. Like it was really happening. Like I might be able to keep it.

"I have some very sad news." He shifted on the bench, his shoulder brushing mine as he leaned to reach into his opposite pants pocket. "I'm afraid we lost a friend." He opened his palm, revealing the nutcracker prince ornament I'd given him yesterday, broken into several pieces. "I think he was a casualty of our fall."

"You still had it in your pocket?"

"Of course. It's the best present I've received in years." He toyed with one of the pieces, twirling it between his hands. "And very fitting too."

"Because you're a prince?"

"Because I can be wooden and rigid, but you bring me to life." He winked, but my breath caught and I could see a self-deprecating truth in his eyes.

"You're not wooden," I objected, but Dom shook his head.

"I'm not very good at letting loose and being myself," he admitted. "My entire life, I've known that I have a role to play, that the figure I represent to my people is more important than who I really am." He held up the remnants of the nutcracker prince and I took them from his hand.

"You can be a symbol to your people *and* a man. Being human makes you real, and your people will love you even more for it." I tossed the pieces into the fire.

"Hey. That's my present you're burning."

"I'll make you another one," I promised, catching his hand. "You don't have to be perfect, Dom. Especially not with me."

"That's a hard lesson to unlearn." He put his arm around my shoulders, tucking me against his side. "You'll have to keep reminding me, Princess."

"I will," I promised—but I wasn't sure how long I would be here. "*I'm* certainly far from perfect."

"You're perfect for me." The words seemed to sink into me with the same warmth as the hot cocoa. He really believed that. In all our time together, he never treated me like I wasn't enough, always more confident in me than I was in myself. I looked at him, marveling at his face, so close and open.

"We're good for each other," I whispered, my throat tight with the truth of the realization. He could give me confidence and I could give him laughter. I'd never really considered that he might need me too. He'd said he'd wished for me like I'd wished for him, but for the first time I comprehended that they weren't just pretty words. That maybe I wasn't the only one getting a dream come true.

If only the wish could last.

Dom looked out over the frozen lake to where the king was chuckling with the French ambassador. "You're magical, you know that?" he murmured. "I can't remember the last time I saw him smile like that." The king's smile was restrained, dignified, but genuine. His majesty was *happy*. "He was always serious," Dom went on, still studying his father. "His duty to his kingdom was always paramount, but he used to find time for joy, for family. Until my mother died. It was like he forgot that he could be a man as well as a king. I think it was easier for him to focus on his work rather than think about what he'd lost, though I didn't realize that at the time."

"It must have been hard for you." I remembered the photo. Dom so young and serious walking beside the casket.

At my side, the prince shrugged. "I followed his lead, becoming the perfect prince and forgetting I could be a boy," he admitted, his gaze still on his father. Then he met my eyes. "Until you. How did you do this?"

My face warmed as I shook my head. "I didn't do anything—"

"Yes, you did. How did you walk in here and bring us all to life?"

I took a sip of cocoa to stall for time, since he really did seem to want an answer. After a long moment, I settled on the truth, "I realized something yesterday. If you'd asked me a few days ago what my favorite Christmas tradition is, I would have said it was sledding with my family on Christmas Eve. And I love that, don't get me wrong, but I realized yesterday that the thing that always made it feel like Christmas was when we would go sing carols at the senior community where my grandmother lived. My parents had to drag us when we were little and we just wanted to play with the new toys Santa had brought us, but those moments when people came together, that's when it felt like Christmas. And I didn't realize how much that meant to me until I started thinking about what kind of princess I want to be. If I could just make a wish and be whoever I wanted to be, who would that be? What would I do?" I looked up at Dom. "What would you do?"

"Are you asking me what kind of prince I want to be?"

"Has no one ever asked you that before?"

"Never." I arched my brows, waiting, and he grinned. "All right. Who do I want to be..." He tilted his head. "Can I steal your answer, about bringing people together?"

"No. No copying. Truthfully. What's your favorite part about being a prince?"

"I don't think anyone's asked me *that* before, either." He took a deep breath, looking around us— and I had the sense he was seeing the entire kingdom. "Sometimes, it feels like the job is all corporate deals and ambassadors and you don't see the direct impact you have on people, but it's the little things that can have the biggest difference. Like the schools."

"The schools?"

"We're a small country, so we're able to make changes and implement them much more readily than our larger neighbors. So when research showed that teenagers' test scores would rise if we actually let them sleep in a few more hours, we changed our school schedule so the little ones started the school day first. It all came from a petition from some sixteen-year-old kids, but we made a difference for the future of this country by doing something small, but practical. Those are my favorite things. The corporations and the state treaties are important. They keep us prosperous. But we need changes like those, too."

He scanned the crowds skating. His people. "I know the idea of the monarchy can feel antiquated, but I feel the people need us to advocate for logic and progress. My father loves tradition and sometimes I'm afraid to go against him, but our people need us as an example, demonstrating that change is good and healthy. That it keeps us strong. We *are* a symbol for our people. They do feel like we belong to them, because in many ways we do. And I'm proud of that."

"So I shouldn't complain when we're on bump-watch and everyone wants a photo?"

He shared my smile. "We have the honor of having a voice. And we can use it to make the lives of our people better."

"And here I thought I was the Pollyanna in this relationship." I took a sip of my cocoa. "Do you know where I was this afternoon? Meeting with local women, because I started thinking that sometimes we do things for people without asking them what they could really use. That we need French ambassadors, but we also need those kinds of advisors. The kind who would encourage a school petition. The kind who want to make sure our seniors are still active in the community. Maybe we can convince your father together."

Dom stared down at me, studying my face. "Where did you come from?"

"Iowa." He laughed, and I smiled. "I wish you'd do that more."

"What? Laugh?"

"We can lead our people by example by being happy too. It's not all about policy."

He smiled. "I'll try to remember that."

"I hope you do," I whispered, wondering if he would remember it after I was gone. I was so scared of the wish ending, the possibility that it might vanish at any moment was constantly hanging over me, but I refused to dwell on it tonight when things were so perfect. My maid skated by and I latched onto the chance to lighten the mood. "Is Amilia really a ninja?"

Dom chuckled. "I don't know about ninja, but she has been trained to protect you. Being a princess's maid isn't all hair curling and tree decorating."

"Are you referring to the fully decorated tree that appeared in our suite this afternoon?"

"You never said if you liked it." He was smiling, all crinkly eyes, but I couldn't give him the praise I knew he wanted.

"It beautiful. It's just not really what I had in mind."

"You were thinking of a palm tree, perhaps?"

I elbowed him and he laughed, lifting his cup to rescue it from being jostled. "I'd hoped we could decorate it together."

"Did they use the wrong ornaments?"

"No..." I shook my head, trying to find the words to explain to a prince. "Have you ever decorated a tree before?"

He shook his head. "It always just gets done."

I sighed, suddenly feeling incredibly sorry for this man in his palace. "I keep forgetting you have all these traditions, but none of them are really *yours*. You light the national Christmas tree every year and you give out prizes for the best gingerbread and listen to concerts, but you aren't a part of any of it. Christmas isn't about the decorations; it's about the decorating. It's not about having a tree; it's about going out and getting one together. It's about taking the time to remember the moment when you got each ornament— and building new memories together as you put them on the tree. That's what makes it special. That's what makes it Christmas."

He frowned, his eyes confused. "Should I have the servants take it down so we can put it back up?"

I shook my head against his shoulder. "No. But maybe we could add a few new ornaments of our own."

"And presents," he urged, his eyes glinting greedily.

I laughed. "And presents."

Though the idea of finding the perfect present for a prince was incredibly intimidating.

Especially when the one thing I wanted to give him was the one thing I was scared I wouldn't get back even when the wish was over. My heart.

Chapter Eighteen

THE NEXT FEW DAYS WERE like a dream... or a wish. I'd fallen asleep on the way back from ice skating and woken up after Dom had already departed again the next morning—but that morning, when I rolled over, a note crinkled under my hand on the pillow. I picked it up, reading the slashing, elegant script.

You aren't the only one with a few surprises in store. Find me in the council chamber when you wake up—and bring Prince Harry.

It was signed with a heart and the initial D.

I flopped back into the plush bedding, squealing at the swoon-worthy note—but that lasted only a fraction of a second before I was leaping out of bed, giggling with an excitement I hadn't felt since I was a kid on Christmas morning. I raced into the closet and Prince Harry picked up on my mood, barking and dancing around my feet.

"What do you think he has planned?" I asked the dog. "Did he tell you?"

Prince Harry simply went into his crouch, wagging his tail, and I laughed.

It was only three days until Christmas. The palace was aflutter preparing for the ball that would be the culmination of the holiday season. I darted around maids carrying centerpieces and footmen hanging garlands as Prince Harry and I made our way to the council chamber. Every inch of the palace would be decked out in Christmas splendor by the night of the ball—and for the first time the long, echoing hallways and massive reception rooms really *felt* like they were filled with the spirit of Christmas and not just the trappings of the season.

Or maybe that was just me. Maybe I felt different.

I hesitated at the door to the council chamber. It was Dom's father's domain, and yes, he had laughed and shown signs of enjoying himself last night, but I was still nervous as I raised my hand to knock.

The door was whisked open almost immediately and Dom stood in the doorway, grinning excitedly, his eyes crinkling. "Good morning," he said, hustling me backward and closing the council chamber door behind him.

"Why do you look like you're escaping before someone can catch you and make you do your chores?"

Dom laughed, wrapping his arm around me to urge me faster, Prince Harry bounding excitedly beside us. "No chores," he insisted. "We've finally agreed on the terms to the trade agreement, and I have *nothing* to do today but enjoy every second of my freedom with you. But we should probably hurry before anyone realizes we're unscheduled."

He caught my hand, breaking into a run, and I couldn't stop the laugh that burst out of me as we ran out of the palace. There was a car waiting in the courtyard and he yanked open the passenger door, holding it for me, always the gentleman even when we were escaping. Prince Harry leapt into the back and Dom raced around the hood, throwing himself into the driver's seat—and then we were off.

"I thought we weren't supposed to go anywhere unguarded," I commented as we zipped through the gates.

"I sent the guards ahead," Dom admitted. "I wanted to be alone with you, even if it's only until we arrive."

"Do I get to know where we're going?"

"And ruin the surprise?"

"What kind of surprise?" I twisted to face him, impatient to know what was in store.

"Don't worry. You won't have to wait long. We're almost there."

We'd arrived in town and Dom pulled into a small parking area near the Christmas market.

"Bringing me back to the ice sculptures to see if I can take out another one?" I asked.

Dom grinned as we exited the car, holding Prince Harry's leash with one hand and taking my hand with the other. "There's a shop," he explained, proving he was just as impatient to share the surprise as I was to learn it. "They make these incredible handcrafted Christmas stockings, mostly for the tourists who come for the season. The children in San Noelle generally put clogs by the fire for *Pere Noel*, but I thought my American bride would like to bring some American traditions to our Christmas—and we could pick them out and hang them ourselves."

My feet slowed as I gazed at him. He could have easily sent out for stockings and had them hung for us, but he'd listened to me. Listened when I said Christmas wasn't about the decorations, it was about doing it together.

"What's wrong?" he asked when he realized I'd slowed.

"Nothing. This is a really good surprise." I picked up my pace, smiling at him.

When we arrived at a stand that was a veritable stocking paradise, he released my hand. "Why don't I pick one for you and you can pick one for me?" he asked, again with that marvelous crinkly grin.

"Deal." I circled the stand in the opposite direction of Dom, examining the wares and mentally noting my favorites. Some were glittering and extravagant while others were simple and traditional.

I debated picking the most magnificently showy stocking, trimmed with sparkling silver threads—a stocking worthy of a prince—but he wasn't Prince Dominic today. He was Dom. And I found myself reaching instead for a simple but lovely stocking of plush red velvet with delicately embroidered snowflakes in sparkling white thread.

I hid it behind my back, coming around the kiosk to where Dom and Prince Harry waited. "Did you find one?" I asked him.

"I found two," he said, still concealing something behind his back as he showed me the showiest, sparkliest stocking I'd ever seen. It was gorgeous— beyond gorgeous—but for some reason my heart started to sink, until he grinned. "This one is for Prince Harry," he declared, and I burst out laughing.

"*This* one," he went on, "is for you." He pulled another stocking from behind his back. Simple.

Elegant. The plush dark green companion to the one I'd chosen for him. "Do you like it?"

I grinned, pulling the red stocking from behind my back. "It's perfect."

His grin deepened when he saw the stocking I'd picked. "They match! Did you cheat? Did you peek at the one I picked?"

"Never," I swore. "Did you?"

"Would Prince Charming do that?" he asked in mock horror.

The vendor smiled, and I had the distinct impression that Dom *had* cheated and enlisted the vendor's aid in picking the perfect companion to the one I'd liked—but I couldn't be annoyed for a second. Everything felt entirely too right in this moment.

We paid for our purchases—Dom plucking some bills out of his wallet like he was any guy with his wife in the market, as long as you didn't pay too much attention to the fact that his father's face was on the bills—and while Dom was paying, I drifted with Prince Harry to the next stall. The vendor there bent to pat my shameless attention-grabbing pooch as I admired the ornaments on display.

No one was curtsying, I noticed—and I had a feeling Dom had sent Franz ahead not just to station the guards but also to tell the townspeople to treat us like any couple touring the market. It was a nice touch. A thoughtful touch. I turned back toward Dom—and a shimmer of gold caught the corner of my eye.

The ornament was small, half hidden behind the larger, showier pieces, but it was perfect. A gorgeously carved and painted nutcracker prince, nestled sweetly among the branches of a display tree.

Did I have time to get it before Dom saw? I reached for it—

"Should we get some more ornaments?"

I could have said yes, I could have shown him the nutcracker, but I wanted it to be special. To be a surprise. I pulled back my hand and shook my head. "Do you mind if we swing by the care home? I thought some of the residents might like to meet Prince Harry."

Dom smiled and took my hand. "I'd love that. I'm realizing it's been too long since I simply talked to my people."

The care home was far more crowded than it had been on my first visit. The residents were laughing and singing with children and adults of all ages. The guards who had closed ranks around us as soon as we left the Christmas market scanned the crowd, frowning.

Franz shook his head. "Sire, the crowds—"

I expected Dom to stage a quick retreat, but he simply said, "I think we can manage," and led the way inside.

The administrator I'd met before spotted us and rushed over with a smile. "Your Highnesses! Welcome!"

"What is this, Marie?" I asked.

The woman smiled broadly. "Apparently, some of the children and their parents from your visit the other day enjoyed themselves so much that they decided to come back to sing more carols today. Is this Prince Harry?" she asked, kneeling to stroke his head.

"Prince Dominic! I remember the day you were

born," the man I'd met on my first visit declared. Dom was quickly drawn away from me and into conversation with Philip—but I couldn't mind the distance.

Dom smiled, moving from group to group among his people, laughing, talking, even joining in a few carols, and I was pulled in another direction, introducing Prince Harry to the children and seniors who were all eager to meet the royal pooch.

Prince Harry was in heaven, basking in all the attention and performing every trick he knew—when I suddenly smelled candy canes. That familiar peppermint cloud.

I straightened, chasing that elusive scent—and there she was. The countess elf. Tucked amid the residents of the care home like the hidden hero of *Where's Waldo?* Smiling at me as calmly as if she didn't have a tendency to vanish on me for days at a time.

I stared at her, momentarily in shock.

I'd forgotten. I'd actually forgotten, on some level, in some corner of my mind—or maybe just in my heart—that this was a wish. It sounded crazy that I could forget, even for a second, that this wasn't real, but reality seemed to have shifted inside me, making room for the wish.

Until I saw my fairy godmother smiling benignly at me.

"Hello, dear," she said cheerfully, bright eyes twinkling.

"You're here," I pointed out, brilliantly. "What are you—where have you been?"

"This is a very busy time of the year for wishes. I

had quite the time finding yours. Like a single star in a galaxy of wishes. It's amazing I found it at all."

"You found my wish?" I shook my head, trying to keep up. "What does that mean? How does the wish work? Can I stay here?"

"Absolutely, my dear," the countess elf assured me—then ruined it by adding, "Until the clock strikes midnight Christmas night."

"What do you mean? The magic will run out at midnight? What is this, Cinderella?"

"It's your wish," she said, as if it was obvious. "You wished for a fairy-tale *Christmas*. When Christmas is over, so is your wish. It was very clear. You didn't say anything about a happily-ever-after."

"So it just ends?" I demanded. "There isn't anything I can do to stay? You said there could be lasting consequences."

"And there can. That's obvious, isn't it?"

"Nothing about this is obvious." It couldn't be over, just like that. I'd finally gotten to the point where I felt like I was where I needed to be. It couldn't just vanish in three and a half days. "How do I stay? Can I make another wish? You granted the first one—"

"It's very greedy to ask for another wish. The one you got is quite nice. Aren't you enjoying it?"

"Of course I'm enjoying it. That's why I don't want it to end. I'm not ready to lose—"

"Jenny?"

I broke off at the sound of Dom's voice, spinning toward him. "Dom!"

Had he heard me talking about the wish? Yes, I had tried to tell him about it before, but now the idea that he might realize this wasn't real was somehow horrifying. Because it felt real. It felt entirely too real.

"What are you doing?" he asked.

"I'm just talking to..." But when I turned back around, she was gone. Again.

Of course she was.

I shook my head. "It doesn't matter."

Dom frowned, stepping close and threading his fingers into my hair. "Is everything all right? You look upset."

"Everything's fine," I assured him, telling myself the same thing.

Because I wasn't going to lose him. I was going to find some way to keep the wish. I had to.

Chapter Nineteen

"I NEED YOUR HELP. I NEED to figure out how to stay."

Margo blinked at me, uncomprehending. We were in the south garden, playing with Prince Harry. It was the day before Christmas Eve, time was running out, and I desperately needed reinforcements.

"How to stay," Margo repeated dubiously.

"Inside the wish," I clarified and Margo nodded slowly.

"The wish. Right."

"I know it sounds impossible, but how else would I end up married to a prince?"

And he was a prince—not just in title, but in all the ways a man could be. And I was falling for him hard—somehow, even knowing my wish had an expiration date didn't stop that.

"You're awesome and he has good taste?" Margo suggested and I rolled my eyes.

She was blinded by loyalty. I'd been thinking about it ever since I'd learned about the expiration date. Back in the real world, I had met Dom, but he was heading back to San Noelle to propose to Andrea and

I was Just Jenny—not the noble daughter of some randomly titled Americans. I didn't speak French. I didn't have any of the connections that had made me suitable for this world. If I lost this wish, I would never get it back.

I would never get *him* back.

No. I refused to think of it. "Things happen for a reason. Maybe this was the reason I was so lost in the real world, struggling to find my purpose. Maybe I was meant to be here. But if this is where I belong then there has to be a way to keep the wish."

I finally felt like I was exactly who I was meant to be. I brought people together. I reminded Dom to laugh. I was making this world *better*. How could I lose that now?

I felt a flicker of selfish guilt that I was asking for help from Margo—the person who seemed to have lost the most inside my wish. But I could fix that. I could find some way to bring Harish here and introduce them. I would put things right between my best friend and the fiancé she'd never met and find some way to convince Margo to chase her Broadway dreams again, but first I had to figure out how I was going to stay until December twenty-sixth.

"O-kay," Margo said slowly. "How did you get the wish in the first place?"

"There was a bracelet with a snowflake pendant. I found it and returned it to this fairy godmother Christmas elf who is apparently some kind of San Noellian Christmas legend who grants wishes—"

"Where's a good San Noellian Christmas legend when you need one?" Margo quipped as Prince Harry raced back with his ball.

"I'm serious, Margo. I have to find some way stay past Christmas."

"Jenny," Margo said patiently, "maybe you should worry less about trying to extend the wish and more about enjoying what's left. You don't want to miss Christmas because you're so busy thinking about what comes next."

Live in the moment. That would have been good advice if this was my real life and I'd been imagining the wish, but... "How can I focus on living in the moment when I know each moment is closer to my last with Dom?"

"Sweetie, he isn't going anywhere."

"No. I am."

"This is just jitters. It's your first Christmas in San Noelle. It's a big deal, but you're going to rock it." Margo ruffled Prince Harry's ears, earning an adoring stare. "Have you thought about what you're going to wear to the ball?"

"I haven't thought about the ball at all," I admitted. I'd been too busy obsessing over the fact that Christmas night was going to be my last night with Dom.

"Sweetie, you need to be thinking about it. This is *the* night. And the dress is key. Don't you want to make Dom's eyes pop out of his head when he sees you?"

Making Dom's eyes pop out of his head did actually sound pretty good. "I guess I assumed Amilia already had the perfect thing stashed somewhere in my closet."

"And she might. But don't you want to see it? And if she doesn't, we are talking about some serious shopping. My best friend is a princess, and she needs to look the part when she's waltzing with the prince on Christmas night."

My heart stuttered—but not at the image she conjured. "*Waltzing.*"

Margo frowned at me as I felt all the blood rush away from my head. "What?"

"I didn't think about the fact that I was going to have to waltz."

"You're a good dancer. Sort of. Or at least not completely terrible. You must have waltzed at some point."

"I'm Princess Graceless and I've never waltzed a day in my life. I can't exactly lead the Cha-Cha Slide at a royal ball."

Margo snorted. "Sorry. I was just picturing the king doing the Macarena."

My own lips twitched at the mental image, but I quickly sobered. "Focus," I reminded Margo—and myself. "If this ball is going to be my last night with Dom" —and I was *determined* it wouldn't be—"then I want it to be perfect. And that means I need to become a waltz expert in the next two days."

Margo met my eyes, reading my determination in them. "Andrea?"

I nodded. "Andrea."

The duchess was, unsurprisingly, an incredible dancer. She floated around the ballroom like the waltz was written into her genetic code, half ballerina, half queen. Once again, I was reminded how perfect she would be for Dom, but I squashed that insecurity, focusing instead on the way Franz—who had been roped into helping us with our waltz lessons—carefully avoided looking at Andrea as she counted out the rhythm.

"One-two-three, one-two-three, back-side-together, front-side-together..."

Franz guided Andrea around the room, his back rigidly straight, his frame as solid as a rock as she floated in his arms like a feather. They looked marvelous together—and I was sure I'd seen them skating side-by-side the other night, but both of them were doing an excellent job of pretending there was no chemistry sizzling between them as they glided across the floor.

"One-two-three, front-side-together..." Andrea ended with a twirl right in front of me. "Now you try."

I blushed, suddenly potently aware of my audience. Margo and Amilia sat at one of the tables bordering the dance floor while several members of the palace staff moved quietly around the room, pretending to adjust the decorations for the ball while they observed the lesson.

But better to look like a fool in front of a few people now than in front of everyone at the ball. Especially Dom. I wanted to be the princess he deserved.

So I stepped forward and took Franz's hand. The majordomo looked as uncomfortable as I felt as he placed his other hand lightly against my scapula. Andrea stood behind me, adjusting my posture with a few deliberate touches. "Shoulders down, head up, back straight... now back-side-together..."

I'm not the worst dancer in the world. I can sort of bumble through the steps of the Cha-Cha Slide at weddings without hurting anyone around me. But waltzing? That was not one of my skills.

I stumbled through the first couple steps, staring down at Franz's feet and trying to predict their direction so I could mirror him. It wasn't *horrible*. I didn't step on his feet and I managed a decent enough box step that Andrea praised, "Good. Just let him lead you."

Andrea stepped back, still counting off the time, and Franz guided me through steps that felt so awkward that I began seriously reconsidering my anti-Cha-Cha Slide stance. Maybe it was time to turn over a new leaf in San Noelle when it came to dancing. Maybe the king would *love* the Macarena, but no one had ever given him the chance to find out.

"One-two-three, don't-look-down, one-two-three, head-up-please..."

"What's this?"

That voice managed to snap my head up when nothing Andrea said nor my own willpower had been able to get me to stop looking at my feet. Dom strode across the floor. He'd had a meeting and was dressed in his princely regalia—looking every inch Prince Charming.

"We're practicing the waltz," Andrea informed him.

"Or trying to," I muttered as Franz dropped my hand and stepped back.

"And no one told me? I do know a step or two." He reached me then and took my hand, twirling me into his arms—though I stumbled and landed against him hard, nearly taking us both down. His face was suddenly close to mine, his eyes crinkling in that way that always made my knees melt. "Perhaps I can be of assistance," he offered.

I'd wanted to surprise him with my grace and prowess, but since grace and prowess seemed to be out the question, right now I just wanted to spend more time in his arms. "Perhaps you can."

"We can't waltz without music." He glanced over his shoulder. "Andrea?"

The duchess tapped a button on her phone and the opening strains of "The Waltz of the Flowers" from *The Nutcracker Suite* began playing through the speakers that had been cleverly hidden around the room.

Dom smiled, taking my hand and guiding me smoothly into the correct position. "How is it we've never waltzed before?"

"Magic?" That was my answer for everything these days.

"Past time we rectified that." He gently placed his hand where Franz's had been on my shoulder blade, but it couldn't have felt more different. My skin felt electrified. I was aware of every inch of him, the strength and confidence he seemed to exude. "The key to the waltz is trust," he said over the trills of the harp, his eyes glinted down at mine. "Do you trust me, Your Highness?"

"It's not you I don't trust. It's my feet."

"Just trust me," he murmured. "We've got this. Look right here." He pointed to his eyes—and I couldn't imagine looking anywhere else. The music picked up the familiar waltz rhythm and he swayed with me, gently guiding me into a few simple box steps, grinning down at me. "You ready for this?"

"Ah..." I *wanted* to be ready. Did that count?

Dom held me closer—

Then we began to fly.

That was the only word for it. He swept me into his arms, into the music itself, and we flew. I'd never felt anything like it in my life. The rush of the music seemed perfectly timed to the beat of my heart. I wasn't aware of my feet or the steps, only of Dom, his hand in mine, his arm around me, the muscle of his shoulder beneath my palm, and the sensation that it would be simply impossible to put a single foot wrong because he had me and together we could do anything.

Only when I saw Franz and Andrea whirling past and Margo twirling with one of the guards did I realize that we had company on the floor, but I still found myself entranced by Dom, incapable of looking away for more than a second. He twirled me out and back in, everything so natural and flawless that I felt I'd been made for this moment.

As the music crescendoed, he bent, looping an arm around my waist and lifting me effortlessly off my feet, spinning me in dizzying circles. I laughed and threw back my head, clinging to him as the only point of stability in my whirling world until the music came to a crashing end and he set me back on my feet, ending with a flourish and a dramatic dip.

I held his shoulders for balance, both of us breathing hard, his eyes crinkling down at me—and suddenly, I couldn't breathe for an entirely different reason.

I couldn't lose this.

The look in his eyes. The feel of his arms. The warm tightness in my chest. Every cell of my body telling me this was where I was meant to be. Right here in his arms.

Dom cleared his throat, straightening and lifting me back to my feet—and I became aware of our audience once again. Andrea had turned off the music. She and Franz had separated as if they'd never been together and now the duchess smiled at Dom and me. "I think you're ready," she said, her eyes glinting.

"That's an understatement," Margo said wryly.

"Thank you," I told Andrea, meeting Franz's eyes as well to include him in my gratitude. I glanced up at Dom, trying to find my equilibrium again. "Did you finish your meeting?"

"I did," he said. "In fact, I was just coming to find you. I have a surprise for you."

"Another one?"

"A better one," he promised—though I couldn't imagine anything making this wish more perfect. It was almost cruel, frankly, the way it seemed to keep getting better and better right when it was about to be taken away.

"Come on," he urged, taking my hand and tugging me along with him, his smile light and eager, worry-free.

I grinned, trotting at his side as we rushed out of the ballroom and down a long hallway. "Are we going somewhere?" I asked him as I realized he was steering me toward the courtyard. "Do I need a jacket?"

"You won't be outside for long," he promised. "Now stop fishing for hints."

I mimed zipping my lips as he threw open a door, and we stepped out into the frosty afternoon.

"Oh, good. We're just in time," Dom murmured as

a trio of dark sedans flying the San Noelle flags from the hood pulled into the courtyard. I glanced at him, frowning in confusion, but he simply nodded toward the cars as the doors began to open—and my family spilled out.

I gasped at the sight of my parents, my sisters, their husbands and my nieces and nephews filling the courtyard. Dom and I were standing at the top of a staircase leading down into the courtyard and none of them had spotted us yet, all rushing around the cars, talking over one another and laughing.

"My family," I murmured, tears pricking my eyes. "You brought my family here."

He slid his arms around me, smiling. "I didn't want anything to be missing on your first Christmas in San Noelle."

I flung my arms around him, emotion welling up inside me. "I love you." The words tumbled out, words I hadn't even been aware of thinking, let alone considering saying. Words that startled me because they felt so incredibly right.

"Merry Christmas!" a shout came from the courtyard and Dom laughed.

"Come on. I think we've been spotted." He ushered me down the stairs—

And I tried not to be disappointed that he hadn't said it back.

Why would it be a big deal to him, after all? We were already married. He must have said he loved me a thousand times—he probably thought I'd said it a thousand times too. But it was a first for me—and even as I rushed forward to hug my family I couldn't stop searching my heart for the truth.

Had I really meant it? The words had spilled out of my mouth, as natural as breathing, and now I couldn't escape the truth of them.

I was falling in love with a prince—if I wasn't completely in love with him already—and I was two days away from losing him forever.

Chapter Twenty

IF I WAS WORRIED THAT my family would be different after our unexpected ascent to the aristocracy, I could definitively put those fears to rest. After learning Margo had never met Harish, I'd wondered what else had changed—would my parents still be the academically-focused matched set who finished one another's sentences and traveled eighty miles every weekend to participate in a quiz bowl? Would my sisters still be with the same husbands? Would I have the same nieces and nephews?

But it turned out they were all exactly the same. Within minutes, my father was providing random trivia about the architectural style of the palace with my mother filling in the words he missed—and my sisters were still just as bossy as ever. I'd been afraid to call them, nervous to see my two worlds colliding, but now that they were here, I'd never been so happy to see them.

When my sisters found out from Margo that I hadn't even picked my dress for the Christmas Ball yet, I'd found myself whisked back to my suite where my sisters, Margo, Andrea, and Amilia decided I needed to try on each of the options and show them off. Dozens of designers had sent over original Christmas-themed gowns for me to choose from for the big event. I don't know who poured the champagne, but before I knew it, I was twirling in my dressing room in ball gown after ball gown, while my sisters, Andrea, Margo and Amilia sipped bubbly and argued the pros and cons of each look.

"I like the blue one. The color is amazing on you," Chloe insisted.

"But it doesn't *twirl*," Margo argued. "If you're going to a ball, you need a gown that makes a statement."

"A statement doesn't have to mean that your skirt takes up three zip codes," Rachel argued.

"Exactly. You want Dom to be able to get close enough to her to actually get his arms around her," Andrea agreed.

"I'm just saying. When else do you have a chance to go full poof?" Margo argued. I suppressed a smile, remembering Margo's wedding dress and the way it had taken up our entire living room. Then I felt guilty all over again that Harish wasn't here. Every second was an emotional rollercoaster today.

"There are still several more options," Amilia interjected, and I was ushered back into the closet to try on Dress Number Four.

I wanted to feel like a princess. I wanted this moment to be fun, but none of the dresses seemed quite right and now that I'd actually started giving some thought to what I was going to wear, I wanted it to be perfect.

Margo appeared in the doorway of the closet as

Amilia reached for another gown. My best friend studied my face, leaning against the doorframe and swirling the champagne in her flute. "Okay, what's wrong? Why aren't you excited?"

"I am excited," I insisted, but even I could hear the lack of conviction in my voice.

"Could you give us a minute, Amilia?" Margo asked my maid.

Amilia glanced at me. I nodded and she departed soundlessly.

"Is it the ball?" Margo asked as soon as we were alone. "Your sisters?"

I shook my head, swallowing, trying to find the words.

"Jenny?" Margo prompted gently, and the truth spilled out.

"I love him." My throat closed and I swallowed hard. "It was supposed to be fun—just a silly wish for a fairy-tale Christmas. A fantasy. But now it's too real. What I *feel* is real, even if all of this is just an illusion or a dream or a wish. I'm in love with him, and it's all going to end. I finally got my chance. I finally got my person. It was finally my turn, and I don't get to keep him."

Margo put her arms around me and I leaned into my friend, fighting not to cry. Because once I started, would I ever stop?

"I'm not sure I believe all this wish stuff, but the way I see it, you have two options," Margo said. "You either let the fear of the end spoil the time you have left, or you live today like tomorrow is nothing to be scared of. Don't they say it's better to have loved and lost than never to have loved at all?"

"I don't think the people who said that knew the loss was coming in advance. I think the hardest part is knowing it's about to happen and that there's nothing I can do about it."

"Hey," Margo gave me a little shake. "All of this is magic, right? Maybe there's more magic left. Have a little faith, Princess J."

I sniffled, eyeing my best friend. "When did you get so wise?"

Margo smiled. "Honey, I was born this way. Now are you ready to find the perfect dress?"

"Ready," I promised, reaching for the next dress, determined to enjoy the moment. If I only had a short amount of time left, I didn't want to waste it. I refused to spoil my last hours as a princess with regret.

Margo helped button me into the next gown and moments later, I emerged back into the dressing room with a twirl. "What do you think?"

"Poof explosion," Andrea groaned.

"Hey," Margo complained, "I *love* this one."

I studied myself in the three full-sized mirrors arranged to display me from every angle. "You don't think it makes me look sallow?"

"Maybe a little," Rachel agreed. "You look lovely, but the gold doesn't do much for your skin."

"You should try it on, Margo," I said, arching and turning for the mirrors. "It would suit your coloring so much better than mine. And that blue one would be better on Andrea, with your figure..." I trailed off and met Margo's eyes in the mirror, then glanced over to my sisters and the duchess. As the idea took hold, a slow smile spread across my face and it was contagious. It caught on Margo, then my sisters, and finally Amilia and Andrea.

Then we were all rushing back to the closet, laughing, tulle flying as *everyone* tried on dresses, Prince Harry barking and leaping around us all. We were all different shapes and sizes, but somehow—I could only explain it with the magic of the wish—we found a perfect fit for everyone.

Fifteen minutes later, after the initial frenzy, Rachel sat on the floor—with a skirt that did, indeed, take up three zip codes pooled around her—and gazed at the designer carnage. "I need a closet like this."

"Our Jenny, a princess," Chloe marveled. "I still can't quite wrap my head around it."

"I'm sure you never thought *that* would happen," I commented, remembering all the times I'd been the baffling James sister who didn't seem to have a purpose.

"Nonsense," Chloe said simply. "We always knew you could do anything. You were the one who doubted yourself."

I stared, startled by the comment as Rachel nodded over her champagne flute. "We just wanted you to *choose* already. You seemed so unhappy before you knew what you wanted—and we only want you to be happy."

I blinked, tears pricking behind my eyes again. I'd always felt like I was somehow disappointing them, failing to live up to the James family name—but had that all been in my head? Me projecting my own uncertainty and disappointment in myself onto them?

"Thank you," I murmured, refusing to think about the fact that back in the real world, I was still that girl who didn't know who she wanted to be. I couldn't have felt farther from that person as Amilia zipped me into another gown and I turned to face my audience.

For a moment, there was only silence as they all stared and I glanced down at myself uncertainly, "Is it...?"

"*Wow*." Margo stared.

"That's it," Rachel declared, the words firm. "That's the one."

"Oh, Jenny," Chloe murmured.

"Don't ever take that dress off," Andrea instructed, from her own position on the floor cuddling Prince Harry. "You should just wear it until they bury you in it."

I plucked up the skirt and flared it wide, turning to face myself in the closet mirror—which wasn't nearly as massive as the dressing room ones, but certainly got the job done.

"Perfect," I whispered.

Now I just had to hope for some extra magic to let me stay.

Chapter Twenty-One

D ESPITE WHAT ANDREA HAD TOLD me, I did take the dress off.

The royal family had a tradition of a Christmas Eve feast, followed by a quiet evening by the fire, and I had a feeling ball gowns weren't quite the dress code the king had in mind. Instead, I donned an off-the-shoulder red cocktail dress that was simple and elegant but also cheerful and festive—making me feel both like a princess and perfectly like myself.

Dinner conversation flowed smoothly, highlighted by laughter and an ease that I wouldn't have imagined I could possibly feel at the palace only a few short days ago. My mother sat to my right. During the soup course, she lowered her voice to speak just to me, our conversation hidden beneath the lively debate over present opening on Christmas Eve versus Christmas morning that was happening at the other end of the table.

"You look happy," she murmured. "Are things good between you and Dominic?"

"So perfect I'm scared it will all go up in smoke," I answered honestly.

"Don't be scared," my mother urged. "With the right person, it just keeps getting better. Even when you want to throw an ornament at his head because he insists Doric columns are Ionic."

I cracked a smile as my mother sent a fondly exasperated look down the table toward my father. He caught the look and blinked. "What did I do?" he asked loudly, and my mother laughed.

"Nothing, dear. As you were."

When my father returned to the present debate, I met my mother's eye. "Dom and I haven't begun debating architecture yet."

"Give it time," my mother said dryly, then her expression sobered. "In all seriousness, it won't always be perfect. Your father and I can't seem to help watching the news pieces about you two and hoping you're as happy as they paint you."

"I am," I assured her. *For now.* "But you shouldn't believe everything you read in the papers," I said as I remembered the furor of Pregnancygate. It had upset me so much only a week ago, but now it seemed like a ridiculous joke. It was so much easier to let those things roll right off your back when you felt confident you knew who you were.

But my conversation with my mother did remind me that Dom and I had never cleared up that particular rumor with his father.

Later, when we all moved into the king's sitting room where a large tree had been artfully decorated beside a roaring fire, while my nieces and nephews were playing tug-o-war with Prince Harry and Dom was embroiled in a conversation with my father, I slipped over to the throne-like armchair where the king sat and nodded to the settee beside him.

"May I join you?"

"Please," he said, with a gesture so solicitous that I instantly felt horrible for not clearing the air before.

I sank down onto the settee and blurted, "Your Majesty, you know I'm not..." I blushed. "That article? I'm not, ah...expecting."

The king nodded, a knowing look in his eyes. "I thought that might be the case. But I've enjoyed thinking you might be."

"You did? I didn't think you..." I blushed, breaking off before I told the king that I thought he hadn't liked me until he believed I might be pregnant. But the king nodded as if I'd said the words, something like chagrin crossing his face.

"I can be protective of Dominic," he confessed. "And resistant of things that are different. I will admit that I was more comfortable with the thought of him with someone like Andrea at first because she was safe, familiar. I did you a disservice by seeing only the ways in which you were different from what we know here—and seeing those differences as flaws."

"I'm not exactly a natural-born princess," I admitted.

"No, but you're a great deal like my queen."

I blinked, startled. "I am?" I'd never heard him speak of her.

Prince Harry rushed over to me to show off his new tug toy and the king smiled. "She could never resist dogs or children either." His eyes grew misty. "She would have loved being a grandmother. And she would have loved you. If only for the way you look at our son."

"I'm so sorry you lost her so soon," I murmured. "I wish I could have met her."

"She was extraordinary. And she'd be so annoyed with me for the way I've gotten stuck in a rut these last few years. The way I've focused on my duty and not my family. It wasn't until I realized we might have a new generation coming that I saw how much I've let down the current one." His gaze went to Dom next to the fire.

"It's not too late. Especially at Christmas. You'd be amazed how much magic is possible at Christmas."

He smiled. "I'm not sure I'm the magic type."

"We're all the magic type," I said, belatedly adding as I realizing I was talking to the king, "Your Majesty."

His smile broadened, until his eyes crinkled, just like Dom's, and my heart warmed at the sight.

My nieces and nephews came to drag me back to inspect the presents beneath the tree, lobbying hard to be allowed to open them Christmas Eve—as was the San Noelle tradition—rather than on Christmas morning as we'd always done back in Iowa. Now that my family was living on an estate in France, I had no idea what our traditions were, so I simply told my nieces and nephews it was up to their parents, which sent them begging in another direction.

Moments later, Dom handed me a hot cocoa and nodded toward his father. "What were you talking about over there?"

"It's a secret."

"Does that secret have anything to do with why

he's smiled more in the last few days than I've seen him smile in the last five years?"

"Are you complaining?"

"Never." He grinned, sliding his arms around me. "So. You never weighed in. Where do you fall on the Christmas Eve versus Christmas Day for presents debate?"

"Christmas Day, of course. Anything else is just sacrilege."

One of Dom's eyebrows arched. "So if I told you, for example, that there was a present waiting for you back in our suite...?"

I bit my lip, unable to hide my eagerness. "Well, I suppose, in the interest of compromise, we could always open *one* present on Christmas Eve..."

His eyes crinkled. "I had a feeling you might say that. Come with me."

Our royal suite, which had seemed so foreign and formal when I first awoke in the wish, had been transformed—or maybe that was just my impression of it. It was still luxurious, but the memories of the last several days seemed to warm the space and the Christmas tree in the corner brought the spirit of the season into the room—even if we hadn't decorated it ourselves. Our stockings hung side by side on the mantel, along with Prince Harry's, making me smile every time I saw them.

Most of the presents for the two of us and Prince Harry were beneath the large tree in the king's sitting room, but two small packages were tucked beneath our tree—the one I had wrapped for Dom and a second, slightly scraggly-looking box.

"I'll have you know I wrapped it myself," he informed me as he plucked up the present and extended it toward me, tugging me over to the settee. "No delegation. No help."

I gently brushed the lumpy, off-center bow with one fingertip. "It's perfect."

"Go on," he urged. "Open it."

I hesitated, suddenly nervous. I'd agonized about what to get a *prince*, but in all that mental wracking of my brain, I'd never once considered what he might get me. "You didn't have to get me anything."

He was already the best present I'd ever had. This Christmas. This borrowed time with him.

"Of course I did. It's our first Christmas." He nudged the box. "Go on."

I tugged at the paper, gently releasing the tape. A jeweler's box, too large and flat for a ring, emerged from beneath the wrapping and my thoughts raced. Earrings? A pendant? Dom leaned closer impatiently, and I slowly opened the lid.

Inside the box, a delicate silver bracelet with a diamond-encrusted snowflake pendant nestled against black velvet. *The* bracelet. The one from the wish. My breath released on a gasp. "How...?"

"Do you like it?" Dom asked softly.

"It's beautiful."

"It was my mother's."

My gaze jerked to meet his as I lost my breath again. "*Dom.* I can't. It's too—"

"She would want you to have it," he murmured, lifting the bracelet out of the box and gently resting

233

it against my wrist. "Franz thought I should select something more extravagant from the royal collection, but this was her favorite and as soon as I saw it again, I thought it just felt like you."

I nodded, afraid to try to speak as tears pressed against the back of my throat and he fastened the clasp. "Thank you," I whispered. I didn't know whether it was magic or not, whether or not it would be able to grant me another wish, but right now all that mattered was Dom.

"Now, mine," he said, flashing a grin—and panic swallowed every other emotion.

"Wait. It's nothing," I protested, reaching for the present as if I could take it back. It seemed silly now. Unimportant. "I didn't know what..." Dom gleefully shredded the paper, sending it flying.

I trailed off as he opened the box and his enthusiasm melted into something softer. "The nutcracker prince," he murmured, gently lifting the ornament out of its resting place. It was more ornate than the one I'd made for him with the schoolchildren, far more skillfully crafted, but it was still just an ornament.

It didn't seem like enough. Nothing could have been enough to show him how I felt. "It's silly..."

"It's perfect." He held up the ornament, letting it spin from his finger.

"I just didn't want you to forget... this." This Christmas. Me. This moment when, however briefly, he'd been mine.

He tipped my face up with gently fingertips beneath my chin. "I never will."

I swallowed, trying to believe him—but the wish would be over soon. I would be gone, back to reality, and how would he remember me then? His lips gently brushed mine, but his phone buzzed and he pulled back, glancing at it with a boyish grin.

He grabbed my hands, pulling me up from the settee. "Come on. I have one more surprise for you."

The sledding hill looked like a fairy kingdom. Twinkling lights bedecked the trees to either side and Christmas music filled the air—as well as the sound of laughter. My entire family was there, along with the king, but I also recognized several members of the palace staff and people I'd met in town over the last week.

"What is all this?" I asked Dom as he led me toward the hill, my mittened hand clasped in his.

"You said you always go sledding on Christmas Eve. I thought it was time for a new San Noelle tradition."

I stopped, staring around at the people who had somehow become my family. Amilia and Margo raced one another up the hill as Prince Harry barked and leapt in the air, trying to catch snow in his mouth. My sisters and their children, along with Cora and her mother, played on the smaller slope, while Andrea dared Franz to catch her on the taller one. And the king surveyed it all with my father—though I had no idea what the two of them could be discussing that had them laughing so hard.

"You did this?"

He shook his head. "*You* did this." He turned to face me, taking both my hands. "You've changed everything. You brought life to this place. Brought *me* to life, the wooden nutcracker prince. I never expected to find someone who made me feel like I could just be myself. I've known what my life was going to be for as long as I can remember—it's the unavoidable side effect of being born the heir to a throne. My duty to San Noelle has always come first. I know the role I have to play as the face of my people, but you showed me that I can be more. With you, it's different. I can be a prince and a man. I don't have to play a part. I can just be Dominic. That's the best gift anyone has ever given me—and I hope you realize how much you've done. And how much I love you."

"Dom..." I whispered. How was it possible to be so happy and so heartbroken at the same time? How was there enough room in my heart for everything I was feeling right now?

This was the fairy tale.

Dom's hands in mine. Laughter ringing in the air. A kingdom brought together by the spirit of Christmas.

But I couldn't stay.

The wish was almost over. After tomorrow, I would go back to the real world and Dom would forget everything we'd shared. The fairy tale would be over. I would be Just Jenny again, and he would be the untouchable prince about to marry Andrea.

"Dom, I..."

A snowball sailed through the air, smacking into the princely shoulder, and the mood was broken. Dom grinned and tugged on my hand. "Come on."

He pulled me toward the hill, moving so fast we were running and tripping in the snow. And I ran as fast as I could. Hoping if I just ran fast enough, I could outrun the ending I knew was coming.

And the heartbreak that was sure to come with it.

Chapter Twenty-Two

CHRISTMAS DAY WAS PERFECT.

We opened presents, sang carols, and Margo even set up an impromptu Christmas scavenger hunt—during which I discovered Dom was incredibly competitive, and a terribly smug winner, crowing in a very un-princely way when he and my brothers-in-law defeated the girls' team.

Laughter echoed in the royal residence all morning and into the afternoon—until everyone retreated to their own rooms to prepare for the ball...

And I realized it was almost over.

I sat at my vanity in my bathrobe, fingering the snowflake bracelet Dom had given me and wondering if I made a wish on it if it would do any good. I twirled the pendant. *Please let me stay*, I begged silently, closing my eyes.

Prince Harry trotted over with his new tug-o-war toy in his mouth and I bent to give it a tug, my throat clogging as I realized yet another part of my wish that I would be losing.

"Is everything all right, Your Highness?" Amilia asked, jarring me out of my thoughts.

"You know just Jenny is fine," I reminded her.

She smiled. "Not tonight. Tonight, you're a princess in every way." She placed a tiara on my head, weaving my hair around it.

By the time she'd finished with me, I did look like a princess, but I felt lost.

I said goodbye to Prince Harry, reminding myself that at least I would see him again in New York, even if I couldn't keep him. Then I glided toward the king's sitting room where Dom was waiting so we could make our entrance to the ball together. When I entered the sitting room, he was standing with his father, the two of them smiling and talking in an easy way that made my heart lift. They both looked incredibly handsome in their formal court attire, purple sashes slanting across their chests and gleaming with medals.

Then Dom looked up. As soon as he spotted me, his expression froze on his face, and it was like the world faded away. It was only us, alone in the room, and he was moving toward me like he was pulled by an invisible string. He took my hand, bowing over it and landing a feather-light kiss on the knuckles of my elbow-length gloves.

"You look... exquisite," he murmured as he straightened. "How did I get so lucky?"

"How did I?" I whispered.

The king wore a crown, but Dom had forgone his and his hair curled over his brow in a way that made me want to brush it back. I gave in to the impulse and his smile crinkled.

"Heaven," he murmured. "That's what you look like. Heaven."

I blushed, glancing down. Amilia had outdone herself.

The gown we'd chosen was a stunning deep red. The sleeveless bodice fit like a glove, hugging my waist before the skirt flared out in a cascade of rich crimson fabric. It rippled around my feet as I moved, the skirt flowing around me like something out of a dream. Or a wish. The glittering tiara and diamond earrings completed the look—but it was the bracelet that made me feel not just like a princess, but like *his* princess.

Dom fingered the snowflake pendant where it rested against my gloved wrist and gave me a special smile. "Shall we?"

I nodded, at a loss for words, and took his arm.

We glided through the halls, the staff members we encountered bowing as we passed. I'd never expected to feel like this. Not just Jenny. But there I was. The princess on the way to her ball.

Dom's father was announced first, and we waited in the antechamber for it to be our turn. I fidgeted with my skirt, trying to keep my head high, and Dom glanced down at me. "Is everything all right?"

How could I tell him that I was dreading this moment? That this ball, this culmination of the season, was going to be the last time I ever had with him and I was finding it impossible not to be twisted up in my head about it? How did you say that?

"Just a little nervous," I said instead.

"Don't be nervous. It's just you and me." His eyes met mine, and I felt it. That zing of connection.

That feeling of the love bubble swelling around us so I wasn't even aware of the eyes on us as the doors opened and the herald called out our titles. It didn't matter how many people were in the ballroom. It was just Dom and I, gliding down the stairs toward the dance floor.

As soon as we reached the base of the steps, the orchestra began to play the opening strains of "The Waltz of the Flowers" from The Nutcracker and I smiled up at Dom. "Did you tell them to play this?"

"Who, me?" he asked with exaggerated innocence before bowing over my hand with a flourish. "Would you care to dance, my love?"

"I would love to."

He swept me into his arms and onto the floor. Just as before, I was flying in his arms. One dance stretched into two, and then three, each moment more perfect than the last—but as soon as each song ended my heart would beat harder and I couldn't help wondering if time had slipped away from me. If the clock would strike midnight and this would be the moment it all ended.

We mingled with guests and drank champagne. Far from feeling out of place and outclassed by the caviar crowd, I felt like I was right where I needed to be. I saw my parents speaking to Dom's father. My sisters laughing with their husbands. Margo flirting with everyone, and Andrea coaxing Franz onto the dance floor. It was perfect. Especially when Dom waltzed me into a nook off the ballroom and angled his chin upward.

I looked above our heads. Mistletoe. A decorative bunch hung directly above us.

"I think there's a rule about this kind of thing," Dom murmured with a smile, but when he looked back down at me, the smile fell off his face at the expression on mine. "Jenny? Are you all right?"

A mistletoe kiss.

How long had I dreamed about a mistletoe kiss that would change everything? About meeting my Prince Charming and finally finding my missing piece? It was painful to think that I was finally going to get my mistletoe kiss, right when the magic was almost up.

"I love you," I whispered—and the concern on his face cleared, even as my heart squeezed tight with all the impossible emotions flooding it.

"I love you too." He lowered his head for the perfect mistletoe kiss. His lips were soft against mine, his arms as warm as home around me...

And in the distance, a clock began to toll the hour.

It was happening. The scent of peppermint rose around us, cloyingly thick. I tried to cling to Dom, tried to hang onto this moment, sure if I could just make it past midnight that I would be allowed to stay—but I felt myself falling through his arms, jingle bells echoing in my ears as that peppermint hurricane gusted around me. In the distance, I heard Dom calling my name, and I tried to hold on, but everything went black, the sounds of the ball retreating and the final toll of the clock echoing like a gong.

Cinderella's time was up.

When I opened my eyes, I was back in my apartment.

"Dom?" I called out, as if I wasn't lying in a heap

on my bed, fully dressed in the outfit I'd worn home after working at Dom's Christmas party. Morning light slanted through the window and I sat up, searching the room, even though I knew what I would see.

No Dom. No Prince Harry. Just the life I'd had before.

A life riddled by the fear of taking a chance.

"No," I whispered, leaping out of bed and grabbing my purse.

I ran through the living room, past Margo who sat at the kitchen counter in her pajamas, sipping coffee. "Jenny?" she called, but I was already out the door, racing down the stairs.

It was the morning after the party. I knew where he was staying. He may be going back to San Noelle today, but I was not letting this chance pass me by. I had to get to the Plaza.

Weekend delays on the E train nearly made me lose my mind. I paced the platform, constantly questioning whether I would have been better off taking an Uber even if it cost a small fortune. When the train finally arrived, I stood beside the door, fidgeting and counting the stops until we reached Manhattan.

As soon as we arrived, I burst out of the subway, running up the steps and onto Fifth Avenue, racing north toward the Plaza, dodging tourists gaping at the window displays and Santas ringing bells for charity.

He had to still be here. I refused to consider any other option. The wish wouldn't have happened if a life with Dom wasn't possible, right?

I was half a block away when I saw it—the black car with the flags on the hood. Flags I had come to know very well. He was still here. My breath caught and I was so fixated on the car that I nearly crashed into a man in a Santa costume. "Sorry!" I called, dodging around the Santa without slowing, my gaze going back to the car waiting outside the Plaza—

And the tall figure in a dark coat being hustled toward that car by his security detail. My heart skipped a beat.

"Dom!" I shouted, though I was still too far away for him to hear me. "Dom!"

I ran to the edge of the street—barely stopping my momentum in time to keep from being run over by a taxi zipping past. The pedestrian signal was going the wrong way. I bounced on the balls of my feet, looking for a break in the traffic so I could race across, but it was wall-to-wall cars.

"Dom!" I yelled again. On the other side of the street he paused with his hand on the open car door, almost as if he'd heard me. "Dom! Over here! It's me!" I waved frantically, but he just frowned, looking as stiff and princely as ever, and folded himself into the car.

A lovely figure in a tailored wool coat stepped up to the car and I screeched, "Andrea!"

But then she was climbing into the car as well. The doors closed right as the light changed and I sprinted across the street, ready to throw myself in front of the car if that was what it took.

But it was already pulling away from the curb.

"Dom! Wait!" I ran after the car, chasing it down 59th Street—but it was too late, and I was too slow. The car pulled farther and farther away from me, turning a corner out of sight, and I staggered to a stop, breathing hard.

He was gone. And my wish was officially over.

Chapter Twenty-Three

"So let me get this straight. You had a dream—"

"A wish."

"—that you were married to the prince of San Noelle and everything was perfect and wonderful, so when you woke up you decided to go chase him through traffic, but that didn't work, so now you want to stalk some weird wish-granting countess so she can send you back to your dream."

"Wish," I corrected again and Margo nodded her patented humor-the-crazy-lady nod. I narrowed my eyes at her. "You were skeptical in my wish too, by the way. You really need to stop being so reluctant to believe impossible things."

"I'll try to work on that." She laughed when I shot her a glare. "Oh, come on, Jenny! You have to know how this sounds."

"I know, but it was real, Margo. It was so real. Ask me anything. I know San Noelle like I know my own hometown."

And it felt like that life was slipping away. He was

going back to San Noelle to propose to Andrea, and I was right back where I had started.

"I've had dreams that felt like they were real too," Margo said gently from her post at the kitchen counter, watching me type my email to our bosses at the catering company. Maybe they couldn't give me Dom's phone number, but even the countess elf lady's email address would help. If magical fairies had email.

My hands went still as I realized I didn't know her name. Or even if she *had* a name, or an identity that anyone would recognize. Nothing about her made any sense. Everyone seemed to know her when she was right in front of them, but she was mysteriously absent in all the pictures I'd seen and people tended to forget she existed when she wasn't in the room. Not to mention the fact that she hadn't exactly proved easy to contact in the world of the wish. But who else would help me? Andrea? Franz? They barely knew me outside the wish. Who would believe me?

"It wasn't a dream," I insisted, frowning at my laptop as I tried to compose the perfect message.

"You went to sleep in your bed. You woke up the next morning in your bed. And in between you were somewhere else."

"Exactly."

Margo's expression was sympathetic. "Sounds a lot like a dream to me. And it makes total sense that you dreamt about the prince. Your subconscious probably took all your regret that you didn't get to spend more time with him and turned it into a fantasy world in which you were married." She waved at the wedding dress that was our third roommate. "With all the fixation on my wedding prep, it's amazing you aren't dreaming about weddings and marriage every night. You're being inundated with the stuff. Really, it's my fault—"

"Margo, you don't understand. This was... this was who I was meant to be."

"Honey, I know you'd be an amazing princess, but this isn't how most people go about it," she said.

"I know how it sounds, but it can't have happened for no reason. There has to be some way for me to get in touch with Dom. To get that life back."

Margo put her hand over mine. "I love you, sweetie, but let's be realistic. It was a dream. Though it sounds like a really good one."

"Then how did I know what the flag of San Noelle looked like? On the hood of Dom's car—it was the same flag."

Margo shrugged. "You must have seen it last night at the party somewhere."

"Did you see it?" I countered. "Because all I saw were Christmas decorations."

"It had to be there somewhere. The party was in his honor. Or maybe it was in that magazine article I showed you." The magazine was sticking out the top of my bag where I had dropped it last night and Margo plucked it out, waving it. "The subconscious is a mysterious thing. It notices all kinds of things we aren't consciously aware of."

I quickly pulled up a browser window and typed a name into Google, spinning my laptop screen toward Margo. "This is Dom's father, the king. *I know him.* How could I possibly know what he looks like if it wasn't real?"

"You probably saw a photo somewhere."

"And the French ambassador to San Noelle? How would I know his name?"

"I didn't even know there was a French ambassador to San Noelle." At my look she sat up straighter. "Fine. If you know all this stuff, why don't you know your supposed husband's phone number?"

"It was programmed into my phone. I know how this sounds, Margo, but something happened last night. It can't have been just a dream—"

A knock sounded at the door, breaking into my protest and I gasped spinning toward the sound. *"Dom."*

"Jenny..."

I ignored Margo, running to the door and flinging it open, holding my breath.

"Surprise!"

My heart sank. It was my family, standing on my doorstep en masse, beaming at me, looking like everything I would have wanted to see just a few days ago. Before the wish, nothing could have made me happier than a surprise visit, but now I just wanted to see Dom. I'd wanted him to be standing there, drawn by a wish or a dream of his own. I knew it didn't make any sense, but nothing about this had made any sense.

And then I felt horrible for being deflated. Crushing disappointment with a guilt chaser.

"We flew out to surprise you. Christmas in the big city!" My mother threw her arms around me and then my whole family was hugging me, crowding around me, hugging Margo, cramming into our apartment and making it feel even tinier.

"We have to see the tree at Rockefeller Center! And go ice skating!"

"I read about a Christmas market at Bryant Park—have you been to that, Jenny?"

"Are you moving back to Iowa, Aunt Jenny?"

"What?" I twisted to frown at my mother, startled by the question from my eight-year-old niece as I was passed from person to person for greeting after greeting.

"There's a job opening for a new secretary at the school," my mother explained, all innocence. "I knew you were worried about whether you could afford to stay here now that Margo's moving on." She flapped a hand. "We can talk about it later."

I frowned, but my mother was already talking to Margo about her dress, congratulating her on her upcoming wedding, and Rachel was in front of me, hugging me tight, with my youngest niece asleep on her shoulder. "I'm sorry about what I said yesterday," she said, pitching her voice low, beneath the hubbub of our family.

"What you said?" What was yesterday? My family could be overwhelming in the best of times and my thoughts were spinning. I couldn't seem to remember a time before the wish. It was all so distant, like *that* was the dream.

"About waiting for your Prince Charming?" Rachel explained. "I blame sleep deprivation. I shouldn't have given you a hard time about holding out for the right fit. You deserve the best. And you'll find your thing and your person, I know it. You wait as long as you want."

But I didn't want to wait anymore. I'd met him.

Prince Charming. And it just so happened he was an actual prince. But how could I get back to him?

"Did you say prince?" Margo echoed, her voice cutting through the din. "Was Jenny telling you about our royal sighting last night?"

"*Royal* sighting?"

Everyone was talking at once, the familiar chaos of my family bringing me back to reality. *My* reality. A reality in which I was just Jenny. And a prince was just someone whose presence livened up a party I had to work to make rent.

My parents weren't nobility and neither was I. I didn't have any useful connections or special qualifications. I was a catering server and a dog walker, and princes... princes married women like Andrea. My gaze caught on the magazine Margo was showing everyone. The magazine with the article about how Dom would be proposing to Andrea at San Noelle's Christmas Ball.

In this reality, that was the truth. Everything else...

Everything else was just a dream.

"When are we going to Rockefeller Center?" my father called over the noise my family generated. "I want to see this tree!"

A week later, I walked into the Manhattan branch of Paws for Love, on my way to see a prince.

Having my family in town for the holidays was wonderful, but it was also all-consuming. Between work—which I still needed in order to pay my bills—and playing tour guide for the Iowa crowd, I'd barely had a second to myself. I'd only managed to find the time to see Prince Harry by sending my family to a taping of one of the morning shows.

I approached his pen and he wagged his tail frantically, spinning in circles of joy.

"Hello, Your Highness," I said, my throat closing. "Did you miss me?"

Prince Harry went into his crouch—which I took to be a wholehearted yes—and I reached for his leash.

"Jenny! Did you hear?"

I paused in the act of freeing Prince Harry, startled by the enthusiastic voice as Mercedes appeared, returning one of the other dogs to his pen.

"Prince Harry has gotten some interest," she gushed. "A family up in Connecticut saw his photo online, and they're thinking of coming down to the city tomorrow to meet him. He might have a home for Christmas, yes, he might. Won't you, good boy? Yes, you will," Mercedes finished by baby-talking directly at Prince Harry—so she didn't notice the frozen look on my face. I had time to plaster on a fake smile before she looked at me.

"That's great," I said, even as I felt like my heart was calcifying. *He's mine*, I wanted to protest. *They can't have him.*

But in this world, he wasn't mine. And my apartment still didn't allow pets. Soon, when Margo moved out and I was forced to try to cover the rent on my own, the apartment would no longer allow *me*.

"Shall we go for a walk, Your Highness?" I asked Prince Harry, but my voice sounded as empty as I felt. Nothing had felt right since the wish had ended.

The countess elf had said that the wish could have

lasting effects. I just hadn't realized they would be on my heart. What kind of a Christmas wish ended in heartbreak?

We walked toward the park, past bell-ringing Santas and harried commuters. The snow had melted in the last few days, leaving only stray piles of graying white as evidence that the city had once been a wonderland. We wandered into the dog park area—and I realized belatedly that I'd forgotten Prince Harry's ball. Sinking down onto a bench instead, I gently ruffled his ears and tried not to think about the fact that tomorrow he might belong to someone else.

"Do you want to go live in Connecticut?" I asked him, stroking his silky head. "I bet it's nice there. They probably have a yard. Though I'm sure it's no south garden. And you wouldn't have the entire palace staff sneaking you treats when they think no one else is looking. But I bet Connecticut is nice... or you could come back to Iowa with me." He cocked his head and I made a face. "I know. I know I said I was going to stay in New York, but maybe it's time to stop trying to be more and accept that I'm just Jenny. There's no shame in that. Iowa is really nice. I bet you'd like it there. We could get a place with a yard..."

Prince Harry whined softly, and I sighed. "I know. I miss him too. But that wasn't reality. Anything between Dom and me... It's just impossible."

I find people are entirely too reluctant to believe in impossible things.

I shook away the memory of the countess elf's voice, focusing on Prince Harry. "Do you remember it?" I asked him. "It didn't feel like a dream, did it?" But neither did it feel real—not anymore.

Things were different in the wishless world.

"If only he remembered too," I whispered.

My phone buzzed in my pocket, signaling a new email—but my heart didn't leap toward the sound. In the last few days, I'd stopped hoping each new call or text or email would be from him. I fished out my phone as Prince Harry sniffed around the bench and I tried not to think about how much I would miss him if he got adopted by a family in Connecticut.

The email was from a recruiter and I frowned as I read it. "It's about a job interview," I explained to Prince Harry. "On Christmas Eve." I grimaced. "I don't even remember applying for this one. It's probably one of those companies where everyone works eighty-hour weeks and no one believes in holidays. But those jobs usually pay well. If I got it, I could stay in New York. Get an apartment where you could come live with me."

It had been something I wanted so badly only days ago, but now, it felt like the consolation prize. Like a huge piece of my future was missing.

"What do you think, Harry? Should I move back to Iowa? Stay here and keep trying to find my place in New York?" Prince Harry cocked his head, as if waiting for a third option. "San Noelle?" I asked him softly, not daring to say the words at full voice.

Prince Harry wagged his tail, scooching forward eagerly.

"That's impossible," I reminded him. "It wasn't real. It was just a wish. And wishes don't last." I stood up. "Come on. Let's get you back to the shelter so you can get all prettied up for your new family tomorrow and I can figure out what I'm going to wear to this interview. We have to take the best of the options we have, right, Prince Harry?"

Chapter Twenty-Four

I COULDN'T BRING MYSELF TO WEAR the standard gray suit uniform on the morning of Christmas Eve. Maybe I was self-sabotaging, stubbornly refusing to play the corporate game, but I wanted to feel like myself more than I wanted to look like the perfect candidate for the job.

The red dress with a white snowflake print made me feel festive and happy—and few things had been making me feel that way since I'd woken up after the wish, no matter how hard I tried to shake off the lingering melancholy. I'd had this great wish and I needed to be grateful for the experience, not depressed because it hadn't lasted. I was *trying* to be grateful, but I still woke up missing Dom. Missing Prince Harry. And Andrea and Amilia and all the people of San Noelle.

Not to mention missing the woman I had become there. I'd loved that version of me.

I stepped out of my bedroom, and Margo blinked at me from the kitchen where she was making coffee in fuzzy reindeer pajamas. She frowned at my dress, the cup she'd made for me frozen in mid-air. "That's what you're wearing? I thought this was some kind of corporate PR gig?"

"Maybe they like Christmas." I accepted the coffee, thanking her. "Besides, it's not like I've had a lot of luck landing a job when I try to be the corporate clone. Maybe it's time for me to abandon the gray suit."

"Excellent idea. They're going to love every festive inch of you," Margo declared, always quick to cheerlead. "Do you know how long the interview is likely to go?" she asked, picking up her own mug. She leaned against the counter and nodded toward her wedding dress where it hung in our living room. "Final fitting today, and as my maid of honor you're required to hold my hand and tell me I look a thousand times better than I do."

"You're going to look amazing. And I'll be there. Right after I rock this interview."

Margo smiled and I toasted her with my travel mug before heading out the front door—but the standard pre-interview pump-up routine felt a little forced. Like I was just going through the motions.

I rode the train into Manhattan, the space surprisingly full of tourists and the unlucky commuters who had to work on the day before Christmas. I couldn't help wondering what Dom was doing at that moment. He'd probably never been on the E train before. What would he think of the subway? The crowds and the smells?

His world was so different from mine. It was six hours later in San Noelle. Early afternoon on Christmas Eve.

In the wish, our families had all gathered together

for an early dinner and the children had shrieked with laughter as they'd played with Prince Harry. Later, Dom had coaxed me into exchanging presents early in front of the little tree in our suite and afterwards, we'd gone sledding, joined by our families, half the palace staff, and the people of San Noelle.

Would he do any of that today? Or would he and Andrea have a somber, formal dinner with his father before he proposed to her at the ball tomorrow?

All the articles about him I'd been compulsively reading over the last few days were *certain* there would be a proposal at the ball. Google had been more than willing to feed my obsession.

The brakes screeched on the tracks, jolting me out of my thoughts, and I realized I'd almost missed my stop. I tucked my bag tight against my ribs and darted through the closing doors, bursting out onto the platform. The subway was less crowded than usual on the morning of Christmas Eve, but I still had to dodge clusters of travelers as I made my way toward the exit.

The interview was in another of those fancy high-rises and I introduced myself at the security desk, showing my ID and getting my guest pass. I watched the employees entering, but visualizing myself swiping my keycard through the turnstiles every day didn't feel as empowering as it had only a few days ago. I found myself thinking about the women I'd met in San Noelle. None of them had fancy keycards or gray power suits, but they were making a difference, each in their own small way, with every change they made to their community. What would they think if they saw me now?

Of course, none of them would remember me. It had only been a wish. But as I ascended the Manhattan high-rise in a crowded elevator, I kept thinking of that meeting in the back room of the community center. The laughter, but also the feeling that I was exactly where I needed to be. That I could make a *difference.*

The elevator doors opened, and I stepped out into the office's reception area. Something about the logo seemed familiar, so I must have heard about the company in some context, but I couldn't place it. Shaking away the nagging feeling at the back of my thoughts, I approached the receptionist with a smile.

"Hi, I'm—"

"You must be Jenny! We've been expecting you."

I blinked, startled by the warmth of the greeting for an interview for a job that was basically an entry-level drone. Maybe the company wasn't as cold and corporate as I'd mentally painted it.

"Right this way." The receptionist stood and began leading me toward a conference room. She opened the door for me, giving me a little thumbs up and I wondered if maybe the red dress had been the correct choice for the cheery company—until I stepped into the conference room and faced a pair of serious faces in very serious suits.

My nerves returned in a rush, but I forced myself to smile through the introductions, shaking hands and handing over my resume, trying to channel my inner princess. The interviewers got right down to business, outlining the position to me.

"You'd be working for our corporate responsibility department," a woman with a *very* serious suit explained. "It's under the PR department, but it handles most of our charity work and social activism initiatives. It's a lot of email and, frankly, a lot of paperwork. We always want to make sure our donations are going to reputable organizations, but you'd really have a chance to do good within that framework."

It sounded better and better the more she spoke, almost too good to be true. Hadn't I just been talking to Dom about how I wanted to make the world better? I'd essentially be getting paid for the volunteer work I already loved doing. But something still didn't quite feel right.

"And, of course, you'd be attending a lot of high-profile functions, interacting with other donors—"

Maybe I could even meet Dom again. I squashed the thought, focusing again on what the interviewers were saying.

"So, tell us, Jenny, what do you see yourself doing with that sort of position? How do you feel you're uniquely suited to be the face of our charity endeavors?"

"I—" This was the moment in all my other interviews when my mind went totally blank. But this time, I knew my answer. I knew myself now, knew what kind of impact I wanted to have. "I've always wanted to make the world a better place. To bring people together..." I trailed off, staring at the warm, engaged faces across the table. "This is exactly the kind of job I didn't know I was dreaming of."

It was the dream job. The kind of job that carried the prestige I'd come to New York seeking. Two weeks ago, I would have leapt at the chance, but now...

I wasn't the same person I'd been before the wish.

For my entire life, I'd been looking for that magical thing that was going to make me feel like I was good enough, that status I could hold up and say *See? I'm not Just Jenny.* But when I'd been a princess, I'd realized that no status or title all on its own could make a difference in how I felt about myself. Those external things can't make you feel worthwhile if you don't feel it inside. I had to know I was worthy. Nothing was going to make me that way. I had to *be* the princess inside.

A princess can do absolutely anything she wants, as long as she does it with confidence. So... who do you want to be?

Margo's voice echoed in my ears. I still wanted to do good. I still wanted to change the world. But I wasn't sure I wanted to do that from an office in a corporate high-rise. Maybe I wanted to do it from a community center in a tiny kingdom halfway around the world. Was that too crazy to even consider?

"Jenny?" the woman across the table prompted and I blushed.

"I'm sorry. I... Two weeks ago, I would have killed for this job. I've always wanted to do something meaningful. I love volunteering at a local animal shelter and taking food to a women's shelter. I would love to be able to do more."

"And with us, you can."

"I know, but..." I shook my head. "You're probably going to think this is ridiculous, but I just have this feeling I'm meant for something else."

Dom was going to marry Andrea. I wasn't going to be a princess—at least not with the title and the palace and the prince—but I could still be the person I'd found inside myself in San Noelle.

"Are you turning us down?" My besuited interviewers frowned at me, visibly confused. "I have to admit, when you were recommended for this job, we didn't imagine you'd tell us no."

"Two weeks ago, I don't think I would have. But now, I have some unfinished business with some community leaders three thousand miles away. There's a senior center and an animal shelter that need me, and I think my talents might be wasted sitting in an office writing checks to deserving groups when I could be getting my hands dirty working with them and really bringing people together." More and more certain that I was doing the right thing, I stood. "I'm sorry to have wasted your time. Especially on Christmas Eve."

The woman in the very serious suit stood as well, coming around the table. "You seem like just the sort of candidate we're looking for, and you came highly recommended, so if you change your mind, I do hope you'll give us a call. Just don't wait too long."

"Thank you. But I think I know what I need to do now."

Maybe the wish hadn't been about fairy tales. Maybe it had been about this. Finding that sense of purpose that was always inside me, waiting to get out.

I opened the door to exit the conference room and the woman turned back to her colleague. "Well. We can tell the prince we tried."

I froze with my hand on the door. "I'm sorry. What did you...?" I turned back. "Did Prince Dominic...?"

Suddenly the familiar logo made sense. This was

the company from the Christmas party—the one that felt like it had happened a lifetime ago. This was the company that Dom did business with.

The woman shrugged. "His Highness felt you would be ideal for the opening, and we like to listen to our clients when they have good advice."

"I... thank you." I picked my jaw up off the floor and stammered my goodbyes, trying to figure out what exactly that meant. Dom had recommended me for a job with a company he worked with... in the real world. He'd remembered me—some random girl who'd mowed him down in the park—and had gone to the trouble of recommending me for a job. A job he would have some contact with, but that was half a world away from San Noelle. And he was marrying Andrea... wasn't he?

I rode down in the elevator, my thoughts spiraling.

I wanted to go to San Noelle for myself because I wanted to get involved with the community—to do what I could with Eleanor and the people I'd met there—but that didn't mean I couldn't also go for Dom.

I'd been scared to take a chance, scared to take that leap because I'd never felt certain, never felt confident, always backing away and playing it safe, but now...

I *wasn't* the person I'd been before. I may not be a princess, but Dom and I had connected. That had been real—in every world. And being the princess inside wasn't just about being confident—it was about knowing what I wanted and going after it. And I wanted Dom. I wanted to at least *try* to tell him how I felt—even if it was crazy—before he proposed to Andrea.

The elevator doors opened and I rushed out into the lobby, driven by a powerful sense of purpose—stepping right into a cloud of peppermint-scented air.

I froze, twisting, looking around for the countess elf who always seemed to accompany that scent, but all I saw were the usual New Yorkers rushing through the lobby.

"Miss? Is there a problem?"

I glanced over at the security guard—and saw a massive candy cane bouquet that must have just been delivered. That must have been the source of the scent. I shook off my fancy, smiling for the guard. "No. No problem. Thanks." I walked out of the building, trying to reclaim that sense of purpose.

I could do this. I wasn't crazy. I was driven. Purposeful.

And I was going to get my dog.

There was no way I was letting Prince Harry go to Connecticut. Dom had been right. When you wanted something badly enough, you made it happen. I couldn't afford to stay in our current apartment anyway after Margo moved out. Soon, I'd either be moving to San Noelle, if things went the way I wanted them to, or I'd figure out what I wanted to do next, but Prince Harry was going to be part of it.

I turned to race uptown to Paws for Love before the Connecticut contingent could steal him away—there were lots of other dogs for them to fall in love with, Prince Harry was mine—and someone slammed into me from the side.

"Oh!" I staggered, catching myself against a giant ornament that was part of the building's Christmas display. I turned to apologize, but the pedestrian who had broadsided me had already disappeared back into the New York crowds.

I straightened my coat, bending to pick up the glove I'd dropped, and there, sitting on the sidewalk, glittering like a star, was the snowflake bracelet.

My breath whooshed out as I picked up the silver and diamond bracelet, my heart suddenly beating thunderously loud in my ears. It couldn't be here. There was no way. But it was. The same bracelet. The one Dom had said belonged to his mother. "It's a sign," I whispered.

I had to return it to him, didn't I?

There had to be a little Christmas magic left. There had to be a chance for us. It might seem impossible— it probably was—

But I was getting very good at believing in impossible things.

Chapter Twenty-Five

"WOULD YOU CARE TO EXPLAIN to me why my maid of honor is flying halfway around the world a week before my wedding? You were supposed to come with me to my final fitting today," Margo said as I threw toiletries into a suitcase.

"I know and I'm sorry, but there's something I have to do."

"Is this about that dream?"

"Wish. And yes...and no. It's about me." I paused, holding up two dresses, neither of which seemed ball-worthy, but one of which would have to do. "It's about who I want to be. Maybe I'll crash and burn, but I finally feel like I know where I need to be and it's San Noelle. Don't worry. I'll be back for the wedding. You know I wouldn't miss it for the world."

"I'm not worried about the wedding."

I shot her a look.

"Okay, not *entirely* about the wedding. What are your parents going to think?"

"Probably that I've lost my mind. Which is why I need you on my side because I'm about to explain to my parents that even though they paid a fortune for that AirBNB and tickets for the whole family and flew halfway across the country to be with me on Christmas, I need to fly to Europe to crash a Christmas ball because I think I'm in love with a prince."

Margo blinked. "In love."

"I know. I know how it sounds. But the wish was real, Margo, and I love him and if I don't at least *try* to tell him that before he proposes to someone else I will always regret it. He's..."

"A prince?" she suggested.

"No." I smiled, shaking my head. "He's so much more than that."

Margo studied me, her eyes going soft at something she read on my face. "You're serious about this."

Prince Harry poked his head out from under the bed where he'd been exploring while I packed and Margo seemed to snap out of her love-conquers-all moment at the sight of him.

"We can't have a dog," she reminded me.

"We don't. I do. And I'm taking him with me. I just need to get a dog carrier. And tickets on the next flight to San Noelle."

"This is insane," Margo reminded me, and I nodded.

"Possibly. Probably. But if there's one thing I've learned in the last few weeks, it's that people thinking you're crazy isn't the worst thing that can happen. And even if Dom rejects me and I'm totally crushed and no one in San Noelle is interested in working with me because I'm not a princess anymore and I come home defeated, at least I tried. At least I went after something and chased it with my whole heart." I looked at my best friend. "I'm not backing away from life anymore."

Margo studied my face. "Who are you and what have you done with my roommate?"

I bit my lip, uncertainty sneaking up and whispering in my ear. "This is insane, isn't it? I can't afford a last-minute flight to Europe—"

"Stop." Margo took my shoulders. "You're finally owning your awesomeness. What kind of a best friend would I be if I didn't help? You know Harish has, like, seven zillion airline miles with all the travel he has to do for work. In one week, half of what's his is mine and I think his wedding present to me should be the miles to get you—and your dog—a ticket to San Noelle in time for that ball."

"Margo, I can't accept—"

"You're the reason I met the love of my life," she said, her eyes dark and serious. "Let me help you chase yours."

"It's not crazy?" I asked nervously.

"Oh, it's crazy," she assured me. "But the best things in life always are. Especially when it comes to love. Just promise me you'll be back in time for my wedding, one way or another."

"I promise," I whispered, hugging her tight. "I wouldn't miss it for anything. Not even a prince."

She laughed. "You'd better not. Now stop getting me all sappy. I need to call my future husband and get you a plane ticket."

The flight to San Noelle was entirely too long—and

gave me entirely too much time to think about the ridiculousness of what I was doing. The only flight available had been a red-eye. It was half empty on Christmas Eve as we traveled the skies alongside Santa Claus, and my fellow travelers sprawled across multiple seats, sleeping the blissful sleep of people who had not just made radical changes to their lives based on a bracelet and a whim.

The snowflake bracelet circled my wrist and I touched it whenever I needed a jolt of bravery and reassurance—which was often. I'd never done something like this in my life and adrenaline fizzed in my blood, keeping me awake and making me feel a little buzzed.

There hadn't been any direct flights into San Noelle on Christmas morning—or afternoon, as it was by the time we landed in Geneva, thanks to time zones. I made my way to baggage claim only to discover my suitcase had somehow gotten lost, but Prince Harry and I were here, so we chose to move on rather than wasting time begging the airline to find it. Instead, we headed to pick up the rental car that Harish had thoughtfully thrown in as his own thank-you for introducing him to Margo. I was going to have to find some way to repay those two.

At the rental counter, it became painfully apparent that I no longer spoke any French at all—which really would have been a very handy carryover from the wish—but the agent and I muddled through and I even remembered how to wish her a *Joyeux Noel* before I headed out and loaded Prince Harry into the car.

I climbed into the driver's seat with my maps— since my outdated phone didn't work in Europe—and groaned when I saw the controls. "Stick shift. Of course it would be stick shift," I told Prince Harry. "We wouldn't want things to be too easy."

My sisters had tried to teach me stick shift on a country road outside our hometown when I was fifteen and let's just say it hadn't gone well. That's so much nicer than saying I panicked, got the pedals mixed up, and plowed our family truck straight through the center of a corn field, sending ears of corn flying in every direction.

But I knew how to drive stick. In theory.

"I can do this," I whispered, and Prince Harry whined encouragingly. "I can do this," I repeated—looking up at the winding, switchbacking road up the mountain that would take me toward San Noelle. The road that was icy and covered with snow.

"The princess in the fairy tale never gets it easy," I told Prince Harry—and turned on the SUV, the diesel engine rumbling to life and sounding exactly like a dragon that needed to be tamed. "San Noelle, here we come."

Night had long since fallen by the time I crossed the border into San Noelle. Prince Harry had fallen asleep and was snoring softly in the passenger seat as French Christmas carols played over the radio. I'd begun to worry, as I drove, that it really had been a dream.

What would happen if I drove into the capital of San Noelle and nothing looked the same? What if the entire wish had been a product of my imagination? What if there was no women's group to join? No shelter to volunteer at and no elder care home to visit with the therapy dogs I had every intention of learning how to train? Would I still stay? Would I still be brave enough to crash the ball if everything I thought I remembered was just the very vivid product of an overactive subconscious?

But then I rounded a bend, and the town appeared before me, the lights like a cluster of stars nestled into the mountainside with the familiar Christmas tree rising out of the town square and the palace spotlighted above it like a beacon of hope. It all looked exactly like I'd remembered it.

It looked like home.

"It's just like we remembered, Prince Harry," I told the sleeping dog, my heart lifting at the sight.

Prince Harry stirred, lifting his head, his tail thumping as we slowed over the cobblestone streets of the town, as if he recognized it just as much as I did. It had begun to snow in the last hour, slowing the drive even more, but now I was grateful for the flakes floating in the air, making the town look like a freshly shaken snow globe.

I pulled up to the palace, earning a startled glance from the valet when I stepped out in the leggings and oversized sweater I'd worn on the plane—and Prince Harry leapt out after me. My bridesmaid dress—which was the closest thing I had to ball-worthy—had been a casualty of my lost luggage, but I'd made it this far and I wasn't going to let a little thing like lack of appropriate attire stop me now.

At least, that was what I thought before two of the guards stepped in front of me, barring my way with their ceremonial lances after I'd handed the rental car over to the valet.

"I'm sorry, miss," Jacques intoned solemnly. "This is a private event."

"I know," I said quickly. "And I know I don't look like it, but I know Dom—Prince Dominic—and I have something I have to tell him. Tonight. Before..." Before he proposed to Andrea and my chance went up in smoke.

The guards exchanged a glance and I could already tell they were silently debating which one of them would have to bodily remove me from the premises if it came to that. But I knew these men. Not well, but they'd always been kind to me. Jacques had danced with Amilia when Dom was teaching me to waltz. There had to be hope.

"Please. Jacques, Alain." They blinked at my use of their names, but neither of the lances barring my way moved an inch. "My luggage was lost and all the shops in town are closed or I swear I'd be dressed appropriately. I just need to see the prince for two seconds. Then you can throw me out if he wants you to."

Prince Harry whined, as if adding his own plea to the argument, but Alain shook his head. "I'm sorry, miss, but without an invitation, there's nothing we can do."

"Please... It's Christmas." The guards were shaking their heads and I was trying to come up with another argument when Prince Harry yipped, leapt up and took off running. "Prince Harry!"

Part of me almost hoped he would run straight to the ballroom and I could chase him all the way to Dom, maybe even accidentally tackle the prince again—but the dog was racing away from the entrance, around the side of the palace, and I rushed after him, my feet slipping in the snow. I heard a jingle bell in the distance and spotted the puppy I'd seen at the senior center in the wish scampering along the frozen lake ahead of me—with Prince Harry scrambling in its wake.

"Prince Harry!" I called again—and this time he heard me, stopping with his ears pricked up as he watched me racing to his side. I hastily clipped the leash to his collar, grumbling at him, "If you were going to pick that moment to decide to go exploring, I wish you'd run in another direction."

"Really, darling, you must be more careful what you wish for..."

My head snapped up and I whirled toward the voice.

The scent of peppermint seemed to swirl in the air the second I saw her. She looked magnificent, more magical than ever in a sparkling white ball gown that seemed to catch each falling snowflake and incorporate it into the dress. She bent, plucking the puppy with the jingle bell collar off the snow and cuddling it into her arms. The magical snowflake bracelet identical to the one I wore seemed to throw off the light of a dozen stars as it flashed on her wrist.

"You're here," I whispered, suddenly breathless.

"Where else would I be?" the countess elf Christmas angel asked, blinking innocently.

I hurried toward her, my feet slipping in the snow. "Please," I begged. "Can you help me? I need to see Dom. I need to tell him how I feel before it's too late. I wished for a fairy-tale Christmas and it's still Christmas—do you think there might be just a little magic left?"

"You believe in magic now?"

"Absolutely," I swore. "Could you please be my fairy godmother one more time? Or my *Tante Arie* or my Christmas angel or countess elf? I love him. And I know he might not feel the same way, but I have to get into that ball. *Please.*"

The countess elf cocked her head, light glittering around her head like a crown made of snowflakes. "My dear, what makes you so certain I'm *your* Christmas angel? What makes you think I'm not his?"

I caught my breath, scarcely daring to hope—and then she smiled.

"No self-respecting fairy godmother would let you go to the ball like that."

With the puppy still tucked under one arm, she waved her free hand with a flourish, and the snowflakes above her fingertips began to swirl in a vortex that expanded and whooshed toward me, that now-familiar candy-cane scent somehow warm around me even as the snowflake cyclone blinded me.

When the storm retreated, I looked down—and found myself in the same magnificent crimson ball gown I'd worn in the wish. A sparkling invitation that seemed to be made of snowflakes and magic was clasped in one of my hands. Even Prince Harry had a debonair bowtie attached to his collar.

"Is this going to vanish at midnight?" I asked, having learned my lesson about asking about expiration dates.

"It will last as long as you believe in it," the countess

273

elf promised and I smiled, tears gathering in my eyes as I rushed forward to hug her.

"How can I thank you?"

She squeezed me, before pulling back and smiling into my eyes. "Never forget the spirit of the season."

"And believe in impossible things?"

She beamed. "Always."

Jacques and Alain didn't even seem to recognize the bedraggled, travel-weary girl who'd tried to crash the ball when I rushed back to the gates, transformed in a dress worthy of a princess, with Prince Harry trotting at my side on a rhinestone studded leash. They barely glanced at my invitation before opening the massive gates for me.

I lifted my skirts with one hand and raced across the cobblestones of the courtyard. I knew the way by heart. This palace had become as familiar to me as the paths of Central Park where I played with Prince Harry. I rushed through the halls and up the stairs until I reached the antechamber outside the ballroom where a herald was waiting to announce the guests.

"Your title, miss?" the herald inquired softly in his deeply resonant voice—and I realized I couldn't be announced as I always had been in the wish. I wasn't Princess Jennifer of San Noelle anymore. And there was only one way I could imagine being announced to the glittering throng in the ballroom below.

I leaned close to the herald and whispered my preferred title. His lips twitched, his eyes gleaming with good humor as he nodded and gestured to the footmen to throw open the doors.

I stepped into the opening as his deep voice rang out over the assembled crowd.

"Just Jenny," he called. "And Prince Harry."

Chapter Twenty-Six

YOU KNOW THAT MOMENT IN pretty much every fairy-tale movie where the princess glides majestically down a staircase while everyone in the room gazes on admiringly and the prince is drawn to her by the sheer force of her beauty and grace?

This was *exactly* that moment.

My head held high, Prince Harry's leash in my hand, I felt like a princess—and it had nothing to do with the dress. Though that certainly didn't hurt.

Just Jenny didn't sound quite so bad anymore. It didn't sound like the James girl who'd never quite figured out what to do with her life. Instead, it sounded like a woman who knew she was everything she needed to be without a fancy title attached.

Then I looked up, meeting Dom's eyes from across the room—and if I hadn't already felt like a princess, the look in his eyes would have done it.

It was that feeling—like something in him was reaching toward something in me. A private moment, even in a crowd.

He smiled, and even half a room away, I felt the

crinkling of his eyes all the way down to my toes. Then he was threading through the crowds, making his way toward me, arriving at the base of the stairs moments before I reached the bottom, his hand extended up to help me down the last couple of steps. He took my hand, bowing over it, the gaze that caught mine full of something that made my throat tight. Every eye in the room could have been on us, but I only saw him.

"Just Jenny," he murmured as he straightened. "I'm delighted you were able to attend."

"Your Highness." I sank into a curtsy.

Prince Harry wriggled at my side, impatient for his share of the attention and Dom smiled, releasing my hand to execute a crisp bow in Harry's direction. "Your Highness," he said with utmost formality, before sinking down onto one knee and ruffling Prince Harry's ears. "Did you change your mind about adopting him?" he asked, looking up at me as he continued to lavish attention on the dog.

"I realized some things are worth going after," I said, meeting his eyes. "If you want something, you make it happen, right?"

Dom straightened slowly as the familiar strains of "The Waltz of the Flowers" began to play and my heartrate accelerated to near-concerning levels. He glanced over his shoulder at the dance floor, looking back to me with something unreadable sparkling in his eyes. "Do you think Prince Harry would mind if I asked his mistress to dance?"

"I think he can spare me," I sighed, wondering who that breathless person borrowing my vocal cords was.

Dom gestured to a footman, who rushed forward to

take Prince Harry's leash. Then he extended his hand, palm up. "Shall we?"

I gently rested my fingertips on his, gliding into his arms. He swept me into the waltz. So effortless. So natural. As if we'd danced together a thousand times—or a handful of other times, to this exact song in this exact ballroom.

He spun me out—and as I twirled, I suddenly became aware of all the eyes on us. Some curious, some suspicious, but all on us. When his arms closed around me again, I realized he was studying me just as intently.

"What are you doing here?" he asked as we waltzed. He sounded more curious than suspicious, but I was suddenly reminded of exactly how ridiculous it would sound if I told him I'd made a Christmas wish and fallen in love with him and now I was here to tell him I wanted to live happily ever after.

"I, uh, I wanted to... to thank you. For the job interview."

His eyebrows popped up. "Really? You came all this way to thank me for arranging an interview?"

"Well, I didn't have your phone number." This didn't exactly make me sound more rational.

"So I take it you took the job."

"Ah. No. Not technically." I swallowed, trying to find the right words. Some variant of the truth. "See, I, ah, I had this really strange dream."

Dom's brow furrowed. "A dream."

"And I..." What was I doing here? Did I really think I could just waltz with the prince once and he would give up his plans to marry Andrea? I caught sight of the duchess and blurted, "I'm sorry I crashed your engagement."

Dom blinked. "My what?"

I blushed, glancing over his shoulder toward where I could see Andrea watching us, her expression curious. "I read an article that said you were proposing tonight."

He smiled, shaking his head. "You really shouldn't believe everything you read in the papers."

My eyes lifted along with my hopes, meeting his. "Really?" I should have known that. Wasn't I the one who'd been embroiled in Pregnancygate on the basis of a craving for shawarma and a gust of wind? But it was somehow much harder to accept that the tabloids were all phony when they played into your own fears. "So you aren't marrying Andrea?"

"Andrea and I are just friends," he assured me. "That's all we've ever been."

"So you never..."

"People speculate. They see us together and assume, but she wants to marry for love." He bent his head, his eyes intent. "And so do I."

"You do," I repeated at a whisper, helplessly caught by the look in his eyes. He was looking at me like he had in the wish. Like he might care for me. Like it might actually be love.

He stopped dancing and I realized he'd navigated us into one of the nooks along the side of the dance floor. I looked up and there it was—a sprig of mistletoe directly above our heads. My heartbeat began to thunder in my ears.

"About this dream..." he murmured, still holding me in the circle of his arms.

"It was actually more of a wish," I breathed. "A Christmas wish—only I don't think I knew what I was wishing for when I made it."

The hand that had been holding mine as we danced slid up my wrist to where the snowflake bracelet he'd given me in the wish rested against my glove. "My mother used to have a bracelet exactly like this one, but it's been missing for years."

"Has it?" I whispered, incapable of forming a more clever response. "I found it. Or it found me."

"Sounds like magic." His mouth tipped up on one side in a half smile. "So in this wish... was there a nutcracker prince who needed to be brought to life?"

My breath whooshed out on a gasp, tears pricking the back of my eyes. How could he know that? There was only one possible way...

"I wished for you," I whispered.

Dom smiled, drawing me closer in his arms. "What makes you think I didn't wish for you just as much as you wished for me?"

He lowered his head, but I didn't wait for him to kiss me. I was done hesitating. It was impossible to think he might remember the wish too, but I was getting good at believing in impossible things. Like fairy tales, Christmas magic, and happily-ever-afters.

I went up on my toes, meeting my prince halfway as the mistletoe magic blanketed us both. His lips brushed mine, and this time there was no peppermint wind whisking me back to reality, yanking me from his arms. This *was* reality. And the purest form of Christmas magic I'd ever experienced—it was love.

My chest squeezed as I kissed him back and the

clock began tolling midnight, and we didn't separate until the twelfth chime had rung.

Christmas was officially over. But this... this was just beginning.

Epilogue

"I CAN'T BELIEVE YOU BROUGHT A prince to my wedding. Talk about showing up the other bridesmaids."

I laughed, swatting Margo with her own bouquet as we stood to one side of the ballroom. Margo was frantically stuffing canapes into her mouth before the next round of the festivities began. She'd grabbed me and begged me to run interference for her with anyone who came over to congratulate her while she loaded up on the calories, complaining that no one had warned her you didn't get a chance to eat the food at your own reception.

"If only you'd known him six months ago," she said between brie puffs. "I could have been married in a palace."

"He did offer," I reminded her.

"I know. And if Harish hadn't insisted it was bad form to force all of our guests to fly to Europe on less than a week's notice, I totally would have taken him up on it."

I laughed, though I had a feeling she wasn't joking.

"I'm just glad the airline managed to get my bridesmaid dress back to me in time."

"Somehow I think a prince could have found you another dress in the right color. Just promise me that when there's a massive royal wedding that's televised around the world, I get to be the maid of honor. And I get to have the kind of dress that will make royals *weep* with envy."

I arched a brow at my best friend. "Don't you think you're getting a little ahead of yourself with the wedding planning? We've only been dating a week."

"Honey, you caught the bouquet," she said, nodding to the flowers in my hand. "It's a done deal now. Besides, weren't you already married?"

"Shh. That was different."

"Sure it was. But I'm still locking down maid of honor."

I grinned. "Don't you mean matron?"

Margo glanced over at her new husband, a smile slowly splitting her face as he caught her eye across the dance floor and made a beeline toward her. "Why, yes," she said, beaming. "I do."

Harish had eyes only for Margo as he swept her onto the dance floor—and I smiled as I watched them, without even a flicker of envy. They were perfect together. But I had my own perfect now.

I was trying to keep my head on my shoulders and not get carried away thinking Dom and I had a straight shot to happily-ever-after just because we'd seen what our lives could be in the wish. But it was hard to be practical and reasonable when you just wanted to float off the ground because you were so happy.

Dom's father was less than thrilled to see Andrea sidelined and an American nobody in her place, but I was confident I could win him over. That zing I'd sensed between Andrea and Franz seemed non-existent now, but maybe once Dom wasn't wedged between them as an obstacle, they'd be able to see one another differently.

My parents had forgiven me for abandoning them at Christmas much faster than I'd expected—due in large part to Dom's efforts to charm them when we flew back to New York two days after Christmas. They were already talking about having him out to Potter's Ferry for the Valentine's Festival—though my father had pulled me aside and informed me in no uncertain terms that, prince or not, Dom had better treat me right or my father would be having words with him.

Thankfully, I didn't think that conversation would ever be necessary.

The opening notes of "The Waltz of the Flowers" began to play as my prince suddenly appeared in front of me, his eyes crinkling. "May I have this dance, Just Jenny?"

"By all means, Your Highness." I glided into his arms, the bouquet in my left hand resting on his shoulder. "How did you get them to play this song?" I asked as Margo and Harish whirled past, waltzing with more enthusiasm than finesse.

"A prince never reveals his secrets."

I arched a brow. "Never?"

He gazed over my shoulder, haughty and regal. "I may have implied there could be a knighthood in it for Harish."

I burst out laughing. "You didn't."

"When you want something, you have to do what it takes to make it happen. And I figured I already owed him a knighthood for flying you out to San Noelle on Christmas. Though I was planning to fly back to New York as soon as my holiday obligations were over to see if I could track down a certain dog walker and catering server."

"Just like a fairy tale," I said, shaking my head in mock dismay. "The princess always has to do most of the work."

"Are you accusing me of hanging out in the background being boringly charming?"

"If the shoe fits..."

Dom spun me in a tight circle, the momentum making me feel like I was flying. Laughter burst out of me, propelled by sheer happiness.

It was impossible to think I'd actually found my person, and he was literally a prince. Unthinkable to imagine that Just Jenny could be the one he looked at like there was no one else in the room, his eyes crinkling every time he caught my eye from across the room. Impossible to actually believe that I'd found my place—in his arms, working to make the world a better place every day.

But I was very, very good at believing in impossible things.

Love made them all possible.

The End

Chicken Shawarma

A Hallmark Original Recipe

In *A Royal Christmas Wish*, Jenny wakes up to find herself married to a real-live prince. As she attempts to navigate the royal lifestyle—with less-than-successful results—she does miss a few things about her old life in New York City, including the chicken shawarma from the place around the corner. Our recipe for it is so delicious, it's fit for a princess. Make it once, and you'll be craving it, too!

Yield: 4 servings
Prep Time: 2 hours, 20 minutes
Cook Time: 10 minutes
Total Time: 2 hours, 30 minutes

INGREDIENTS

Spice-Rubbed Chicken:
- 1 teaspoon ground cumin
- 1 teaspoon smoked paprika
- 1 teaspoon kosher salt
- 1 teaspoon black pepper
- ½ teaspoon dried oregano
- ½ teaspoon ground cardamom
- ½ teaspoon ground coriander
- ¼ teaspoon ground turmeric
- ¼ teaspoon crushed red pepper
- ¼ cup olive oil
- 2 tablespoons fresh lemon juice
- 2 garlic cloves, smashed
- 3 large or 4 average boneless, skinless chicken breasts

Garlic-Cumin Sauce:
- 1 cup plain Greek yogurt
- 2 teaspoons fresh lemon juice
- 1 garlic clove, fine minced
- ½ teaspoon ground cumin
- ¼ teaspoon kosher salt
- ¼ teaspoon black pepper

Marinated Cucumber Salad:
- 1 cup halved grape tomatoes
- ½ cup thin sliced cucumber
- ½ cup drained chick peas
- ¼ cup thin sliced red onion
- 1 tablespoon olive oil
- 1 tablespoon fresh lemon juice

- ¼ teaspoon black pepper

- 8 bamboo skewers, soaked in water
- 4 naan (or pita or flatbread), warmed on grill, in oven or in a skillet
- ¼ cup spicy hummus
- As needed, flat-leaf (Italian) parsley, chopped
- 4 grilled lemon halves (optional)

DIRECTIONS

1. To prepare spice-rubbed chicken: combine dry spices, olive oil, lemon juice and garlic in a large bowl (or ziplock bag) and stir to blend.

2. Slice chicken into thin 2-inch pieces: place in bowl with spice rub and toss to evenly coat. Cover and refrigerate for 2 hours, stirring occasionally.

3. To prepare garlic-cumin sauce: combine all ingredients in bowl and whisk to blend. Refrigerate.

4. To prepare marinated cucumber salad: combine in ingredients in bowl and toss to blend. Refrigerate.

5. Heat grill to medium heat. While grill is heating, thread spice-rubbed chicken pieces evenly on bamboo skewers.

6. Grill chicken skewers for 10 minutes, or until fully cooked, turning frequently.

7. To assemble chicken shawarma: spread each piece of naan with hummus. Top evenly with marinated cucumber salad, spice-rubbed chicken skewers and garlic-cumin sauce.

Garnish with chopped flat-leaf parsley and a grilled lemon half, if desired.

Thanks so much for reading *A Royal Christmas Wish*. We hope you enjoyed it!

You might like these other books from Hallmark Publishing:

A Down Home Christmas
The Christmas Company
A Timeless Christmas
At the Heart of Christmas
Christmas in Evergreen
Christmas In Evergreen: Letters to Santa

For information about our new releases and exclusive offers, sign up for our free newsletter at hallmarkchannel.com/ hallmark-publishing-newsletter

You can also connect with us here:

Facebook.com/HallmarkPublishing

Twitter.com/HallmarkPublish

About the Author

Contemporary romance author Lizzie Shane was born in Alaska and still calls the frozen north home, though she can frequently be found indulging her travel addiction. Thankfully, her laptop travels with her and she has written her way through fifty states and over fifty countries. Lizzie has been honored to win the Golden Heart Award and HOLT Medallion, and has been named a finalist three times for Romance Writers of America's prestigious RITA Award®, but her main claim to fame is her recent appearance as a contestant on Jeopardy! For more about Lizzie and her books, please visit www.lizzieshane.com.